One Spell

BRIAN JAMES HILDEBRAND

Dedication: To every writer struggling to finish their first book. It won't be easy, and it will take longer than you think it should, but you can do it.

1| BLAINE

I NEVER THOUGHT I WOULD MISS THE PSYCH WARD, BUT STARTING HIGH school in a new city was certainly making me reconsider. At least there I knew I was around people who wanted me to get better, even if I did have to lie to them to get released. I don't really think I could say the same about high school. Those people would rip me apart if they found out the truth. They'd all think I was crazy. To be honest, I'm not too sure they'd be wrong.

I took a look out the window as my mom drove me to school. Being here already felt a little overwhelming. I knew that I had come from a small farming community, but moving to the city really made you realize just how different things are. And school was definitely one of them.

My mom pulled the car over about a block from the school after spending a couple minutes trying to find a closer spot. "You sure you'll be okay to take the bus home?" She asked as she parked the car.

"Yeah, Mom, I'll be fine."

"Okay, good luck. Have a nice day."

I closed the car door and headed for the front entrance. The place was enormous. At least, it felt that way to me. A two-story building for just high school? We had one floor and less than ten classrooms for everything from preschool to grade twelve at my old school. Just how many people went to school at this place?

I swear it felt like a jungle in there. There were people everywhere. It was nigh impossible to get anywhere without nudging or bumping someone.

At least it was the first day of classes for everyone. I'd be ignored in everyone's rush to say hi to all the people they didn't see over the summer, the question of the day being, 'What did you do over summer?'

I decided a week earlier that if anyone asked about my summer I would lie and say I spent it up at my family's cabin. Who would admit, in high school no less, to being in a psych ward for six weeks? My family didn't actually have a cabin, but I have an aunt who does, and we usually go up there for a weekend every summer.

I wasn't exactly keen on lying, but if my time in the ward taught me anything, it was that people would rather hear a comforting lie than the truth. Better a lie than ruin their welcome-back day with my depressing story, a story that would probably make me a social outcast.

I headed to my first classroom. My mom had grabbed me a map of the school when she registered me. I had taken some time to look at it. I didn't want to be using a map or asking for directions on my first day. No better way to show that you're the new guy than not knowing your way around.

Just walking through the hallways seemed all but impossible. It felt surreal having to twist and swerve my way through the crowd. I think I bumped into more people in the ten minutes it took to get to my classroom than I ever had in my fifteen years back in my hometown.

I was about to walk in the door when I smacked into a blonde girl wearing the same short shorts and tank top that half the other girls seemed to be wearing. She had green eyes and skin a lot paler than I would have expected. I thought all city girls tried to get tanned during the summer.

"Hey, watch where you're going!" she shouted, in a huffy, full-of-it voice. I had just bumped into one of the school divas.

"This guy bothering you, Sheila?" I heard a guy say as a hand clamped down on my left shoulder. I looked behind me to see who had grabbed me.

He was tall, over six feet, so, a solid half-foot taller than me. He was wearing a muscle shirt and shorts; overall, he looked like he was more prepared to hit the gym than the books.

"I was just trying to get to class," I said as I tried to walk past and get out of the guy's grip.

"Oh, leave the guy alone. Dressed like that he deserves a break at least once. I mean, plaid and a ball cap?" a brunette girl said, "he's got to be new to the city, if not the entire planet."

Should have known that the plaid shirt was a bad idea.

"Oh my god, I know, did he like come straight off the farm or something?" the blonde girl added.

I tried to slink away from the group, but with the big guy's hand still on my shoulder, I couldn't.

"So, what's your story, new guy?" the big guy asked, holding me tight so I couldn't escape.

"I'm Blaine. My dad got a new job in the city," I lied. My dad had not gotten a job yet, neither had Mom. We had just moved a couple weeks earlier so that I could go to a new school where no one would know that I'd been locked in the loony bin.

"What's he do?" the brunette said, trying to sound like she was nice and cared, but I'd been around far too many doctors lately who had to fake that they cared. I could tell when someone didn't actually care. She was probably hoping for me to say something that she could make fun of.

"He sells stuff," I responded, feeling bad for having to lie.

"What kind of stuff?" the brunette dug harder.

"Farm equipment, tractors, that kind of hillbilly-farm-hick stuff."

I felt dirty for saying it before the words even left my mouth.

They laughed for a few seconds before the jock said, "You're okay, Blaine. I'm Grant, this here is my girl Sheila, and her friend Natasha."

I nodded politely at all of them before slipping away to find a seat in the classroom.

"Catch you later," Grant shouted as he and Natasha walked off. Sheila walked into the room and took a seat, with a half-dozen other girls immediately flocking to her position.

There was a guy in the seat to my right who leaned over and said, "Just tangled with the queen bees, huh? Hope they didn't sting you too bad."

"Nothing too serious," I replied.

"Cool, I'm Jake. You new around here?"

"Yeah, actually just moved to the city a couple weeks ago."

"Yeah, you're kind of fresh off the boat."

I looked down at my clothes and said, "That obvious?"

"You look like you should be working the field. The only thing missing is a piece of straw in your mouth," he replied.

I was starting to think I should burn and replace my entire wardrobe. But as long as they were focused on my wardrobe they weren't digging into my past.

An older man, mid-forties or so, with a solid beer-belly entered the room. He was wearing a muscle shirt, blue jeans with a hole or two in them, and a blazer. I thought there was no way that this man was the teacher. He must have been someone's parent.

I took a quick glance over at Sheila and her posse, expecting some kind of snarky remark.

My mind blew a fuse when the first word out of any of their mouths was, "Wow, who is the *hottie*?"

I looked back at the fat man in the room, and then back to Sheila and her posse who were all checking him out. I tried to piece it together, but it just did not make sense.

"Does that guy look good to you?" I asked Jake

"What?" Jake said, his head spinning around like I had just asked him if he had ever dated a werewolf. He then said, "Dude, its cool if you're gay, but seriously, don't ask that kind of stuff."

"No, I'm just . . . ." I paused to collect my thoughts. "The divas seem to think he's good-looking, but all I'm seeing is an overweight, balding man."

Jake raised an eyebrow and said, "Okay, you need some glasses. Also—divas?"

"Isn't that what you call them?" I asked.

"Oh, you have so much to learn. You are not leaving my sight," Jake said as he patted me on the shoulder.

The supposedly attractive man went to the front of the room and said, "Hello, everyone, my name is Mr. Brown. I will be taking over this class for Mrs. Elms for the year."

"What . . . but she's on our syllabus," Sheila asked.

"I don't know, um . . . ."

"Sheila."

"Sheila, right. I'm sorry, but I don't know. I was interviewed for the job only a couple days ago. If I find out anything, I will let you know."

Sheila looked slightly disheartened, but nodded.

"Okay, so you have decided to embark on learning about journalism," Mr. Brown said to begin the class. "Uncovering the truth, no matter how daunting. It is an exciting field to be working in. And not the easy credit that I'm sure some of you were hoping for."

I was really looking forward to that class. I hadn't really made up my mind about what I wanted to be when I grew up, but journalist was in the top ten. Back in my hometown I spent a semester being taught science by a man who admitted he hadn't taken a single science-related course since he was back in high school. I guess in the city they can afford a specialist.

Mr. Brown was kind of cool. Still, it was weird that he looked different to everyone else.

Class ended when it felt like it had barely started. The bell rang and I was about to head out when Mr. Brown said, "Blaine, can I get you to stay behind for a minute to help me out?"

"Sure thing, Mr. Brown."

The door closed as Mr. Brown looked at me and said, "So, you are new around here."

"Does everyone know that?" I asked, slightly frustrated.

"I read the files of all my students, to make sure that I know about them and any concerns that may come up," Mr. Brown replied, "I'm barely started, but . . . ."

"But my last name is Allan," I finished for him.

I didn't want to hear where this conversation was going; I already knew.

"Blaine, I understand you were in psychiatric care for six weeks this summer. Is that correct?"

I didn't give him a chance to say anything else. I turned and headed for the door. No way was I going to let one of my teachers go all shrink on me.

"I'm sorry," Mr. Brown said from behind me, "I just wanted you to know that I am here if you need someone to talk to. Trust me, I can empathize with you more than you think I can."

I pulled the door handle and walked out. I didn't want to

5

hear anything more that he had to say.

Jake had been waiting for me outside of Mr. Brown's room. Together, we headed to second period. Sheila was heading that way too, with a chunk of her girl posse from last class still around, and a few fresh new faces to replace the ones that had left.

As we walked into the room, there was a projector that was displaying a picture of the classroom, all of our names on specific desks.

"A seating plan?" one of Sheila's friends shouted. "Seriously? We're not in the third grade anymore!"

"Totally," I heard another one of them say.

I couldn't really argue with them. Maybe growing up in a small town was different, but we never really had a seating plan.

The teacher walked into the room. She was into her late fifties and glared at all of us as she said, "Everyone will please take their assigned seats."

I was about to sit down in my desk when the teacher looked at me and said, "Hats are not to be worn inside the school!" She came over and ripped my hat off of my head and took it to her desk before I could even begin protesting.

But begin protesting I did. "Mr. Brown didn't mention anyth—"

"Mr. Brown should have made himself better acquainted with our policies," she replied as she shoved my hat into her desk, "You can have this back at the end of the day."

I ran my hands through my hair quickly, knowing that it looked terrible without the hat on, and I went to take my seat. There was a note taped to the top of the desk. It had on it each period of the day, the student to be seated in that desk for that period, our partner for paired work, and our group for group work.

"We don't even get to choose who we work with?" Sheila said, upset.

The teacher glared at Sheila and replied, "Ms. Bennett, you will control yourself in my classroom. Outbursts like that will not be tolerated."

I took a close look at my list. My partner for paired work

was the diva herself. Wonderful.

"We will begin the year by joining our partner and talking about our summers. You will then write a page about what your partner did for the summer."

Sheila looked at me, waiting. So I moved my desk over to her instead of her meeting me halfway.

"Well, I suppose this could be worse," Sheila announced. "You have at least some semblance of cool."

"Um, thanks," I said. "So would you like to—"

"No, you first."

"Okay," I replied. I started to think hard. I needed more details than just being up at the cabin. What else could I say?

"Well, I spent most of the summer out at my parents' cabin. I did a bit of water stuff, water skiing, wake-boarding, tubing, that sort of thing. It was pretty nice."

"Oh, do not expect me to write a page out of that. Where is the cabin; who was there with you? Details. This thing needs to write itself."

"The cabin was up at Emma Lake," I replied. "It's this nice but small place, two bedrooms, one for my parents, one for me, a bathroom, and an open living room and kitchen area. Not a lot of room for anyone who wants to stay inside. It also has a very nice deck and is lucky enough to be right on the lake. I know a lot—"

Sheila stopped me as she said, "My family has a home at Emma Lake too. And I've certainly never seen you there."

"It's a big area," I replied, cautiously.

She caught my lie. I had to come up with something fast. She was one of the last people I wanted to find out. It'd be all over the school before the day was over.

"Okay, it was my Aunt Mary's cabin. I just wanted it to sound cooler and say that it was my parents', but yeah, I spent most of my summer up there."

"Your aunt Mary? I literally babysat for her a couple times over the summer. Why are you lying to me?"

I didn't know what to do. Didn't know what to say to her. So I said nothing.

That was the wrong choice.

"What did you really do this summer?" Sheila asked me, slightly angry, and slightly inquisitive, like she was digging for gossip.

I wasn't going to tell her. No way. No chance.

"Okay, I spent the summer at my dad's farm, helping him out. Planting crops, getting ready for harvest, that kind of thing," I said. It wasn't too far from the truth. It is what I did for the week or two before I went to the psych ward.

"So you spent most of your summer outside, helping at your parents' farm?" Sheila said, pen at paper, ready to write.

"Yep."

"Then why don't you have a tan?" she asked.

I looked at my hands—they were very pale. Dang it. Now she knows I'm lying for sure. She's definitely not as dumb as she seems.

"I . . . ."

"Must be pretty bad if you're trying to lie about it," Sheila replied.

I clammed up, turned my head away from her, and said, "I told you what I did for the summer. Your turn."

She didn't take that well. But instead of arguing, she smiled and replied, "What I did for the summer is see a boy who was supposed to be at his aunt's cabin, but was constantly coming back drunk, or on drugs. His arms were full of holes from all the spots he had injected to shoot up."

"You wouldn't."

"Roll up your sleeves and show me I'm wrong," Sheila said.

I couldn't. While in the psych ward they had taken my blood a couple of times, for testing. And I had been given drugs a few times, to keep calm. 'Cause there were some nights where I did nothing but scream. The drugs helped. They made me stop thinking about everything crazy that happened that night. And everything crazy that happened since. If I pulled up my sleeves, she'd think she was right.

"No," I said, firmer than I expected. Why did this have to happen to me, I thought. I just wanted to try and get back to a normal life.

"Tell me the truth,"

I couldn't take it. I wouldn't let her ruin my life anymore than it had already been ruined. I grabbed her arm and whispered, "You want the truth? Fighting got me expelled from my last school."

It wasn't a lie. Not entirely.

She looked terrified. My first instinct was to apologize. But I couldn't do that. I needed her to be afraid of me. Afraid enough to stop digging into my past. I hated doing this her. But what choice did I have? I couldn't tell her the truth.

I let go of her. She started writing. She wouldn't say much of anything; my paper wasn't going to end up very good. But that was okay. I had dodged a bullet there.

Or so I'd thought. I knew that Sheila had been talking about me to other people, about how I had threatened her. I saw her group looking over at me at lunch. Fortunately for me, Sheila wasn't the type to tattle to a teacher.

Unfortunately, she was the type to tell her boyfriend.

At the end of the day, I was walking to the bus when Grant shouted from behind me. "You threatened my girl?"

I tried to ignore it and kept walking, but a quick glance over my shoulder told me that Grant and his friends were coming towards me. I turned around and looked them in the eyes.

Maybe I should have just walked away, but I decided to stand my ground.

"I don't want her spreading rumours about me," I said.

"So you threaten her?" Grant shoved me to the ground.

My instincts kicked in. I jumped to my feet and decked Grant right in the jaw. If he thought he could intimidate me, he had another thing coming. My arms were up in a boxing stance as Grant stood there in shock. My punch more of a surprise to him than actually hurting. I could see it getting red though, I'd be leaving a nasty mark at least.

"Not used to someone who fights back, huh?"

Grant's friends surrounded me. I couldn't hope to take them all. I started wishing a teacher, even Mr. Brown, would come and save my hide.

"STOP!"

My head whipped toward the sound, as did all of the football players'.

There was a thin redheaded woman in a green t-shirt with blue jeans, sneakers, and a small black leather jacket. She looked a bit like Sheila, but slightly older.

"Amber? What are you doing here?" Sheila said, stepping away from her girl posse and towards the redhead.

"Came to pick you up, sis," Amber replied. "Mom and Dad had to head out of town last minute. I see you're still dating this loser."

Amber's movement was swift. The crowd parted for her as she walked right towards Grant. She stopped less than three feet away from him.

She had certainly grabbed Grant's attention. While still holding me with one hand, he glared at Amber. "Get lost!"

"No," Amber replied, staring him down, "I think you're going to leave the boy alone."

"Or you'll do what?" Grant replied as he tossed me to the ground. I picked myself up quickly.

"Beat you up," Amber responded. She brought her hands up in front of her face and cracked her knuckles as she added, "again."

"Get her!" Grant's football friends went after Amber. The first one got a punch in the face and fell to the ground.

Grant was focused on me though. I was ready for a fight. But not the way he was going to fight. Covered in his football gear, he didn't throw a punch, he charged, ready to tackle me. But right before he would have made contact, I disappeared.

I reappeared a couple feet away.

Not again, I thought. It couldn't be happening again. It hadn't happened in over two months. Why was it happening again? I thought it had just been a dream, a hallucination.

I didn't have time to think about that. Grant took a swing at me and almost knocked my head off, but I disappeared again.

This time I was a good thirty feet away. Grant was getting angry, and confused. Though I can promise I was definitely the one more freaked out.

Grant charged at me again. At least, it seemed like he was charging at me. He was moving like he was in slow motion. But why would he be moving so slowly? Could I have been doing that too, like I had disappeared?

That was a question for another time. All I knew is that this was the opportunity I needed to win a fight against a football padded brute. So as Grant charged, I punched.

I hit him square in the chest. The punch dropped him flat on his back. He wasn't getting up.

Sheila screamed, "GRANT!"

She raced towards him, falling to her knees beside him, trying to wake him up.

I was ready to get out of there. I wasn't even looking at the crowd as I started walking away.

"Hey kid, want a ride?" Amber shouted at me, I saw that there were several guys on the ground around her. Guess she had won her fight too.

My bus was gone. So I nodded at Amber and headed for her car. Anything that would get me out of there faster than walking.

"Sheila, come on, we're leaving," Amber shouted. I cringed at the thought of having to be in the car with her, but I guess it would be worth it to get out of here.

The look on Sheila's face was one of pure hatred and disgust, "I'm not going anywhere with him!"

"Your boyfriend started the fight," Amber said, "Now get in the car or I tell mom your boyfriend started a fight. See how long he stays your boyfriend after that."

"You wouldn't!"

Amber pulled out her phone and pushed a button or two, Sheila was in a furious silence before she said, "Fine. I'll go."

She marched to the car, taking the front passenger seat. Arms folded across her chest, she refused to say anything.

I hopped in the back of the car. It was pretty clean. Cleaner than my dad's truck had ever been, anyways.

"Let's go," Amber said as she put the car in gear and drove off.

As we drove off, the fight kept playing again and again in

11

my head.

I had done it again. Disappeared and reappeared. And maybe even done something to make Grant move really slow. How did I do that? Why did I do that? And no one else noticed? What was wrong with me? Was I losing my mind?

It had all started with that night.

That night in the alley . . . .

No. Don't think about it. It wasn't real. You remember it wrong. You didn't disappear. None of that happened. You just won a fight, that's all. You're not crazy.

You're not crazy.

2| AMBER

I HAD NEVER FELT SO CONFUSED IN MY LIFE. NONE OF IT MADE SENSE.

The boy had used magic. A clear teleport. And the way he punched Grant? He was using time magic.

But that was impossible.

No one new to magic could do anything that powerful. They'd pass out. So he couldn't be new to magic.

But he couldn't be from Atlantis . . . .

I was the highest ranked mage in the province. I should have been told if any new mages had moved to my region. Had Atlantis simply forgotten to send me the details?

But that didn't explain my readings. I had scanned him the instant I saw magic. Nothing. I'd seen it show that a person doesn't have magic, but he didn't even show up. Like he didn't exist. But he was clearly there; it wasn't an illusion.

So how?

I knew my history. All mages are from Atlantis; all of the other magic cities were destroyed.

Just who was this kid?

"Thanks for helping me," the boy said as he leaned forward.

"Any time, I can't stand that Grant jerk," I replied.

"I'm Blaine."

"Amber," I wished I didn't have to focus on the road; I didn't like having to take my eyes off of him.

"My house is the other way," he said as I made a left turn.

I needed an excuse to not take him home. I needed to keep an eye on him until I could contact Atlantis.

"I was going to take you to our place," I said, trying to fill the silence that had been looming after his question.

I almost slammed my head into the steering wheel for the sheer stupidity of that line. I didn't want him at my house.

But, the acreage was isolated. As long as I kept Sheila away, there would be no witnesses.

I had a plan. I hated it, but I had a plan.

"You're taking him to our place? Why?" Sheila demanded.

We were at a stoplight, so I took a second to turn around and said, "Plaid gets me hot."

Sheila gave me a look of pure disgust. Typical, coming from her. Blaine? I think his eyes just about shot out of his head.

"Oh my God, pedophile much? He's like five years younger than you. I can't believe you would do this to me!" Sheila shouted.

Why did my sister have to be such a drama queen?

I didn't even turn to look at her, "And I can't believe that you would get back together with Grant. How many times has he cheated on you by now? I stopped keeping track after the time he made a pass at me."

"He's the captain of the football team! And I don't sleep with him!" Sheila shouted back at me, as if being a star football player was enough reason to excuse being a horrible person. Sometimes I just want to scream at her to grow up, but then I remember that I was exactly the same at her age.

"And that makes it okay for him to treat you like that? God, the fact that you are even dating a football player at all is just . . . !" Okay, I do yell at her. So sue me.

"Right, because I should be dating some slut I picked up at a bar. Oh, wait, I forgot; I'm not a lesbian freak."

I knew she didn't mean it. She was just trying to get a rise out of me. I wish it hadn't worked.

"Better a slut than a narcissistic jerk," I shouted back. "I did not spend three years at that school fighting against the holy football team just to have my sister get in bed with their saviour."

I wish I hadn't gotten so angry. I guess there were other things on my mind, like whether or not I had a ticking time bomb in the form of a teenage boy sitting in my car with me.

"Yeah, well, maybe I actually want people to like me. But I guess that's something you'd never understand," Sheila replied in anger.

"Oh, I did understand. But then I grew up. I just pray to God that you will too, Lord knows it's taking you long enough."

"Well, not everyone is going to 'see the light' like you did," Sheila said.

"Yes. But I didn't have a mentor—you do."

Sheila scoffed at that, but finally shut up.

We drove out of town in relative silence. Sheila steaming, Blaine confused, and me trying to keep it all together.

It felt like eternity had passed before we arrived at the acreage. I could see Blaine's eyes looking at it in wonder from the backseat. The place can almost seem like a mansion sometimes.

Before I could even get the car into park, Sheila stormed out, shouting, "I'm calling Grant."

Sheila stomped off with big deliberate steps as she walked up the stairs to her bedroom.

Well her leaving on her own sure worked in my favour.

I smiled at Blaine and grabbed his shirt as I said, "Come on, sugar boy, we're gonna make some magic."

I still cannot believe I said that.

Blaine didn't fight me as I dragged him into the house and upstairs to my bedroom. I could feel his head swivelling around a bit, trying to get his bearings and check out the place.

I followed his gaze. He saw the photos of my high school graduation, Sheila's cheerleading competitions, Dad's business deals, and clips from Mom's court cases. Dad always said that if you want to be successful, you have to keep constant reminders of your previous successes around. Beside every single one of the photos or clippings was a quote. They varied, but they all boiled down to one simple message: keep succeeding—keep working hard.

I could see Blaine get visibly nervous after one set of the family 'trophies,' the award for when I earned my black belt. I felt Blaine stop resisting after that.

I dragged Blaine into my room, and closed the door behind us. Blaine started looking around, deliberately avoiding my gaze. If he'd known I was on to him then he wouldn't take his eyes off of me.

My room isn't exactly girly. Yes, some makeup, a walk-in closet full of clothes, but other than that, nope. I had a bookshelf full of my textbooks and my own personal reading materials. Then there were the posters around the room. Dad hates those things. Blaine saw one of the posters in my room and looked down uncomfortably.

The poster was of a wedding cake, with two grooms at the top instead of a bride and groom. The line underneath said, "Does anyone object?" My dad wanted to rip that poster down, but I was pretty firm about getting to keep my space the way I wanted. It's still a bit of an ongoing fight, because he 'doesn't want that kind of filth' in his house, and I refuse to let him control how I express myself. Half the time I expect that he wants to throw me out of the house for how much my beliefs don't align with his, but he also believes in family above everything else.

Blaine looked at me, awkwardness all over his face, "So, um, I, uh . . . ."

He was stammering! It was hard to believe someone like that could be dangerous. But he was, and I could not forget that.

I locked the door to my room. Now I just had to hope I was strong enough to deal with him and get some answers.

"Okay, Blaine," I said, "how do you know magic?"

Blaine's body twisted around. His face had the stupidest stunned expression I had ever seen, jaw dropped, eyebrows raised.

"What?"

Fake surprise wasn't going to fool me.

"At the school, you teleported. How?"

Blaine's eyes widened, a level of innocence in them that could not have been sincere. "You saw that? So I'm not crazy?"

Did he actually think he could convince me that he didn't know about magic?

"I don't know what kind of game you're playing, but it ends now," I stepped towards him.

He tried to get past me, to the door. I wasn't going to let that happen.

I threw a punch at him. Before it could connect, he vanished and reappeared on my bed.

"Where did you learn that?"

"I didn't," he almost shouted, "It just happened!"

"You're lying," I said, my fists clenching. "No can do that kind of magic by accident."

I thought back to high school, back to the time I was sent to the principal's office for my article in the school paper, and how strong I was when I stood up against him. Passion and strength, the cores of my best magic. I opened my left hand and a fireball formed out of thin air.

"How did you . . ." Blaine started to say, his eyes transfixed on the orb.

You'd think he'd never seen someone conjure a fireball before.

"Like you don't know. You're not leaving until I get some answers. Who do you work for, and what do you know about Atlantis?"

"Atlantis? I was just hoping for a ride home. I don't know anything about magic or Atlantis, and I'm not really okay with the whole sex thing either."

He almost sounded believable. But what he said couldn't be true. The magic he used takes months to learn.

I thought back again to my investigation at the school that led to that article in the first place. Digging out the truth, the core to another of my magics. I used my detection magic, felt the room around me, the flow of the air, the sound of my heartbeat. I focused, listening for the sound of his heartbeat, to see if it was racing too fast for him to be telling the truth.

There was nothing there.

But that was impossible. I could see him. But my magic couldn't. I couldn't feel his heart beat, couldn't feel him breathing. Like he wasn't there. I'd never seen anything like it.

"I just want to go home," Blaine muttered.

"Not happening. Not until I know my sister is safe."

"But don't you hate your sister?" Blaine asked. Spoken like a guy without siblings, or a sociopath.

"The people you love can drive you crazy," I thought to when Sheila became a cheerleader and started dating Grant. How she cried on my shoulder because Grant had cheated on her, only to forgive him the next day because 'he's the star of the football team. He gets to do what he wants.'

My fireball diminished until there wasn't even a spark in my hand. Stupid, amateur, rookie mistake. I had let myself get caught up in a memory that didn't focus my magic.

Blaine saw that the fireball was gone and he raced for the door again. He rushed me, hoping I would get out of the way or something. I threw a punch.

He disappeared again.

My watch beeped. It was about time someone from Atlantis got back to me. I took a look at who was on the other end. It was an older man in a decorated military uniform, gray hair, but in no way balding, and with a face just starting to show wrinkles. Emanuel. As if the day hadn't been hard enough already.

"Amber, what business do you have using the emergency frequency?" Emanuel asked. Sexist, ageist pig. I've never seen him give trouble to any other warden, but because I'm female, and one of the ten youngest wardens alive, he gives me grief.

"I have a situation," I replied, trying to remain cordial. "A boy with magic who I can't scan or detect."

Emanuel replied in the condescending tone of a teacher reprimanding the student they hate. "The emergency channel is for real emergencies, Amber. This isn't something to be joking around with."

I started to think about that time with the principal again and almost burned the watch in my sheer frustration.

"As the ranking officer in my region, I demand to speak to a superior about a potential threat and security breach."

Emanuel laughed, "This sounds like just another one of your crazy ramblings, Amber. Like that one about mind-wipes causing permanent mental damage."

He cut the call. I swear if anything happens I am holding that old man responsible.

Blaine was opening the window. I don't know where he thinks he could go, we were on the third floor. He would break his legs if he tried.

Except he could teleport. I tossed a fireball. He teleported and the fireball hit the wall, starting the curtains on fire.

I cursed and quickly pulled the flames off of the curtains.

I spun around to see Blaine behind me, running for the door. He opened it and raced out of the room.

I ran after him into the hallway and down the stairs. He wasn't going to get away. I couldn't let him.

I tossed a fireball at him in the middle of the hallway.

"Oh my god, what did you . . . how did you?"

I turned around to see Sheila in the hallway. I'd spent the last six years being careful with my magic and I had just screwed it all up. How could I have been so stupid?

They would have to wipe her memory. I couldn't let them. Not my sister. I couldn't let them mess up her mind like that.

I had to fix all of it before it was too late; and to do that I had to stop Blaine. He couldn't escape.

Sheila had her cell phone in her hand. She shouted, "I'm calling 911!"

"NO!"

I pulled the flames off of the walls, into a fireball, and made it disappear. Sheila's knees buckled and she fell to the floor.

"How did . . . ." she started to say as she tried to get back to her feet.

She didn't get a chance to finish. "No phone calls. Go to your room and pretend none of this ever happened, Okay?"

"But . . . ."

I recreated the fireball, and tossed it at Sheila, stopping it about a foot from her face, "Okay?"

Sheila nodded, terrified.

"Good," I pulled the fireball away.

I raced after Blaine, down the stairs and towards the front door of the house.

The door was already open and I could see Blaine running to the highway. He was moving too fast for me to catch him on foot.

But I had to catch him. He knew too much. He had to be stopped.

3| BLAINE

SHE THREW FIRE AT ME. I COULDN'T BELIEVE IT. COULDN'T UNDERSTAND how she could do it.

There was no time to get an answer though. I needed to get out of there before she burned me to a crisp.

I ran as fast as my legs would carry me. Faster than I had ever run in my entire life.

I ran to the main road, tried to signal for help, only for a car to whiz past me.

I kept running down the road as I tried to get the attention of oncoming cars. But there weren't any. The road was dead.

Finally, I heard the sound of a car coming. I had to pray that this car would stop for me. I turned around to try and grab its attention . . . only to realize it was Amber.

I ran off the road straight into the bare empty field beside it. Amber followed, driving after me.

I couldn't look back, not when I needed to be running. I cursed the field for being so barren. There was nothing to hide behind.

It was getting very hot. Suddenly the field looked different, sounds seemed to be coming from my left. I had teleported again.

I looked over where I was. The earth was scorched, and the grass was on fire. I glanced back and saw Amber, one hand out the driver's side window tossing fireballs at me.

I could see a patch of trees ahead, probably half a football field away. It wasn't much, but it was the only thing I could hope would stop her.

I could hear her car getting closer to me and I felt it getting really hot again. Then the heat was gone. Another teleport.

Now there were a couple of trees off to my right. Nothing

too huge, but hopefully big enough to stop a car. I ran for them.

Amber's car sped at me, and she tossed another fireball. I turned around just in time to see the fireball coming, and then be completely out of the way. Teleported again.

Amber's car rammed into the trees. One of the trees fell over and toppled onto her car. Amber opened her door and tumbled out to safety, her eyes glowing with flames.

Now that she was on foot, I didn't think I'd have any problems. I could teleport and she couldn't. I was going to get away.

I ran for it. I was pretty sure I could outrun her, but that didn't mean I could slow down.

A fireball nearly fried me, sending dirt up in its wake.

But this latest fireball had shot down.

I looked into the sky. Amber was there.

She could fly. Of course she could fly. Because why would anything actually work in my favour?

My old plan came back. That patch of woods would be a good place to hide. She'd have to burn the whole thing down or come in after me. I could lose her in it.

I kept running, fireballs hitting the ground around me, shooting up dirt and grass and ashes. I started to cough and covered my mouth as I kept running.

I finally made it into the trees and took a moment to catch my breath. I needed a plan.

A fireball shot right by my shoulder, smashing into a tree and setting it on fire. Sparks trickled down to hit the ground, lighting up dry leaves and twigs.

She was on foot in the forest. The trees made it difficult for her to be flying.

It was time to see if I could get this magic to work for me for once.

I focused on trying to get time to slow down like it had before.

And it did work . . . kind of. She seemed slower. But not by much.

In the time it took her to raise her hand to shoot a ball of flames, I tackled her.

"Leave me alone, I don't want to hurt you!"

"You're lying!" she shouted back in slow motion.

I was sitting on her chest, trying to pin down her arms. As I did, her body started to burn me.

She was trying to light herself on fire. I let go of her arm and was about to punch her in the face. But I stopped myself. I wasn't going to hit a girl.

I jumped off of her and bolted out of the woods.

That might have been one of the stupidest things I ever did. She was going to kill me, but did that change whether or not I was willing to hit her? Nope, not in the slightest.

She wasn't moving slowly anymore, my spell had worn off. But I had a head start on her, and I was pretty sure I was faster than her on foot.

I was wrong.

Amber's hand reached out and grabbed my shoulder, I felt her yank me to the ground. I didn't teleport away this time. Why didn't I teleport? I really, really wanted to.

This time she was on top of me, sitting firmly on my stomach.

"Looks like even you have some limits," She placed a hand on my chest. I started to feel sweaty and thirsty. I tried to teleport, but all I could think about was that it was so hot.

I grabbed her arm with both my hands and tried to push her off of me. With one solid push, she fell to the side.

She was already in the air though, and I felt her foot in my face before I saw it.

I fell to the ground, my jaw hurting, my lips red. I spat some blood out of my mouth and looked over at Amber, who had taken up a fighting stance as she hovered six inches off the ground.

"I don't need magic to take you down," Amber said.

I struggled to get back onto my feet.

Before Amber could strike again, a white flash came from the distance.

"Stop!"

There was a group of nine people approaching us. They were wearing white jackets with hoods up. The jackets had two flaps on the back that went down to the knees while the front stopped at a proper shirt length. Along the length of the arms of each one were gold stripes of varying amounts from three to six. Each jacket had a stripe going diagonally down it from right shoulder to belt, and for each of them the stripe was a different colour.

The ninth and final man looked similar, though his outfit looked far more formal than theirs. Where theirs had a diagonal stripe, his had a gold and red symbol that took up his entire torso. It looked like a dragon. The man had lightly-tanned skin and black hair and brown eyes.

"Amber, report," the dragon-crested man said.

Amber paused and landed carefully. She was nervous. That could not be a good sign.

"General Cabrera, I . . . he doesn't show up as having magic."

General Cabrera glanced over at me, pushed a button on his watch, and nodded.

"I didn't know what to do," Amber continued, trying to sound official but clearly scared. "I called in, and I was just laughed at and—"

Cabrera had a calm expression on his face. "I know. You were not briefed for this."

"Not briefed? This has happened before?" Amber asked him.

"Yes," Cabrera said, "Now both of you, listen up."

I had no idea what was going on, but no one was attacking me, so I figured that was a good sign. "Uh, does this mean I'm not going to die?"

General Cabrera chuckled at that. "No. You are not going to die. Cortez, see to their wounds"

The man with a black stripe approached me. He placed his hand on my cheek. I felt a weird tingle on my face, and my lip healed. I put my hand to it and there was no blood there.

"What the . . . ." I shouted in shock. I felt fine. Even my breathing was fine, and I had been running like mad.

"Cabrera—" the man in light blue started to say.

"Not now, Ramirez."

"But," Ramirez continued, "There is a car approaching."

Reaching the edge of the woods, a car that was probably worth more than my parents could ever make in three years came to a stop.

"Why aren't we stopped?" Cabrera demanded, shouting at Ramirez.

"I don't know, sir. But I suspect it's him." Ramirez pointed at me.

General Cabrera looked at me with a look of deep scrutiny on his face as he said, "He's disrupting your magic?"

"Yes."

Cabrera walked over to meet whoever was in the car.

Sheila stepped out and shouted, "Oh my God. What is going on here? Amber, you totally trashed your car. And you did that thing with the fire . . . and who are these people?"

"Johnson," Cabrera commanded, "do it."

The man in purple approached Sheila.

"What are you doing? Stay away from me!" Sheila shouted.

Amber flew faster than ever before and took up a position between Johnson and Sheila.

"Please don't do it, she's my sister!" Amber cried.

"She has seen too much," General Cabrera said as he put his hand on Amber's shoulder.

Sparks came out of Amber's hands. She looked ready to fight. She also looked terrified.

"You know how unreliable these things are, General. Even with the best telepath, there is still a chance that the person will become mentally unstable!"

Cabrera glared right in Amber's eyes. "Johnson is an expert. Nothing will happen. Now stand aside."

One of Cabrera's men shouted. "Wait. A mind-wipe may not be necessary."

The General glanced at the soldier clad in pale green. "Explain."

"She has the spark."

General Cabrera raised an eyebrow and said, "Are you certain, Madhava?"

"Yes," Madhava responded.

General Cabrera moved past Amber towards Sheila.

Sheila trembled, and curled up into a ball beside her car as she said, "I don't know who you are, but my dad will make you pay if you hurt me."

Cabrera pushed a button on his watch. Everyone was silent until he said, "It is there. But we've never accepted someone with a spark of magic so small before."

"But it's her choice," Amber said triumphantly, "She has the spark. She can learn magic if she wants to."

General Cabrera examined Amber with the face of a skeptical parent. He looked like my dad does when he thinks I'm about to do something very stupid, but not stupid enough that he needs to stop me.

"Very well. Men, return to base. Amber, give them their orientation. But first, you need to be debriefed."

Cabrera gestured to me and so I walked over and stood beside Amber. I wasn't really comfortable with that, who would be comfortable standing beside someone who had tried to kill you minutes ago, but I was trying to make sense of it all.

"Blaine here is what we call an aberration."

My lips reacted before my brain did, "So even among people with magic I'm the odd one out?"

"Yes."

That felt absolutely great. I finally got an explanation for all the weird stuff that happened to me only to find out that, even among people with magic, I'm the freak.

"What makes him so special?" Amber asked.

"As an aberration, he will be far better at magic than anyone with his amount of training should have," Cabrera began.

"Doesn't feel like I'm good at it. I just keep bouncing around." I muttered.

"Most people take months of training to do what you are already doing," Cabrera said, "Assuming that Amber's report was accurate."

It took me a moment to process that. I was already as good as someone who had been training for months?

"Any other differences?" Amber asked, her voice calm and respectful. Deference coming from her did not seem right. I'd seen her room and her attitude; treating someone as her boss wasn't her.

"Yes. An aberration is only gifted at one school of magic. But they have mastery over it, no one can use the same type of magic around them unless they allow it. At least, that's how it is with our other aberration."

"Our other?" Amber asked.

"There is only one other known aberration, probably because they are utterly undetectable."

"Would I know them?" Amber asked.

"Better than anyone else I'd imagine. The other aberration is Drake. Your Ex."

4| SHEILA

So, I OFFICIALLY HAD NO IDEA WHAT THE HELL WAS GOING ON.

My sister had thrown a fireball at me. There were these weird people in white who just disappeared. And they all were talking about magic like it was real. It was just too weird for me.

Something else had to be going on, and I had a hunch I knew. Blaine had roofied me. That's the only thing that made sense. There was no way magic was real.

"This isn't real. This isn't real. Wake up!" I said to myself, pinching my cheeks to try and snap out of it. That hurt. But who knows how things are supposed to be when you've been roofied; not this girl.

My hallucination of my sister glared at me. "Sheila, this isn't a dream. Now get in the damn car."

"Nuh-uh," I said to her, "I'm not going anywhere with him."

For a second, I thought that maybe I wasn't going crazy. But wouldn't my crazy-acid-trip hallucination of my sister act just like I think she would?

Blaine headed for the car and got in the backseat. He was just sitting there, acting totally normal. It didn't make any sense.

Amber grabbed me and looked me straight in the eyes with her 'serious-business' face. "Magic is real. I've been learning it for over five years—and now you get to."

"What if I don't want to?" I muttered as I let my sister walk me to the car.

"You know what," Amber said, raising her hands in the air and walking to the driver's door of my car, "I don't care. This is not the time for you to be a whiny, entitled princess, so get in the car and shut up."

I got in the car, taking the front seat. I grabbed the rearview

27

mirror and turned it so that I could watch farm-boy the entire time. I wasn't going to let him do anything to me.

Amber sighed as she started up the car, even though it was mine and I should be the one driving it. Who cares if all I have is my learners license, it was like some kind of emergency.

Amber tore through the field and got back on the road. She glanced at me and farm-boy as she said, "Magic stays a secret. If I don't clear someone, you do not tell them about it. Got it?"

"So what," I shouted, "you're our boss?"

Amber smiled, the smile that tells me I won't like what she's about to say.

"Well, I think guardian or mentor would be a better word. But yes."

My eyes literally burst out of my head. I wondered if there was a spell for that.

"Oh no, no way," I said, crossing my arms and taking a look back at farm-boy to make sure he wasn't up to anything, "You don't know the first thing about anything."

Amber's voice was in that, like, calm anger she gets when she is trying to not explode on me, her hands gripped the steering wheel so tight that I thought she might break it. "I am the most powerful and educated mage in the province and am, thus, the warden here. I have been for the entire last year."

"Warden . . . how many magic people are there?"

Amber turned the car into the driveway to our home, "About one hundred thousand worldwide. Seventeen in province, including you two."

"So when do we get to meet them?" I asked. "At least some of them have to be cool."

"If by cool, you mean at least ten years older, then yeah," Amber replied with a smirk. God, I hate it when she smirks like that. "The youngest other mage in the province is twenty-seven."

"You're the youngest, and in charge?" Farm-boy asked. I wish he'd just shut up, he was talking like way too much.

"Age doesn't mean much when it comes to magic," Amber turned back to look at Blaine, right as she was heading into the garage. She wasn't even watching where she was going.

"You're gonna crash my car!" I shouted at her, overtop of

whatever useless drivel she was trying to say to the psycho farm-boy.

Amber hit the brakes, gently, and the car stopped, like, perfectly. And she was being completely reckless with my car, so you know it's a big deal when I say it was perfect.

"How did . . . ." farm-boy said, surprised, "You weren't even looking."

"I took a couple classes on detection magic. I'm pretty good at sensing what is going on around me without needing to look."

"So what," I said, "you're like Santa Claus, 'see's you when you're sleeping knows when you're awake' and all that?"

"I'm not that good," Amber replied. "But sure, something like that."

No wonder I couldn't get away with anything around her. She, like, knows what I'm doing even when she's not looking. Big sister? Ha, more like Big Brother, constantly watching and controlling your life. I wonder if that show is still on, I haven't watched in years.

While I was sitting in the car, going over the horror of this discovery, Amber had already opened the door to the house, stepped in, turned around, and flashed an impatient 'are you coming' look my way.

Farm-boy was calmly and quietly walking inside. I could not understand why he was so calm. My sister had tried to kill him; you'd think he'd be out for revenge.

That shifty jerk was just biding his time. I was sure of it. Well, I would be watching him. And he wouldn't do anything, not with Amber here. I felt pretty confident he couldn't beat her. Besides, she'd know before he does anything. I guess that her seeing everything could be useful sometimes, even if it was, like, a total invasion of my privacy.

Amber walked into the living room and took a seat in Dad's favourite chair.

He wouldn't like that. Nobody's supposed to sit in his chair. Not that it really stops anyone. He can be so uptight sometimes.

Amber gestured for Blaine and I to sit. On the same couch. There was no way that was going to happen. Blaine took a seat on the far corner of the couch.

"Sit," Amber said, talking all forceful and demanding.

"No way, not near him," I said.

Amber sighed, and then a fireball burst out of her hand and shot toward my face.

"Sit down," Amber said, in that 'I am tired of dealing with your bull' way that she had perfected.

I took a seat at the other edge of the couch. The fireball shot back towards Amber. She squeezed her hand around it and it disappeared.

"Going to Atlantis is...complicated," Amber began.

I couldn't help but laugh. It just kept getting weirder and weirder. Magic was real, and you only had to go to the lost city of Atlantis to learn how to do it—right alongside the money-growing trees in the enchanted forest of flying pigs.

"Is something funny?" Amber snapped.

"Yeah," I said, "you can't seriously expect me to believe that you are getting trained in *Atlantis*."

Amber started to hover above the couch and said, "You have no problem with me flying. But when I say that Atlantis is the last of the great cities of magic, you think I've gone too far?"

"The last—" Farm-boy began before Amber cut him off.

"I wasn't around. I don't know the details, and the government seems to keep them pretty close to the chest, but apparently there used to be a dozen or so magic schools. There's only one now, Atlantis."

"Why would they keep that a secret?" Farm-boy asked.

"'Cause Atlantis practically runs on secrets," Amber said, a bitterness to her tone, "They keep so many records private and personal, if they even keep these things on record at all. It's part of why I've been working so hard to become one of the best mages. Under Atlantis' archaic system, those who know magic best are more likely to be placed into leadership positions, without any requirements on actual skill as a leader half the time, and those leaders get to know more of the truth than most people. I didn't know about aberrations until today, and I used to date one!"

Talk about being right under your nose. Guess my sister wasn't as Big Brother as I thought.

"Should we even learn magic then?" Farm-boy asked.

"Yes," Amber said, "You know about Atlantis, so they'll wipe your minds if you don't become a resident. Besides, if you can overlook the fact that you're living under a secretive dictatorial regime, Atlantis is a nice place. Most people are friendly, there's plenty to do, and you get to learn magic. The government just really sucks."

"Doesn't the government always suck? I mean, that's what Dad always says," I said.

Amber laughed, "Yeah, I guess so."

"What would happen when we go to Atlantis?"

"We get you into training." Amber replied casually.

"Whoa, I'm in grade ten, and have cheerleading, and a boyfriend, and, like, a social life, though I know you don't understand what that actually is. I don't have time to be taking another class on top of all of this."

Amber grinned. "Fortunately, time is something we don't have a problem with."

"What do you mean?" I asked.

"Thanks to Time magic, and a healthy dose of technology and know-how, the city is in a completely separate time bubble. Every day you visit Atlantis and stay in the city for twenty-four hours, only five seconds will pass by in the real world. You also don't age when you're in Atlantis. Learning magic means you get to live two lives, and you get to live much longer, one life here, the other in Atlantis."

Having two lives sounded pretty awesome. I could, like, have extra time to practice my cheerleading and become really good at it. Or, have more time to do my homework so that I don't fall behind. This magic stuff was weird and freaky, but if it actually gives me more time, then it would be great.

I must have been smiling and hadn't noticed, because Amber said, "Yeah, extra time really comes in handy. Big exam coming up—extra study time in Atlantis. Falling behind on your magic training? Find a private place and get in some practice in the mundane world."

"Yeah, that does sound nice," Farm-boy said, acting all nice. I was surprised he hadn't made his move. Wasn't he going to attack? Or had he realized that he can't mess with my sister, so he was going all spy and pretending to be a goody-good?

"So, what else is there to say?" Amber said, more to herself than to me or farm-boy. "Oh, right. Atlantis has people training in magic from literally all over the world."

"All over the world? So wait, if you take in everyone with magic, don't you have, like, terrorists?" I asked, my mouth reacting before my brain could catch up.

"Mildly racist, but a reasonable question," Amber replied. "We keep an eye on people. We don't bring in anyone with any kind of criminal behaviour. We also don't tolerate any kind of racist behaviour or anything like that in the city."

"What, you jail people for being racist?" I asked.

Amber looked a touch uncomfortable and wouldn't meet my eyes.

"They do mind-wipes, don't they?" Farm-boy asked.

Amber looked at farm-boy and nodded. "Yes. You don't treat your fellow citizens with respect and dignity, they wipe your memory of magic and Atlantis completely and send you back to your normal life."

"How dangerous is it?"

"Dangerous enough," Amber replied. "Look, we don't have perfect studies on it. Some say that one in every hundred people who has a mind-wipe performed on them has something go wrong and they go mentally unstable. I've heard rumours that as many as half of the people in psych wards around the world are people who had a mind-wipe done on them that didn't take well."

That's totally creepy.

"That's why you didn't want them doing it on Sheila?" Farm-boy asked, as if he was actually concerned for me.

"Exactly. The government keeps mind-wipe records confidential," Amber replied.

"Golly, a secret magic world that keeps secrets from its people, who would have guessed?" I replied.

Amber ignored my quip, like she had every single time I saw something that she didn't want to talk about. "Now, what do you say you see this world for yourself?

"It's almost six. At six, I am going to be teleported to Atlantis for a day, and will reappear back here in five seconds. That's how it works. Everyone around the world enters at the exact same time. Now, if you want to grab onto me, then you can join me in Atlantis. You'll get your first look at just what the city is like."

"And when we get back it'll be like no time has passed?" Farm-boy asked.

Amber nodded.

Well, I definitely wanted to see what all the fuss with Atlantis was about. Maybe the place would actually be cool. I grabbed my sister's hand and Farm-boy carefully placed his hand on Amber's shoulder.

Six o'clock came a couple seconds later, and we were gone.

5| BLAINE

THE TELEPORT TO ATLANTIS FELT DIFFERENT FROM ANY OF MINE. IT took longer. I know that sounds weird; how can you tell that disappearing and reappearing somewhere else takes longer? But that's how it was.

I blinked a few times when I arrived, as though the rapid change in scenery was taking a couple seconds to register. Like how it takes a few seconds to focus after you just went to sleep.

As my eyes started to focus again, the first thing I saw was Amber and Sheila. Then the background started to come into focus.

Where could I even begin to describe what I saw? It was like every building ever built was all in one place.

There were skyscrapers, new ones that looked like they were made mostly of glass, older ones with statue and stone architecture. Flanking them you could see a pyramid. I kid you not. There was literally a pyramid. To my right, there was a castle out of the Middle Ages jutting into the sky a couple blocks down. There was even an ancient roman coliseum. Then there were townhouses, malls, and small corner shops.

It felt like an odd mishmash of buildings, yet somehow, it all flowed together.

And the roads! They looked normal, but there was not a single car. I saw a few people run by, running as fast as a car.

A quick glance upward showed me people flying around. Not all of them the way that Amber had though. In fact, many of the people flying around seemed to have something on them, like a weird metallic backpack, or a hover board. And there appeared to be traffic lights in the sky and proper lanes that people were supposed to fly in.

"Aren't you worried that people might fall and die?" Sheila asked as she looked up.

Amber walked us to the corner of the nearest building and pointed at a hollow black glass crystal, about as big as my head, imbedded in the building wall, "This takes care of it. Just watch."

Amber pointed at a skyscraper across the street where a door, not a window, opened up on the twentieth floor and a man stepped out. I was sure he was falling to his death with how fast he was falling. But when he was just a couple feet from the ground, he stopped almost entirely, and he delicately landed on the ground and walked off like it was nothing.

"We can put our magic into a vast assortment of objects. And with those objects, people can do things that they are not able to achieve with their own magic."

"Like using a hover board to fly?" I asked.

"Among other things," Amber said as she clutched at her necklace.

"Oh yeah, you got that necklace like a year ago. What's it do?" Sheila asked.

Amber looked at it and said, "It's a self-control crystal. It keeps my mind my own."

"Wait, people could be, like, reading my thoughts right now?" Sheila sputtered, aghast. "I, like, need one of those right now!"

"Nobody is going to care much about the minds of new students. Besides, self-control crystals are very hard to make. It took me forever to get one. Now come on, I need to get you both your watches."

We followed Amber to the pyramid. It looked like it was just made yesterday, instead of looking as old and ancient as you would expect a pyramid to look. I was about to walk in the door when I heard Sheila scream.

I turned my head immediately, ready to deal with whatever danger was approaching, and noticed that the air around me was shifting and felt a little weird.

I then realized that Sheila had screamed because she saw some clothes in a shop window across the street. Great. Sheila ran over to the building, "Ooh, can I buy some stuff here?"

Amber looked exhausted as she followed. She grabbed Sheila's left arm and started to drag her back.

A woman stepped out of the store. She started speaking, and Sheila just looked confused.

I couldn't hear what anyone was saying, so I moved closer.

Sheila stammered, "What the . . . what's she saying?"

The woman raised an eyebrow. Amber raised Sheila's arm. "New student."

The woman nodded and said something, which I also couldn't understand, but it seemed clear the woman could understand Amber.

"Come on, Sheila,"

As they came back towards the pyramid, Sheila asked, "What just happened?"

"I told you there are people from all over the world here and it didn't occur to you that some don't speak English?"

"How can we get taught if we won't understand each other?"

"Your watch has a universal translator. It will even translate text. But it only translates for you—it doesn't make everyone else understand you. So both people need a watch to communicate."

A universal translator? And hover boards? I wasn't sure if I was learning magic or going to a space academy.

Inside the pyramid, there was a lot of open space with plenty of seating and an impressive desk with an older lady stationed behind the hand-carved and sleek mahogany. Amber led us forward. "Hi there, I have a couple of newcomers. I need a pair of watches."

The receptionist raised an eyebrow. "Two at once? How odd."

The woman walked off to get the watches, her heels clacking on the marble floor.

"Oh, before I forget," Amber began, "I should tell you rule number one about the watches."

"Oh, what's that?" I asked.

Amber looked at me, then at Sheila, to make sure that she was paying attention. She was, for once. "The watch is your way into or out of the city. Take care of it. Should anyone lose their watch, you must help them get back to Atlantis."

Sheila looked at me and said, "So, if farm-boy here loses his watch, I have to help him? Sheesh, as if."

A head or two in the lobby turned at those words. Amber grabbed Sheila and pulled her over to the side of the building. I followed. Amber whispered, "Listen up and listen good. That is one of the most important rules in our society. If you don't comply, the city will banish you. And you know what banishment means."

"A mind-wipe."

"Exactly. I don't want that to happen. Even suggesting you would refuse to help a fellow mage is cause to consider banishment. You are on ridiculously thin ice right now. You haven't proven your loyalty to the city, your willingness to keep its secrets, protect its citizens, or anything. You will be watched, and I mean watched closely." Amber turned her head towards me and narrowed her eyes, perhaps a bit worried. "Especially you, Blaine."

""Cause I'm an aberration," I commented, sighing inwardly.

I heard the clacking of heels on the floor. The receptionist had returned with our watches. She had two small white boxes in her hand, about the right size for a watch, and not much else.

"You have to leave the watches on at all times," The receptionist said as she passed them to the two of us. "This button enables the watch to look how you desire. You can have it look like a bracelet, a watch, a tattoo, or even make it look and feel like it is not there. You will feel a pinch when you put it on. That is the magic of the watch connecting and registering you as its user. It will not work for any other wearer."

Amber smiled. "Alright, lady and gent, strap them on."

I pulled the watch out of its box and placed it on my arm. My eyes bulged. I blinked, and Amber was nowhere to be seen.

"Right behind you."

I spun around to see Amber almost at the door already. "How did?"

"The watch takes a few seconds to set up. You stood there, eyes bulging, mouth wide open. Here," she pulled out her phone, "I took pictures."

Sheila and I looked at the pictures. "Oh my god, I look

terrible, delete it!"

"Never," Amber replied, laughing as she pulled the phone out of Sheila's reach.

"Give it here," Sheila shouted, trying to reach for the phone.

Amber backed away and pocketed the phone. "Please," Amber replied, "I have way worse photos of you than this."

Sheila was pretty angry. How petty can you get, worked up over a couple lousy photos?

"Come on," Amber said, as she led us out of the building, "I want to show you something fun. Maybe get you flying. So, follow me ple—"

Amber stopped short. I looked at her for an explanation.

I should have just looked forward.

There was a man standing in our path. Early-twenties, probably, older than Sheila and I, at any rate. Maybe around Amber's age. Clean-shaven, with black hair, and his eyes were a deep blue. He was wearing a simple black outfit, black dress pants and a black dress shirt. He smiled. Felt like the smile was directed more at me than the girls.

"Hello," the man said as he walked over to us.

Amber was not pleased to see this guy. She stepped in front of Sheila and I and created a fireball in her hand. "Get lost."

The man laughed at the fireball. "Such a wild temper on you, isn't there? I would have said fiery, but, well, that would have been too obvious."

"You heard me the first time—get lost," Amber repeated, the fireball growing in size.

"I'd rather not," the man replied smoothly as he approached, "After all, your friend Blaine and I have much to discuss."

"Leave Blaine alone," Amber replied, placing herself in front of me.

"No," the man said, "Now please, let me talk to him."

"I said no," Amber created a fireball in her other hand, "Leave him alone Drake."

Drake . . . General Cabrera had mentioned that name. Drake was the other aberration.

That's why he wanted to talk to me. I kind of wanted to talk to him, too. Get some answers about just what I am. But if Amber hates him, maybe I shouldn't talk to him.

Drake chuckled as he stared at Amber's chest. I thought he was just being rude until he said, "Nice pendant. Blocks all mind control and mental suggestions, I'd wager?"

"Tired of having people in my head," Amber replied coolly. "I'm sure you can understand why."

Drake shrugged, "A good idea, in theory, but it needs to be more secure. And perhaps better hidden."

The pendant's clasp came undone, and the pendant shot through the air and into Drake's waiting hand. He held the pendant and said, "My, my, this is quality work. Not an easy thing to make. Probably took a few months of crafting just to make this little gem. Now, I know your daddy is rich on the outside, but your money doesn't count for anything here. How did you get it?"

"A friend," Amber replied, her voice terse, angry.

"And how many times did you have to spread your legs for this friend to actually help?"

I decked him.

Drake fell to the ground, a hint of surprise evident on his face, "Huh, chivalry isn't dead, then. Didn't expect someone to defend your . . . hmmm, well, I would say honour, but I don't really think you have any."

I was shaking, but Amber almost looked bored. "More than you'll ever have," Amber replied. "I still don't understand why they don't banish you. Or is it that they don't want to banish an aberration? Is that the secret you've had all these years?"

"Oh, trust me, they want to banish me."

Then why wouldn't they, I thought. And then the pieces clicked in my head. He had used some kind of telekinesis, and Amber was pretty specific about not wanting people in her head, "Your aberration is mind magic. Telepathy, telekinesis and probably mind-wipes. If you're like me, then no one can use your type of magic against you. You literally can't be wiped."

Amber's eyes widened briefly, and her fireballs went away. "So that's why you're still in this city. Well you'll toe over the line soon enough."

"You doubt my ability to charm people," Drake replied, walking over to her now that her guard was down.

"You, charming? Don't make me laugh."

"I was charming enough to get your pants off once or twice. Oh, wait, never mind—that's not hard to do," Drake said dismissively as he passed Amber's pendant back to her.

"I was young and stupid. I grew up."

"Yes," Drake said, "Now you're older, and stupider. Aren't you one of the crackpots who started the whole 'mind-wipes are harmful movement'?"

A fireball flared to life in Amber's hand. "I'm telling you one last time . . . get lost."

"No. I want to talk to Blaine," Drake said, crossing his arms.

"I don't want anything to do with you," I said to him.

"Oh, I doubt that," Drake began, taking a step towards me, "You are just itching to find out what aberrations are like. And I am your only peer in that arena. But, let's not take my word for it. Let's look into your head and find out."

He reached towards my forehead.

Amber tossed a fireball at him. It bounced away, like an invisible wall was protecting Drake.

I tried to stop time, or to teleport, but it didn't work. Drake forced his hand onto my forehead. He seemed focused on something, but nothing happened. I grabbed Drake's arm and pushed him to the ground.

"Don't do that again, ever," I said to him.

Drake looked at me, then at his hand, and said, "That was interesting." What a piece of work. He completely ignored that I had shoved him, or that he was on the ground. He was absorbed in his thoughts as he stood back up and looked at me, wonder and excitement in his eyes.

"What?" I asked, because my curiousity got the better of me.

Drake got to his feet and dusted off his pants. "My magic didn't work on you. I can't get in your head. Now that was a worthwhile discovery. I wonder if that will hold true if other aberrations are ever found? Are we incapable of affecting one another? Fascinating."

Drake turned around and walked away. He shouted back at me, "Blaine, thank you. Today was most educational. Come find me when you decide you want to know more about being an aberration."

6| BLAINE

AMBER WAS DETERMINED TO MAKE SURE THAT MEETING DRAKE WAS not the impression we had of Atlantis. So it was less than twenty minutes after that encounter that I found myself in a driving range sized dome, strapping on a backpack that was supposed to let me fly.

"How does this even work?" I asked, taking a look at the backpack Amber was still carrying.

"Someone else infused it with flight magic. It has to be recharged if it gets used too much though. It's not easy to alter an object to accept magic, but once it has, anyone who knows the right type can recharge it."

"So you could refuel these backpacks if you wanted to," I asked.

"Yeah," Amber passed Sheila a backpack.

"I want a hover-board," Sheila said, not taking the pack, "Come on, I use a snowboard all the time at the mountains, and I know how to use a surfboard and a wakeboard too. I can handle a hover-board."

"Backpacks are for beginners, company policy" Amber replied, and shoved it in Sheila's face. "Trust me, I'm just as good with a snowboard as you, hover-boards are not like that."

Sheila griped a little, but eventually said, "Fine."

We stepped out of the lobby and into the dome proper. There were a few other people around flying. Some were up really high. As the dome went higher, the colours on the wall changed. It started off in red, then went to orange, yellow, green, blue, and violet. The red zone ended about twenty-five feet off of the ground.

It was then that I realized that both mine and Sheila's

backpacks were red.

"Come on and get up here," Amber said as she let herself hover up ten feet off the ground.

She didn't need to tell us twice. I jumped into the air, hoping that I would fly. And I did. I was flying. Or at least, hovering where I was. It felt a touch different from what I expected. The backpack wasn't dragging me around with it, it was letting me control the flight as though I was the one with the power. I shot upward, and then my bag stopped. The rest of my body came to a jerking halt, because the bag would not budge. I looked over at the wall and saw that I was at the top of the red zone. I thought about going down a couple feet, give myself some room, and the backpack was quick to do it. I started off moving slow, but then I got the backpack moving faster and faster. It wasn't all that fast, I could probably go faster on my bike, but it was fun. I was flying! Sheila and I collided a couple of times while flying before we learned to try up and down instead of always going left or right to try and avoid crashing into each other. But, man, was it fun to fly.

Before I knew it, Amber was telling us to come in so that we could have lunch. Which seemed odd, 'cause we had arrived closer to suppertime.

"Look at your watch. We came into Atlantis at six in the morning. Your body adjusted for that."

We ate lunch at this brilliant café, Small World. Small World served every food you could imagine, and then some, several times over. The lunch menu by itself was pages long. It would be the restaurant of nightmares for an indecisive person.

Amber leaned back in her seat, replete after her bowl of shrimp scampi. "I'm glad you got to have some fun this morning, because this afternoon is going to be the most fun of all. Paperwork."

"What?" I could feel the excitement leaving my body, a slow scream ready to erupt.

"The next Intro to Magic class starts tomorrow, and I want to make sure you're both in it. So, paperwork."

And, unfortunately, aside from a break for a nice supper, paperwork was the rest of the day. Filling out forms about family history, if I had any relatives with magic, a detailed account of how I was discovered, the list just went on and on. I was actually relieved to just lie down on the floor for the night when it was over. Sheila and I were stuck spending the night at Amber's small place, and she only had one bed and one couch. Sheila was quick to grab the couch. Not that I would have let her sleep on the floor, regardless of how annoying she was.

I woke up back in Amber and Sheila's house, sitting on the couch, like we hadn't even left.

"So, hope you enjoyed your first day, in spite of all the paperwork. You'll be starting classes tomorrow. Come on, Blaine, I'll give you a ride home."

I didn't argue.

The ride home was particularly quiet. I'd already figured out that Amber was not the type of person to act all childlike and excited around.

My parents were a little surprised when I finally made it home.

"Blaine, where have you been?" My mother asked as I came to the door.

"I made some friends today, we hung out," I said, trying to sound casual, "I thought it wouldn't be a big deal. I made sure I was home for supper."

"You made some friends? Already? Well, that's great! Your father and I have made some friends as well. Father Orson from the church will be coming by for supper on Saturday," my mom said, and didn't ask anything else as she went to go and finish making supper. Not surprised she didn't ask anything else. After the last few months, my mom wants to believe I'm fine. She won't question anything that makes it seem like I am.

Dad was a bit more skeptical, but he didn't want to push it either. I'd wager he would have asked more questions if Mom wasn't around, but he never wanted to worry her.

Over supper, they asked how my first day of school was, and who these friends of mine were. But, after Atlantis, trying to talk to my parents about my day at school over supper wasn't the easiest thing in the world. How can you make math and journalism sound interesting when you were attacked and run

44

down by a flying girl tossing fireballs, shown a mystical lost city, told that magic was real and not only are you going to learn it, but you are going to be one of the best there is? Going to regular old high school sounded like a prison sentence now.

I didn't sleep well that night, my mind far too focused on magic. I would start learning magic tomorrow. Who could sleep with that on their mind?

The next day Mom dropped me off at school. I must have been fidgeting in the car a lot, because she asked me what I was so excited about.

"Uh, no reason," I lied.

I slipped out of the car and headed up the sidewalk. I grabbed Jake as I headed in. "Hey, how you doing?"

"Not too bad," Jake said as he patted me on the back. "You? Everyone knows what you did yesterday. I hear the principal is downright furious that you hopped in a car and raced off."

"Oh great," I said, sarcastically. In all the hassle about magic I had completely forgotten about the fight I'd been in the day before. Well, two days before for me.

"How did your parents deal with it?" Jake asked.

"Huh?" My parents hadn't mentioned anything to me. I guess they hadn't been told. The principal probably wanted to see if he could deal with this before he had to call anyone's parents.

Speaking of the devil, the principal stuck his head out of the main office when I neared the doorway. "My office, now." he said, waiting for me to step in.

I sighed.

Grant was already there and he looked fine to me. There was a woman standing next to him, older, probably his mom. "So, this is him? This is the monster that hurt my boy?"

Oh, great. Grant was one of those kids: they act all tough, but if someone stands up to them, they have an overprotective parent they can whine to.

"Shouldn't my parents be here for—" I started to say, but

the principal cut me off, "Blaine, when we let you into this school it was under the assumption that you would behave differently than you did at your last school."

From the door, a voice said, "He did, Grant started the fight, and Blaine did nothing but run away until Grant showed he wouldn't back down."

That wasn't what had happened. Grant shoved me, and then I punched him in the jaw. I didn't run away. Who would say that? And why would they lie in my defence?

Mr. Brown stepped into the room, a laptop in his hands. Oh great, now he was lying to save me and try to make me forget that he read my files and tried to go psychiatrist on me.

"I have the security camera footage of the incident," Mr. Brown said, flipping open the laptop and pressing enter. A video of the fight started playing. It showed Grant shove me. And then it showed me scared on the ground, getting back up slowly, and trying to walk away. It showed Grant come after me, and had Grant stumble and fall when I dodged his tackle. But that wasn't what had happened. I punched Grant. Twice. Yet the video didn't show that.

Grant's mom exclaimed, "He punched my son!"

"Cameras don't lie, ma'am," Mr. Brown replied, "And the video shows no evidence whatsoever that Blaine fought Grant in any way. He tried to leave the fight, and simply dodged when Grant charged at him."

Grant's mom was absolutely livid, "Are you calling my son a liar?"

The principal was very apologetic in that moment, "Of course not..."

"Your son's account of the events does not match what the video shows. So, yes. Your son is lying," Mr. Brown replied, cutting off the principal, "In fact, with this video as evidence, Blaine should be the one bringing charges against Grant.

There was absolute fury in Grant's mom's eyes, and a look of shock on Grant's. Our eyes locked for a moment and the look of shock on his face turned to anger. I could tell from his eyes that he blamed me for why the video wasn't showing what it was supposed to.

"I have never been so insulted in all of my life," Grant's mom said, furious.

"Miss," the principal said, standing up, "I believe this issue has been resolved. You and your son may leave now."

Grant and his mother stood and began to leave. At the door, Grant's mom turned and glowered at us all. "This isn't over."

Mr. Brown nodded to the principal and said, "Hope that settles that."

Mr. Brown left the room. I looked at the principal, waiting for permission to leave.

"Go..." the principal said, more exhausted than anything.

I raced out the door after Mr. Brown. I needed to know what he had done. How had that video shown something that had never happened?

"How did you . . . ." I started to say as I walked down the hallway behind Mr. Brown.

"I was in a similar boat when I was your age," Mr. Brown said. "Never did anything wrong, but the popular kids picked on me, and when I pushed back, I got punished instead of them. It felt really good to be able to stop that from happening to someone else."

"But that video...it wasn't what really happened."

"I know," Mr. Brown replied as we stepped into his classroom, "It was magic. But a student of Atlantis should know all about that, right?"

My heart stopped. My breathing halted. How did he know about that?

"Relax, Blaine," Mr. Brown chuckled. "Is it that weird that I know magic?"

I thought about it, and it helped make sense of a few things.

"Is that why you look different to me than everyone else?"

"You see through my illusions, because we aberrations cannot affect one another" Mr. Brown replied, "Try looking again, and this time, focus on the fact that there is an illusion to see."

Cabrera had said that Drake was the only other aberration. To have Mr. Brown say that he was one too didn't make any sense. Regardless, I tried to see the illusions he claimed he had; and I finally saw what everyone else was seeing. A man in his mid-twenties wearing a classy suit, and looking like he should be a movie star more than a teacher.

"Why didn't Amber tell me about you?" I said, "She's the warden for the area, she's supposed to know everyone in the area who goes to Atlantis."

Mr. Brown gave a small chuckle as he rested his chin on one of his hands. "You didn't really think that Atlantis was the only magic city, did you?"

I felt time stop. Not magic. Just my brain freezing up. There was more than one city of magic? But Amber had said Atlantis was the last one. It made no sense.

But it did answer one question.

"That's why Amber doesn't know you? Why no one mentioned that one of my teachers knows magic . . . because you are from a different city?"

Mr. Brown nodded as he said, "Yes. New Asgard is a smaller city. Atlantis doesn't even know we exist. Which is why you weren't told about us."

My mind slowly caught up to me. I realized that there was something not right about this.

"You knew about my magic before I did, didn't you? You killed Mrs. Elms, the woman who was supposed to be my journalism teacher."

Right after the words left my mouth, I realized how stupid I was for saying that out loud. If he had killed Mrs. Elms, then what would stop him from killing me?

Fortunately, Mr. Brown had a look of genuine shock on his face, as he shouted back, "No I didn't!"

"Well, you did something to her, all to get at me. What do you want with me?"

Mr. Brown held his hands up in a defensive gesture as he said, "I want to help you. Look, you're right. I did manipulate myself into this position. We mentally altered Mrs. Elms and set her and her husband up by giving them their dream jobs. She had wanted to run an inn on an island resort in the Caribbean ever since she visited one on her honeymoon. Now she does."

I didn't know how to feel about that. Is it right to alter someone's perception of reality? Right to make someone think

48

their life is something it wasn't until then? Even if that something was their dream job?

Then again, Atlantis banishes and mind-wipes people just for disagreeing with the law.

Neither sounded perfectly moral. Neither sounded good. Was magic worth learning with all of this involved? My parents had always told me that there was right and there was wrong. I didn't like all of this 'shades of gray' stuff.

"How do you want to help me?" I asked.

"I want you to switch schools. I want you to join our city."

I was already registered in Atlantis, so I felt I kind of owed them. But I guess it would be nice to have a backup plan.

"Okay . . . so, what's the speech?"

Mr. Brown smiled and said, "We believe in using magic to make the world a better place."

"And Atlantis doesn't?"

"Atlantis believes in magic for the sake of magic. They believe in not interfering with the real world. They just want magic to be something you do for fun, like a hobby in another world or something you use when no one can possibly notice," Mr. Brown said, walking over to the door to respond to a knock he had heard. After telling whoever was at the door to wait a minute, he came back to me.

"So they don't interfere? What's wrong with that?" I said, deciding to stand up too.

Mr. Brown sighed. "The Holocaust, Chernobyl, Nine-Eleven."

"What about them?" I asked, fearing the answer.

"Atlantis mages predicted all three of those events months, if not years, in advance. And because of their noninterference policy, they did nothing. They could have stopped World War II, Chernobyl, Nine-Eleven. They could have stopped them all from ever happening, and by doing so, eliminated part of the reason for the war on Iraq. No, not could have. They should have stopped those things from happening."

My mind seized up there. Some mages could see that far into the future? And they wouldn't do anything to try and change what they saw? That couldn't be right. If they knew something

49

bad was going to happen, they would act. I wanted to be sure of it, but I was starting to have doubts.

"My city does not believe in non-interference. We are small, just under twenty-thousand people. But we believe that magic should be used to protect the world, to make it a better place. We believe that those who have magic ultimately have a calling—a calling to be guardians of the world."

I liked that idea, being a guardian. Helping people who need help. Why learn magic if I can't help people with it?

"So, tell me, are you interested?" Mr. Brown asked, extending his arm to offer me a handshake. He detected my nervousness, put his arm down and said, "You don't have to decide right now. Take your time. I just wanted to make the offer. Let you know that Atlantis is not your only option. Let you know that there are people who disagree with the way Atlantis does things, and are using magic the way it was meant to be used."

I was about to head for the door, I needed some time to think, when I realized that I needed to be in this room for my next class. "Yeah, I just need some time to think about this."

"Of course," Mr. Brown said, "I'm going to guess that you will be going for your first lesson in Atlantis today?"

"Yeah," I admitted cautiously, wondering how he could know that.

"Well, how about this. You spend your first day with them, and this evening you and I can meet up and I will give you some more details about New Asgard after you have experienced more of Atlantis firsthand. No pressure. We'll even meet somewhere public. How about at this mall?" Mr. Brown whipped out his phone. "They have a lovely indoor mini-golf course. What do you say?"

I wanted to say no. He had been hiding what he looked like to other people. And that can't be a good thing. At any rate, it didn't seem like very normal behaviour. Then again, Amber did try to kill me. Perhaps I should hear him out.

"Okay," I said, "I'll be there."

"Excellent," Mr. Brown said as the bell rang to start class for the day. "Seven O'Clock."

7| SHEILA

ENTER NATASHA, BREEZING INTO THE CAFETERIA LIKE SHE OWNED THE place. Temporary queen bee. For the thousandth time, I cursed the fact that I was only a sophomore. She was totally glaring at me. She snapped at me, her face pinched as she rudely asked, "What's wrong with you?"

"What?" I said, pretending to not know what was going on.

"You went with your sister and that loser after they beat up our boyfriends."

"In case you haven't noticed, I don't exactly have control over my sister, like, in the slightest. I know I'm not the only one of us who has a totally lame sibling. Isn't that right, Val?"

"Hey, my little brother is a total dweeb, but at least he knows to act like he's not related to me at school," Val said, totally slinking back and not wanting to have to pick a side in this fight.

"Yeah, well, that's 'cause he's a younger sibling," I said, crossing my arms. "Try being the younger one. They never listen to you."

"Look," Natasha replied, sitting down and speaking in that mind-numbing, bossy tone. "You have to do something about her. Get some dirt, threaten her, I don't care. The guys are embarrassed and we can't have that kind of morale on the football team. Besides, you're not looking too hot yourself, leaving with them."

I wanted to scream. At Amber and that stupid farm-boy for everything they did, and at Natasha for using this as an excuse to knock me down a peg. 'Cause she and I both know that was the only reason she was making this tough for me.

"What dirt could I possibly have on her? She's already out of the closet."

Natasha didn't even look at me as she replied. "Figure something out. If she causes any problems again, you're off the squad."

I almost laughed. There was no way she could back up that threat.

"Off the squad? Natasha, you're barely half the cheerleader I am. I've been doing this stuff for years, longer than any of you. You couldn't hope to win without me, and Coach knows it."

Natasha looked bored. "So she'll find drugs in your locker, or maybe when you do a flip, someone will mess up trying to catch you."

I couldn't believe what I was hearing. I grabbed my stuff and stormed out of the cafeteria.

I raced to the basement. There's a broom closet down there that the janitors never use until after school, and they never bother to lock it. It's the perfect place to go when I need some alone time.

I slid into the closet and cried. Amber was ruining my life. All of this magic junk wasn't worth that. I pulled out my phone and called her. "Hey, Amber, don't pick me up today after school." I meant it to sound angry. How dare she ruin my life with her stupid magic. But I'm pretty sure she caught a bit of sobbing in my voice.

Amber sighed heavily into the phone. "The broom closet?"

Stupid, she was the one to tell me about this hiding spot in the first place. Why did I even call her? It wasn't like she cared about me at all.

"Yeah."

"What happened?"

I don't know why I told her. I mean she was the cause of all of my problems. Things wouldn't get any better, not with her as my mentor.

A mind-wipe might not have been a bad idea.

"I just, I can't believe my friends would do this to me," I said, holding back tears.

"Natasha isn't your friend. Not if she's making threats like that," Amber replied, "And the others, well, if they're more concerned about staying popular than defending a friend, then screw them."

"She said she'd kick me off the team . . . ." I said as I tried to get comfy in the broom closet. Not an easy thing to do, but I curled up and it wasn't too bad.

"And that would be bad, because—wait, don't answer that. I get it. You're good at this stuff, the flips and splits and whatnot. You know, I'd bet you could get into a gymnastics course or two if you wanted. Heck, I bet you'd be pretty good at it."

I hissed quietly into the phone, "You think that's going to solve everything? Just go join gymnastics? I've wanted to be a cheerleader my whole life. I'm not giving it up. You're ruining my life."

I could feel Amber's impatience over the phone, "Look, I'm not going to apologize for defending Blaine, or for thinking your boyfriend is a jerk. But if you want me to stay away so you can protect your reputation, then fine, I'll do it. But make sure you're alone at six."

"Fine," I grumbled as I got out of the closet and headed back upstairs. I wiped the tears off and slipped into a bathroom to check my face and make sure it wasn't too red. I was fine, so I stepped out of the bathroom and dropped back into the cafeteria.

"Okay," I calmly said as I took a seat, "it's dealt with."

Natasha looked skeptical, but all she said was, "Spill it."

"Huh?" What could she want now?

"If you've dealt with your sister, what's your dirt on her?"

"None of your business, that's what," I said angrily, she was really trying to put me in my place. I couldn't give her an inch, she'd totally take a mile right now.

"How do we know she won't come back?" Natasha huffed, insisting on being a total pain.

"Because I said she won't, and I've never broken my word to any of you. Which is more than most of you can say."

I looked Natasha right in the eyes, daring her to step up or say something. But I had her—and the rest of them. While all of them were constantly lying about why they missed practice, cheating with each other's boyfriends and whatnot, I was the one that wasn't backstabbing the others, and all of them knew that.

Natasha left it alone after that, but I could see from the look in her eyes that I was on thin ice. Not that I was surprised. Pulling the holier-than-thou card was only going to work for me once. I just hoped I hadn't wasted it.

The rest of the school day went by slowly, and not just because I was excited to learn magic. I was constantly checking to see if one of the girls was watching me. I caught the rest of the girls talking at least twice without me around and they went silent when I approached. Twice they were clearly talking about me. Great.

After school, I was about to head out, get myself ready for learning magic in a few hours, when Grant came by. He was in his football uniform.

I dashed over and gave him a kiss on the cheek, like a good and dutiful girlfriend.

"Hey, babe," Grant said as he put his arm around me.

"Hey, hot stuff," I said back to him, giggling a little bit. The giggle was fake. Not like he knew the difference, though.

"What are you doing here?" I said. "I didn't see you at lunch."

"Just got here, couldn't let the team down," Grant said.

"Wow, that is so noble of you," I said, the words rolling off my tongue easily enough even though I didn't believe them.

Truth is, I don't love Grant. Not in the slightest. But he's the star quarterback, and he chose me. I can't really stay popular if I turn him down. And hey, he's not completely horrible. I mean, he tried to defend me against Blaine when I thought Blaine was trouble. And he is here for the football team, even though he totally did skip all of his classes today. Not that his coach will care, or the principal, or anyone, really. Isn't that the stuff my sister was always whining about?

"Hey, babe, stick around and watch me practice. We'll grab some food after."

Ugh. Watch him practice? Don't get me wrong. I love to watch the games. But practice? Gag me now.

But I didn't say that. I said, "I'd love to, Grant, but I have to get the house cleaned and everything. My parents are back in town tomorrow, and I did throw that big back-to-school party at my place. If I don't get that cleaned up, I'll be grounded for so long that I'll be lucky if they ever let me go to a game."

It was a lie. My parents weren't coming back for a week. And I'd told Grant that a few days ago. Not that he actually listened.

"I thought your parents weren't coming back for another week?" Grant said.

He actually listened to me before? Colour me totally impressed.

"Come on, babe," Grant begged. "That won't take you that long. Stick around. We'll grab dinner and a movie afterward."

Translation: we're gonna go to the restaurant he wants to go to, I will pay since I have the rich parents, then I'll pay for us to go to a movie which we won't actually watch 'cause we'll be making out and he'll be groping me the entire time. Totally want to pass on that. So glad he graduates this year. I am so totally going to dump his ass and find myself some nice piece of meat on the football team to take his place.

Watching him practice was so boring, but I cheered and did all that stuff that makes him happy. Can't have Natasha and the other girls thinking I'm not helping out team morale.

Then Grant took me to the same old place that was stupid expensive for crap food. I honestly don't know why he loves it so much. I swear, it's like the fact that the food is expensive makes him think it must taste good. What an idiot.

We had taken a seat at the table and were about to order food when my phone buzzed.

I pulled it out of my pocket to take a look. My sister had sent a text: We jump in 5. You ready?

I looked at the time. Dang, it was 5:55, I totally forgot that I was going to vanish in five minutes.

Okay, well, this is a fancy restaurant, the washroom won't be too bad. I looked at Grant and said, "I'll be back in a minute."

"That better not be that dumb sister of yours," he said. He's gotten that way around her even before she beat him up. I was tempted to tell him that it was none of his business, or so what if it was my sister. Or even tell him that only I got to call my sister dumb. Instead I lied.

"Nah," I replied, "Just Mom. You know how she worries."

Grant laughed and said, "Yep, okay, go talk to her. I'll get you a salad. Chicken, right?"

Ugh, maybe sometimes I don't want a stupid salad. I wanted to shout at him that I do eat normal food, like a human being and all. It was a small consolation that while he was using me, I was using him, too.

I walked into the bathroom and headed for one of the stalls. At least they were clean.

I sat there, waiting for a couple of minutes for the magic to kick in. I was so glad that there was nobody around. It was kind of a miracle that there was no one in the bathroom with me. That would have been terrible, have someone banging on the door to the stall, only to look down and not see anyone there. I swore that I would never be stuck in a bathroom stall during teleport again.

That was my last thought before I arrived in Atlantis, waking up to find myself on the couch in Amber's apartment, farm-boy sleeping on the floor less than ten feet away.

"Where were you?" My sister demanded, as she walked in.

"With Grant," I replied.

She rolled her eyes, but didn't say anything.

"I checked with the head office, and your apartments are ready. I'm going to take you to them now."

Had I really filled out paperwork for my own apartment? It all seemed like such a blur, there had been so much paperwork yesterday.

"They're not very big," Amber said. "Well, certainly not compared to what we have, Sheila. It's basically a one bedroom apartment. But it's yours. You should already have a bed, a table and chairs, a desk, and basic amenities like a stove and fridge."

I'll admit it, I loved that I was going to have my own place here. Somewhere to be away from Blaine, my sister, and everyone else.

"Aren't we a little young?" Blaine asked as we walked to

our places.

"We don't take people under twelve to learn magic, and even at that age, we're okay giving them their own place."

Amber led us into the lobby of a totally fancy hotel. The ceiling went up, like, three floors and I could already see off in the corner that there was a weight room and a swimming pool. Oh man, I do not go swimming anywhere near enough these days.

"This one is yours, Sheila," Amber said as she passed me a card key, "and this one is yours, Blaine."

I took a look at the keys. We were neighbours. Both on the second floor. Why couldn't I get away from this loser?

Amber took us up the stairs, 'cause why would we ever use an elevator? She brought us to our rooms. I took my keycard and opened the door to mine. Amber came in with me to take a look around while Blaine walked over to his own room.

It was awesome. Yeah, Amber was right. It was pretty small, but hey, I don't need a lot of space to have a me-zone.

"I could stay here all day."

"Doubtful," Amber said.

"What, why not?" I asked.

"Well, why would you miss class?"

"I don't know, maybe I'm sick or something."

"Call the healers, have them come by and fix it," Amber replied as she walked over to the phone in my room. "Seriously, Sis, have I been sick even once in the past five years?"

No, she hadn't. It felt like my mind was playing catch up as I realized that living in Atlantis would mean that I would never be sick again. Atlantis just kept getting better and better.

"Now, I need to go show Blaine his place. Do you want to chill here for a bit, Sheila, maybe get some sleep?"

"But I'm not . . . ." I started to say, right before I yawned. "What the?" I said.

"It's six in the morning, the watch adjusts your body for that" Amber replied, "I'll show Blaine his place quickly and then I'm gonna crash for a bit. 6 A.M. is not a time that should exist. Get to the school by 8:30—you don't want to be late."

Amber left me alone in my room.

I crashed into the bed and smiled. My own place away

from everyone. A place to recharge from all those annoying girls and my stupid boyfriend.

Who cared about the magic? Having my own place and the extra time was what rocked.

8| BLAINE

I ARRIVED AT THE FRONT ENTRANCE TO THE SCHOOL AT 8:30 SHARP. There was no way I was going to be late to learn magic.

The school was massive, more like a university or college campus than a school. There were at least a dozen buildings, and they were all at least six floors high—most of them more. And once again, the architecture was all over the place, from glass wall skyscrapers, to stone buildings with gargoyles and lion-head stone work, to a stadium, and a castle.

Amber and Sheila were already there. Sheila was rubbing her eyes like she had just gotten out of bed.

"Good," Amber said, "at least, I didn't have to go and get you." She looked pointedly at Sheila and then said, "Follow me."

Inside the first building was a slightly futuristic feel. Not like a sci-fi movie, but like, you're used to every building you are in being years if not decades old and yet this building felt like it was brand new and innovative design. The floors were a sleek marble, and every wall seemed to be glass.

Walking up a flight of stairs, we arrived at a classroom that I could already see into thanks to the clear glass walls. There were four people already in the room and desks for about a dozen people total.

"I see that half of the class is already here. Feel free to mingle," Amber said.

Sheila and I took a skeptical look around the room. Mingle? Easier said than done. Sheila and I were easily the youngest two in the room.

There was an elderly woman in a simple robe, her dark skin rich with wrinkles. There was an overweight man with a full head of black hair. He looked to be about Mr. Brown's age, if I had to guess. There was a professional-looking Asian woman who looked to be in her thirties or so, wearing glasses. Not too professional though, more like a teacher. The last person in the room was a dark-skinned man in a green military uniform. He was even wearing the formal military cap. On one of his shoulders I saw an American flag. He was also the person here closest to mine and Sheila's age. I'd put him at maybe mid-twenties. I don't know much about military symbols, mostly just what I've seen on TV, but I was pretty sure he wasn't the lowest rank.

Sheila took a look and muttered, "I, like, having nothing in common with any of these people."

Amber nodded as she glanced over the sheets on the clipboard in her hand, "We've got a typical crowd here, you two are probably the only ones under twenty. Oh, no, I was wrong, there is a girl from Brazil who will be joining the class. She's the same age as you. Her name is Jasmine."

"And everyone else?"

Amber scanned the list again and replied, "Late thirties, at the youngest. Jasmine and Mr. Military back there are the only two even close."

I figured it was better to just jump in instead of waiting around, so I grabbed a seat in the back right beside the military fellow.

"Hello, I'm Blaine," I said, offering a handshake.

The look he gave me had me reconsidering talking to him. Like he was analyzing me. I didn't like it, I got too much of that back in the psych ward. After a second or two that felt like an eternity, he smiled, shook my hand, and said, "Matt."

"Hi, Matt, you excited for this?" I asked, trying to drum up a conversation, and knowing in my head that I was kind of sucking at it.

Matt glanced around the room instead of at me as he said, "Still trying to figure out if I'm dreaming. Magic being real just seems too ridiculous. They told me it's been around for thousands of years, but I find that hard to believe. Secrets get out, no matter how hard you try to keep them."

"Oh, well, they use magic to wipe the memories of anyone

who knows about this place but shouldn't," I replied, trying to be friendly. "At least, that's what I've been told."

"Hmm . . . ." Matt looked me up and down again. "Still in high school?" He was changing the topic. I hoped I wasn't doing that bad at chatting.

"Yep, grade 10."

"Country?" Matt asked. I could tell that he was trying to be polite, but it felt like he was drilling me at the same time. There wasn't enough of a casual tone to his words, too formal.

"Canada," I said, "from Saskatoon."

"New York City," Matt said, going back to looking around the room at the new students who had popped in.

I tried to bring the conversation back, touching the symbol on his sleeve, "I don't know my military very well. What rank is that?"

"Senior Airman," Matt replied, his eyes continuing to scan the room, "I've been with the Air Force for three years now, joined right out of high school."

I glanced up to see Sheila talking with a girl around her age. The girl pointed over at Matt and I and started to walk over to us. Sheila did not seem happy with that, but she put on a fake smile and followed behind the girl.

"Hey, guys, this is Jasmine. Oh, and I'm Sheila," Sheila said, directing the latter part to Matt.

I said hello and Matt nodded a greeting.

"I'd heard the class would have people of any age and culture, but I don't think it really hit me until now," Jasmine said as she took a seat beside us.

"Yeah," Sheila said, clearly wishing that Jasmine hadn't walked over to join us. "My sister told me that everyone else in our class is, like, in their late thirties, at the youngest."

A bell rang to let us know that class was supposed to start. But there wasn't anyone else in the room, just Amber and us twelve students.

"Alrighty, class, I guess it's time we get started," Amber said as she stepped up to the front.

Sheila's eyes bugged out of her face, and I'd wager mine did the same. She was going to be teaching us?

"Where is our teacher?" the older businessman asked.

"You're looking at her," Amber replied.

There was a murmur from several of the other people in the room, a murmur that was capped off by one man, a middle-eastern look to him, who said, "I will not be taught by some western whore."

My fist tightened at the whore comment. I didn't care who this man was, you don't talk to someone else like that.

Matt saw and whispered, "Don't."

Amber glared at him as if daring him to challenge her, "If you have a problem, there's the door. Of course, right outside are several mages ready to wipe the mind of anyone unwilling to follow Atlantis law. Your choice."

"This is an outrage."

The man stood up and headed for the door.

When he opened it, a pair of men dragged him back into the room. A woman came in, placed her hand on his forehead and said, "He would rather take the mind-wipe than be taught by you."

Amber shuddered, turned away and said, "Then get on with it." You could tell from her voice that she was angry, but that she didn't think she could do anything about it.

I didn't see anything, but suddenly the man screamed, louder than I have ever heard anyone scream in my entire life. I clutched at my desk and bit into my tongue to stop myself from screaming alongside him. A muffled yelp still managed to escape my lips, and it was accompanied by the screams of almost everyone else in the room. Matt being the only stoic face to what just happened.

When it was done, the man was unconscious, maybe dead? Amber looked at the two men holding him down, a look of disgust on her face. "I trust you will send him back home?"

The men carried him off. Amber took a moment to compose herself before she said, "First rule here in Atlantis: you leave the rest of the world at the door. We don't care about your religious beliefs, political opinions, gender, sexual orientation, whatever. When you are here, you follow our rules. I don't care if your country is at war with another country, it stays out. We don't tolerate hatred or bigotry here."

Everyone in the room was trying to avoid Amber's fiery and passionate gaze, looking down, out the window, at each other, anywhere but at her. I could almost feel a cold sweat coming over me as Amber glared, and I'm pretty sure I wasn't the only one. Without realizing it, my hand started to clutch around the tiny crucifix that I wore around my neck under my shirt. I thought about Amber's place, that poster about same-sex marriage. My parents had always told me that kind of stuff was wrong, and I'm not too sure what I think about it. Could I get kicked out for that?

Amber could read the room pretty well, and after death glaring us for a few seconds she relaxed and smiled at the class, "Relax. No one's perfect. The fact that you're all staying is a good first step. It either means you're going to work towards being appropriate while in Atlantis, or that you think you can trick us. Which you can't. Now, any questions?"

Matt asked, "What can you do?"

Amber smiled, and hovered a foot off the ground as she created a ball of fire in her hand, "Flames and Flight are my specialties. But I also know a bit about detection magic, so I guess you could say that I do have eyes in the back of my head. Anything else?"

"Yeah," the businessman said, standing up to try and seem stronger and intimidating. "Why are you our teacher? And why am I in the same class as kids and the elderly?"

Amber looked at him curiously and said, "With magic, age doesn't matter. A person's magic can become powerful enough to need training at any point in their life. So we take you the moment your magic is strong enough, provided you're over twelve. Although I am only twenty, I have been learning magic since I was fifteen, and will be finishing my master's degree this year."

The man sat back down before Amber continued, "We are going to be dealing with your placement in this class. Over the next two months, we will test you in every school of magic and every sub-school within them to determine exactly what types of magic you are skilled at."

"So we can't just take whatever we want?" Sheila asked.

"You can, but it won't be easy," Amber began, leaning

against the whiteboard as she did. She seemed kind of restless. "I know someone from my intro class six years ago who is still taking first year courses because she chose magic that doesn't suit her. I'm not saying it's impossible, but trying to learn magic you aren't skilled at will take five to ten years just to learn what a skilled person could learn in one. Oh, and before I forget, no using magic in the real world for financial gain. No becoming a celebrity, winning the lottery, joining the Olympics, and so on. Magic stays hidden."

The businessman said, "Then what good is this?"

It was a good question. I mean, Amber drives a car everywhere when I know she can fly. Yeah, maybe she would have to be careful. But, she lives in the country; she could fly to city limits.

I was starting to see Mr. Brown's point. If magic can only be used here in Atlantis, then what good is it in the real world?

Amber decided to outright ignore the question. "Before we begin today, I'm going to take you on a tour of the school. Get a chance for all of you to see just what magic there is."

Amber walked out the door, and from the sound in the hallway, she wasn't waiting for us.

I got up and headed to the door to follow, as did many of my classmates. There were a couple of stragglers, who didn't like that they had to get up, probably people who didn't like Amber for one reason or another. I could understand that. Her aggressive attitude takes some getting used to.

Once out of the room, I walked quickly to catch up with Amber. The rest of the class caught up pretty quickly as well.

Amber, noticing that we were all following, with her magic probably, turned around and hovered backwards as she said, "Right now we are in the main building. It has all the offices, and classrooms for intro and first year courses. From here, we are going to visit each of the twelve schools."

We followed Amber through a connecting passageway that led us to another building. The building seemed more business than magic school. Tile floors. Large glass windows. There was a set of chairs at the side, almost couch-like. They had a sign by them that said, "For those with diminished mobility."

It took me longer than I would care to admit to realize that the chairs were hovering a few inches off the ground.

The sign as we entered the new building said: Welcome to Alteration.

Amber turned around to talk to us again. "Alteration is all about changing your body. In this school you'll find invisibility, silence, phasing, shape shifting, and flight. Now, come with me and we will check out the invisibility wing."

Amber walked into what looked like an opening in the building that would leave us falling four stories down to the ground below. There was nothing there, but she had just walked out onto it.

Amber stood there, impatiently, "Is no one going to follow?"

Sheila was quick to reply, "You can fly—we can't."

"Oh for the love of—" but Amber stopped herself short. She lowered herself and kicked at what must have been the floor.

"The invisible wing is invisible itself. It's designed so that if you walk through it when not invisible, everyone can see you. It's kind of a way of shaming people who haven't mastered the craft."

Some people were mumbling, but we eventually followed her down the hallway. It didn't take too long before we were back on visible ground, at which point Amber held a key above her head and said, "We are now in the silence sector. People here are learning how to manipulate sound. The hallways are designed to forbid any sound not produced by magic."

Everyone had to try it. But not one of us could get a word out; even clapping made no noise.

The silence ended as we came across a locked door. Amber pulled out a key and unlocked it, only for a loud, blaring alarm to go off for a couple of seconds and then stop. Amber muttered something under her breath that would sound more appropriate coming from a sailor before continuing

"This is the phasing wing. These doors set off alarms if you have to use a key to open them instead of walking right through."

Amber took us up the stairs to the top floor. There was no roof. There also were not as many doors as you would expect.

"Top floor, flight magic," Amber said, pointing at what was clearly a classroom of students in a room blocked off by a glass wall and no visible door, and no roof "Advanced flight classes. If you can't fly into the room, then you shouldn't be in the class."

Our tour continued onward to the next building, which felt pretty underwhelming by comparison. It was the creation school, so I think we were all expecting it to be covered with all kinds of artwork, or something. But the entire building was actually really drab and boring. We walked by an open room that had absolutely nothing in it.

"You would think that people learning creation magic would actually create something," Sheila said. I couldn't help but agree.

"They do," Amber replied, "But what they create goes away when they stop focusing on it. The rooms are empty because if a student wants to have a seat they better know how to make a chair."

The buildings all had their own quirks to them, quirks that made them fitting to the type of magic taught there. In the Detection building, classrooms teleported around, changing locations in the building, so you had to use your magic to find where your room was. In the Elemental building there were rooms underwater, rooms surrounded by fire, and rooms with dirt floors, to name a few. The Emotion building was quite different. It seemed like people needed to know how to control their own emotions before they could manipulate others, because the building sent us through feelings of sadness, anger, and joy. That part was not fun. And the Fate building? One corridor had locked doors that would only open if you could successfully roll two sixes on a pair of dice, and another split into two or more paths and only one of them would lead you where you wanted to go.

I started to pay a bit more attention when we made it to the school of illusions. Mr. Brown had been using illusions. I wanted to know more about them.

When we arrived in the Illusion building, my first thought was that it seemed like we were at the beach. And there were naked people. I closed my eyes pretty quickly. And yet, closing my eyes didn't seem to help, I could still see them. What was going on?

I was trying to leave, but it felt like I wasn't moving at all. The air around me started to swirl, to feel odd.

But then I remembered what Mr. Brown told me. Look for the magic. I focused. I reminded myself that it was not real. That it was just an illusion.

And I saw it flicker. Amber was walking around to everyone and put some weird sunglasses on their faces, muttering something about 'stupid illusionist pranks' as she did.

I moved over to the table the glasses were lying on and quickly put a pair on myself, struggling to focus on the table and not be distracted by the illusion. Focusing on the illusion being a lie was a lot harder than I thought it would be. It had been so much easier around Mr. Brown. I couldn't help but wonder if he had made it easy for me.

Amber glanced at me briefly as she put the final set of glasses on Sheila's face. "You saw through it?"

It wasn't until that moment that I realized my mistake. I shouldn't have known how to see through an illusion. I hated having to tell a lie, but I did. "Well, um . . . I figured that it's an illusion, and all those times you see illusions in sci-fi it often seems like if a person knows it's an illusion, they can see through it. So I just kept telling myself that it's not real."

Amber had a skeptical look on her face, like she wasn't sure she could believe. It confused me at first, but Amber did have detection magic, she could probably tell when someone was lying. Except for me. That must frustrate her. But instead, a small smile appeared on her face. She turned to the rest of the class and said, "Did everybody get that? Because that is exactly how to see through an illusion. They rely on you accepting them as true."

"So, with these glasses, we could see through any illusion?" Sheila asked.

"No, but they help. You all knew you were entering a building of illusions. The glasses tapped into that part of your brain and put it forefront in your thoughts. There is no way to outright stop someone from using their magic, or having it affect you. If they are good enough, then they can do it. Seeing through illusions is a battle of your willpower against their magic."

"So people who are really good with illusions can trick us whenever they want?" I asked.

"Sort of, Making you believe that your lifelong crush likes you back is far easier than making you think you are being attacked by dragons. If you can't believe it, illusions usually fail."

We kept the glasses on as we travelled through the Illusion building. At times it looked like wolves were going to attack us, another time, it felt like we were in a western, then we were the crew of a space ship. But the glasses helped. Kind of like how Amber's pendant helped her ward off mental influences.

The next building was for the college of Life. It looked like a hospital. There were patient wings, doctors running around, and sick people waiting for treatment.

Jasmine had the hugest smile over her face as she looked around the building, "So, can life magic heal anything?"

"If you're good enough, yes," Amber replied, "Most can fix a cough or cold that up in minute or two. But more complicated things, like cancer, or brain tumours, aren't so easy. Our best can cure those things. But that's our best. There's only about twenty to thirty in the entire city who are that good."

From the look on Jasmine's face, you could tell that she was determined to become that good.

"You're excited," I said. I know, brilliant line.

"I've wanted to be a doctor ever since I was a little girl. But my family can't afford to have me go to school and learn. Coming here, learning this? It's like a dream come true."

I'm pretty sure that she wasn't actually speaking English. But not only did it sound like English to me, her mouth also seemed to be moving to say the exact words that I was hearing. I wonder . . . .

"Could you say that again?" I asked, pretending I hadn't heard her the first time.

She did, but this time I focused on her lips, and I focused on looking for the magic. Her lips moved differently, out of sync with the English words I was hearing. It looked like our watches were designed to make communicating easier in more ways than one. No sensation of watching a badly dubbed movie.

Amber was quick to scurry us along to the next building.

68

We had a schedule to keep, she said; we couldn't waste our entire first day just touring the school.

The Mental building was interesting. We walked in on a class that seemed to be having a deep discussion without doing any talking, and another class where every single chair was missing its legs and needed to be held up telekinetically so that the student could sit.

From there we visited the Physical building. It was a gym. Weights, track, those kinds of things. Except that the weights involved lifting a few thousand pounds, the tracks had people running at speeds clocked at over three-hundred kilometres, some people were punching right through foot-thick blocks of steel, and scariest of all, there was a shooting range where people who were learning how to be invincible let other people shoot them. That seemed ridiculously dangerous until the time when one of the people getting shot at stumbled, and a barrier instantly appeared around them to prevent them from actually getting hurt. Everyone hear was training, some in ways that were without magic and looked completely normal.

"Why train without magic?" Matt asked.

"Physical magic doesn't make you strong or fast, it just amplifies your natural abilities. Someone with strength magic might be able to make themselves one hundred times stronger than they normally are, but that doesn't mean much if they struggle to lift fifty pounds."

I could see Matt taking a look around the place; he liked it here.

"Found what you like?" I asked.

"All that fire and illusions and stuff is right out of fairy tales. But this? Making your body stronger? This I can believe in," he said with a smile.

The next school was called Protection. The place was dangerous. Amber had all of us staying close to her as arrows shot out of the walls, weird screams came from nowhere, and the floor buzzed with electricity. The Protection school was all about keeping yourself safe, both physically and mentally. The best thing they had going for them was anti-magic. They could literally just stop all magic from working around them.

Finally, we arrived where I had wanted to be in the first place: the Time and Space building, last one on the tour.

It was incredible. I could see different pockets in the building. In some of them, time was moving by incredibly fast, in others, it was down to a crawl. I saw no stairs, elevators or anything up to the higher floors on one of the wings. Must have been for people who teleport. I guess this building was my turn to smile, 'cause Matt said to me, "This stuff excites you?"

"Well, yeah. I mean, being able to go anywhere I want just by thinking about it? Slowing down time so that I'm never late or run out of time. Why wouldn't I like it?"

"Heh, weirdo," Matt said. But I could tell from his tone that he was just bugging me.

"Musclehead," I said back to him.

For a brief moment there was a look of downright fury in his eyes, and I was scared that I had crossed a line, before Matt smiled and said, "You're too easy."

With that, the tour had come full circle, and we were back in the Administration and Beginners Building. Amber led us back into the classroom we were in before. Which, oddly, now had a desk in it. There was also a man in a doctor's coat at the back, here in case we screwed up and hurt someone, I guess.

"Alright, class," Amber began, "now that your tour is complete, it is time for your first lesson to begin."

At those words, Amber smiled and the desk at the front of the room transformed into an older man, balding, but healthy otherwise.

He looked at all of us and said, "Good morning, class. I am Master Tantalo, one of the six leaders of the city, and the best mage in the city, hence the title Master. Today we are here to learn about my specialty, alteration."

We had all started to head back to our seats in the room when Master Tantalo said, "I should warn you, it can take a lot of concentration to use magic your first time. Do not be surprised if it takes you ten minutes of concentration just to get the slightest effect. Turning one finger invisible is impressive for someone new to magic."

I think my jaw almost hit the ground. I knew I was better

than average, but this made it seem like I already was months, if not years, ahead of everyone here.

"We are starting with invisibility," Master Tantalo said. "Think back to times when you were completely ignored, when no one was paying attention to you. Let those memories flow over you, and use them to fuel your magic."

The businessman in the room shouted, "That's all it is. Just wish for it to work?"

Amber barely restrained her voice, but managed to sound informative instead of volatile as she responded, "Magic runs on memories, so you're good at the magic you have the strongest memories for. This is why some people become good at a new type of magic later on in life, or struggle to use magic they were once good at."

"So, what are some other examples of the memories that you need?" I asked.

"I'm a bit of an activist, very passionate. And passion mixes well with fire." Amber created a fireball, "I'm pretty good at flying. But I didn't take a single course in it until my third year, when I was seventeen."

Sheila blurted out, "That's when you came out of the closet!"

A few people in the class looked around awkwardly at that. Glad to know I wasn't the only one who was a bit uncomfortable.

Amber nodded. "Flight magic works best for those who can cling to a memory that made them feel free and uncontrolled. But enough chitchat, start becoming invisible."

We were all asked to stand, and to remain standing as long as we wished to try. And try I did. But I couldn't think of much for it. I'm an only child, so I get lots of attention from my parents, and I'm from a small town. There were about five hundred people total, and even with the kids bused in for school, and the parents of those kids, the population didn't crack six hundred. For the most part, everyone knew everyone. It was next to impossible to feel alone.

But I did as I was told and I focused.

After some time, the instructor said, "Okay, Blaine, you've been at it for about five minutes now, have you felt anything?"

"No, not really," I admitted.

"I did not see anything coming from you either. You are welcome to continue trying, but I wouldn't get your hopes up too high."

After about nine minutes, there was only one person the Master had not tapped out. The old woman held up her hand, and we saw that one of her fingers was missing. She smiled as the finger reappeared, and then passed out.

Jasmine jumped out of her chair and over to the old woman so fast that I thought she must know speed magic. Jasmine kneeled down beside the woman and said, "Okay, she's breathing, she's not having a seizure or anything."

"What just happened?" Matt asked as he moved in beside Jasmine, double-checking Jasmine's assessment.

"She earned her Zs," Amber replied. "Most people pass out the first time they use magic successfully. If you overexert yourself when performing magic, you pass out, and the first time always requires overexerting yourself."

That made everyone nervous, but it was a couple seconds later when the old woman woke back up and said, "I'm fine, everyone. Don't worry about me. Weirdest thing. I don't think I really passed out. I could hear all of you. I just couldn't do anything."

The lesson continued with another type of Alteration magic. At the rate we were going, and the order we were starting, I was getting the feeling that we wouldn't get to Time and Space for over a month. And if I wasn't going to be good at anything else, it was going to be a very long month.

"Next we will be working on phasing. The ability to walk through solid objects. This one can be particularly dangerous," the Master began.

"We have several bowls of water here. Place a finger into the water, and try to think about the water going through your finger instead of around it. Think about a time you wanted to escape. Think about a time where you wanted to or did run away."

That was easy. I thought of the time when I saw the man gunned down in front of me in the back alley. I was so scared, absolutely terrified. I focused on the memory, pushing past the fear. I remembered the two women in their suits and shades, each holding a gun on the man in the trench coat who was lying in a pool of his own blood. I remembered the women in the suits looking over at me, 'A witness,' one of them said as the other pointed her gun at me. I remembered screaming. I remembered that somehow, in an instant, the two women were gone. And I remembered running to the man who was dying. I remembered trying to help him, I remembered wishing I had a phone so that I could get help for him. I remembered him pushing me away, and telling me to run, 'Kid, get out of here. Now!' But I didn't, I couldn't leave him.

And then he died and . . . .

"Blaine! BLAINE!"

I was on the floor. Shaking. Why had I done that? Why had I let myself think about that?

I couldn't breathe, couldn't . . . .

"BLAINE!"

I came back to the present. Covered in sweat, my body shaking. I tried to calm myself down. Relax. Think about something else. You're in Atlantis. You're getting to learn magic. How awesome is that?

Amber was screaming at me while the medic was looking me over, a flashlight out and checking my eyes. I brushed him away.

I struggled to get back to my feet, Jasmine and Matt helping me up.

"What just . . . ."

Amber addressed the class, "Be careful with the memories you choose. Make sure that they are ones you can handle thinking about," then to me she added, "you going to be okay?"

"I . . . think so . . . ."

But my pity parade ended pretty quickly, not that I wanted one in the first place. Some people were still trying to phase. And it looked like Sheila had just succeeded.

Her eyes bulged, and she shot back and fell onto the floor. Her body was in spasms.

Jasmine raced to Sheila. "She's convulsing, does she have epilepsy?"

Amber shook her head. The medic stepped in and pressed his hands onto Sheila. He was focused, I could see light leaving his hands and entering Sheila, but it wasn't helping, not fast enough, anyways. Five minutes passed before Sheila was actually back with us, breathing. She looked up. "What just happened?"

Amber pushed the medic and Jasmine out of the way, grabbed and hugged her sister. "I am so sorry, Sheila. So sorry."

The medic was not happy. He looked directly at Amber and said, "That's your sister? The one who has magic lower than anyone we've ever admitted into this city before?"

"Yeah, what of it?"

The medic's hand trembled, he started to raise it, and I thought he was going to hit Amber, then he muttered, "Do no harm," put his arm down and yelled at Amber, "You are unbelievably stupid. A mind-wipe would have been kinder. Her body can barely handle using magic at all."

"She'll train," Amber replied, "she'll get better."

"She doesn't have the reserves to start properly. Every time she uses magic she may as well have smoked a couple packs of cigarettes for how much harm it will do her body. I don't care if she gets better. By the time she does, she'll have shaved five years off her life, at least."

The medic headed for the door, "Find someone who is willing to watch a murder for your next class. Or do the smart thing and get her wiped."

Sheila looked at Amber, fear in her voice, "Amber, is learning magic going to kill me?"

9| AMBER

"YOU WANT ME TO WHAT?" SHEILA SHOUTED AT ME, GETTING UP OFF the couch in my apartment. She stormed through the living room, headed for the door. Typical of her, trying to walk out the moment I say something she doesn't like.

I went through the kitchen and beat her to the door. She glowered at me, arms crossed, but didn't try to get past me.

"Look," I said, leaning against the door. "You heard what the doctor said."

"Yeah, it'll be like smoking a pack every time I cast a spell. I get it. I'm still going to do it."

"But you don't have to. You could just stay here in Atlantis, enjoy the free time it gives you. Practice your cheerleading. Fly around with the backpacks."

Sheila scoffed at that and walked back to the living room and plopped down on the couch. "Yeah, and be the loser who quit after just one lesson? If I'm not going to learn magic I may as well get wiped. No way I'm sticking around as the loser."

My body tensed up, almost shaking. She couldn't possibly mean it.

"No, sis, you don't . . . ." I followed her back to the living room.

"Of course I don't want to get my mind–wiped," she said, looking at me like I was an idiot. "I saw that guy screaming. I'm not stupid. But I'm also not going to be the pity party. I can do this. I can get to the top, even if I'm starting at the bottom. After all, I've done it before."

She looked me right in the eyes when she said that last line. Back when I went to high school, I caused a lot of problems in my grade twelve year. I came out as bisexual, had a girlfriend, fought against the special treatment that the football team had in the school. Sheila became a freshman there the year after I graduated. To become popular she had to fight to get to the top, because everyone was expecting her to be as much of a problem as me.

I almost smiled. Even if everything she had done in the past two years undermined what I believed in, I couldn't argue with how much we had in common. Nothing can stop us from achieving our goals. Tenacious, we both were.

"Okay," I said, "you never listen to me anyways."

Sheila left the apartment, feeling like she had won a fight. I wish I could say that this fight would be over between us. But she was determined. So the best thing I could do was help her in whatever way I could.

My watch started beeping. Shoot, I was supposed to meet Dwayne in five minutes at the dome. I raced into my room, grabbed my lightning suit, and sped out the door.

I ran to the dome, my suit still in my hands.

"You're running behind," Dwayne said as he caught sight of me.

Dwayne was a pretty nice guy, and if the way other girls looked at him is any indication, he's also easy on the eyes. I can kind of see it. He does have almost-movie-star good looks. Strong chin, dark hair, blue eyes, and he was powerfully built. But I've never seen him like that. In part because he was my teacher five years ago when I was in Intro to Magic, and part because I used to date his sister. Dwayne taught me a lot of what I know, and last year when I started my master's degree, which caused me to outrank him in the city's opinion, he was proud to hand over the title of Warden to me. Not that most of the others in the province were. All of them liked Dwayne. Well, except for Jesse, but Jesse just hates cops with a passion, and Dwayne was a pretty good cop.

Dwayne had on his orange fire suit when I saw him, and he had his hover board in hand, an orange fire sleeve wrapped around it.

"Yeah, sorry about running late," I said, "First day of teaching, and my sister . . . ."

"Talk is for after we spar."

I threw my lightning suit on over my clothes. The yellow suit making me looking like I was leaving a contaminated area. Atlantis protective gear will never win any fashion awards.

We walked into the dome. The man operating didn't even bother to look up; he knew it was us, here for our weekly sparring match.

The arena we were in was one hundred metres wide, fifty metres high, nice for a good fight.

"Fifteen seconds," Dwayne said as he set himself on his hover board. He flew up to one side of the dome. I flew to the other and checked the marker on the wall. Thirty metres up. Our starting point. I pulled the hood and mask of my suit up over my face.

"Ready," he shouted.

"Set," I confirmed.

"Go!" we shouted together.

I tried for a direct approach, sped straight at him and tossed a fireball his way. He dove, and my fire hit the wall.

Dwayne returned with a shot of lightning. I slid to my left and the blast went right past me.

But that lightning of his was too weak. He was going easy on me, the jerk.

I pulled in my fire, made two balls, and pulled them together around my hands. I dove at him, flaming hands first. He fired a bolt of lightning at me. I amped up my flames so that they consumed his lightning.

I used that to my advantage. I lit my entire body on fire and continued my dive, the lightning going around my body instead of hitting me.

I got within a couple feet of Dwayne, and then my magic died. The flames disappeared, and I was falling through the sky.

Dwayne hovered down, keeping pace with me as he said, "Gotcha."

He pushed his hand right into my chest and hit me with a bolt of lightning that sent me flying into the wall. The suit absorbed the electricity, keeping me safe from it entirely. It also saved me from the impact. That would normally hurt a lot.

"First point, me," Dwayne laughed as he pointed at himself.

"Oh, you won't be laughing for long," I said as I flew back up at him.

"Twenty-three to eighteen," Dwayne said as we sat down to eat supper, "You clobbered me in there today."

"Yeah, well, you did pretty good yourself, a bolt of lightning with anti-magic spiraling around it? Stroke of genius." I pushed my menu to the side, I already knew what I wanted to eat.

Dwayne laughed. "It might have been, if you hadn't seen it coming."

"You shouldn't have tried to blindside me before pulling off a trick like that, you know I start detecting the moment you catch me off guard," I replied, giving his arm a gentle slap as I did.

Dwayne laughed, "You really needed to let off some steam, didn't you?"

"Yeah . . . ." I said. I was about to tell him what was going on with Sheila when our waitress came up and asked, "Hey, Amber, that meeting still on for tomorrow?"

"Huh? Oh, yeah, it is," I said without evening thinking about it.

Our waitress, Alicia if I remember correctly, smiled at me. "Awesome, see you there. Now, what can I get you to eat?"

Dwayne muttered his order, but she picked it up pretty quickly anyways. I gave her my order and looked over at Dwayne, who was refusing to meet my gaze.

"So, you're still doing those meetings?" he asked after Alicia walked away.

I felt myself tense up instantly. I could not believe he was going to start this fight again.

"Don't give me that look," Dwayne said to me, "I've told you before that those stories are completely bogus. The only so-called expert to say mind-wipes cause mental damage wrote his paper five years ago, and no one has been able to duplicate his results."

"And how would they know," I said back to him, the anger rising in my voice. "There's no public record of who has been mind-wiped. Heck, I had to turn in all of my papers from today's class to the Atlantis central office, and you can bet that mind-wiped bigot won't show up in any files. The only reason there aren't any more studies is because when Atlantis has someone wiped, they don't tell us anything. One day your neighbour is there and the next they're gone."

I should have known better than to say that in front of him. Dwayne stood up, and said, "If you'll excuse me I have some stuff to do. You can get the bill, right? It was your turn, anyways."

He turned around and walked away.

I shouted after him, "Dwayne, look, I'm sorry. I know that!"

He stopped but would not look at me. "Amber . . . just don't."

He left without another word. Why did I do that? Why did I make him think about his ex, Charlene? I should know by now that he's still hung up on her.

Her being banished was kind of my fault. Dwayne started dating her here in Atlantis, at the same time that I was dating his sister. I made a comment to him about looking forward to my date with his sister. Charlene was a homophobic idiot. She said she was disgusted by me, and by Dwayne for being okay with it, and she said all of that in public. It was less than an hour before she was mind-wiped and expelled from Atlantis. She was screaming the entire time that being homosexual was wrong and that I should be the one being expelled, not her. Back in the day it made me love Atlantis. I mean, who wouldn't love a place that banished the people who were rude to you? But nowadays, it just seems like a bad idea. Of course, that could be because my opposition to mind-wipes might get me wiped any day now.

Dwayne just didn't understand. He'd never noticed the problems in the system before. He found following the rules too easy. Or maybe he was in denial, refusing to believe that mind-wipes cause harm because he'd seen one done to someone he loves and he needs to believe she's still fine. But that wasn't me.

I ate my supper in silence. My waitress, wisely, chose not to comment on Dwayne's absence.

I finished the meal with time to spare before my meeting would begin. Yeah, I was going to be talking at it, but I still didn't want to arrive too early.

I walked back to my place, in part because I wasn't sure I would have the energy to fly there.

I saw Mr. Folstad at my door. He was in a suit, nothing fancy, the kind of suit you would expect from a classy teacher. Appropriate, since he is the Teacher, head of the school and one of the six leaders of Atlantis. He had just finished knocking and was about to leave a note under the door. I'll give Atlantis credit for one thing, it does not believe in having other people do things for you, even the leaders of the city have to do work themselves instead of having personal staff to deal with it.

"Hello, Mr. Folstad," I said as I approached.

"Ah, Amber, you're here. Good, then I can just give this to you," he passed me a sealed envelope.

"What is this?" I asked as I ripped it open.

"You're not going to like it," he said.

I took one look at the note. He was right, I didn't like it, not in the slightest.

"Are you serious? I know that Blaine's special, but pulling him out of the intro class for two hours every day? What for?"

Mr. Folstad shrugged, "He may not have the best control, but he is already more skilled at magic than most people who have half a year of training. He doesn't need to be wasting his days in a beginner class when he should be doing more advanced work."

"Fine, so he'll be joining a couple first year classes on Time and Space?"

Mr. Folstad shook his head. "That was our initial plan. We were, ah, persuaded to take another course of action."

"Persuaded? By who?"

"Finish the note," Mr. Folstad said as he started walking away. Walking very quickly away.

He was out of sight by the time I finished the note. Lucky for him, because I practically shouted as I finished it.

"Private lessons? From Drake?"

10| BLAINE

THE EVENING IN ATLANTIS WAS A BLAST, EVEN IF SHEILA WAS THERE the entire time. Jasmine suggested that the four of us, her, Matt, Sheila, and I, grab a meal together. Sheila and I told them that they had to try Small World. I swear there was a moment after we both suggested it that we looked at each other in shock over actually agreeing on something. After that, the four of us went browsing around the city, checking out all of the cool stuff. We stared at hover-boards for over an hour, and Sheila actually convinced a shop owner to let us try them. The shopkeeper was happy about that, and muttered something about how it was nice that the broomstick fad was finally starting to die. It was a great way to spend an evening.

Going to bed is kind of the weirdest part about Atlantis. I go to bed at ten or eleven at night, and before I wake up, it's six in the morning in Atlantis and I teleport back to Saskatoon, where it's six at night instead of morning. Amber explained it's 'cause Atlantis takes people at midnight on Coordinated Universal Time.

Amber gave me a ride home after I left Atlantis. She told me that this would be the last time she would give me a ride, 'cause I could handle going to Atlantis myself. She was very quiet for most of the drive, like she wanted to say something, but didn't know how to put it. I asked her what was up.

She was about to avoid the question when she instead said, "Look, Blaine, 'cause you're special . . . they decided you should have some special training."

"What?"

"Private lessons. I don't know what exactly their plan is, but from nine until eleven every day you're going to be going off for some separate lessons."

"So, wait . . . who's going to be teaching me?"

"Drake," Amber said, I could feel the anger in her voice. I did not want to touch that anger with anything less than a ten foot pole, so I just nodded and said, "Okay."

As we arrived at my place, I hopped out of the car, and saw my parents opening the front door and coming out.

Amber sped off as my parents rushed out into the driveway. They really wanted to figure out why I had been late getting home for the last two days, but Amber left before my parents could talk to her.

When I got inside, a late supper was on the table. Mom and Dad had waited for me, like they always do.

"How was school?" my dad asked after we said grace.

"It was a good day," I replied. "Classes were kind of boring, but it was a nice day."

"Who was that dropping you off?" my mom said, "she seems a bit old for you."

"Her name is Amber, she's Sheila's older sister, one of my classmates."

"So, are you dating this Sheila?" my dad asked.

"No," I said, a bit too quickly. I mean, dating Sheila, can't see that ever happening. But my parents are going to hear that and just think I was denying it. I swear, they grew up so long ago. They can't seem to buy that guys and girls can be just friends. That's what I get for being the child of high school sweethearts. They think I'm going to find the love of my life before I graduate.

"Well, we were thinking we could play some cards tonight," my dad said, a usual thing for our family. We play cards after supper most nights when none of us are busy.

I was about to say yes when I paused, "Actually, I need to go to the mall. I'm meeting a friend of mine."

My dad gave me that concerned-parent look. "Well, Blaine, I am happy to see that you are making so many friends, but I am worried about your schoolwork. You seem to be really busy already, and we just moved here."

"Dad, it's the second day of school, there isn't really anything to do yet," I said. "Besides, isn't it a good thing that I'm fitting in so well already?"

"I suppose," my dad replied, "as long as you have enough time for your schoolwork, church, and some family time, everything is okay."

"So, can I get a ride?"

"Yes, I'll take you once we finish supper. Is that okay?" My mom said.

"Yeah, that's great."

We ate supper quickly and quietly. I told them about my day at school. Just boring talk about my classes. I kept everything about Grant, Atlantis, and Mr. Brown to myself.

After supper, my mom gave me a ride to the mall. She wanted to come in and meet my friends, but I told her to not embarrass me, so she just dropped me off and drove away. I think she was a little hurt, 'cause I've never been private like this around her before, but I guess she just figured that it was a part of me growing up. Or it was her not wanting to dig too deeply into anything going on with me.

I walked into the mall and wandered around a bit looking for the mini-golf area. Not that it was hard to find. Mr. Brown was there. He was wearing nice pants, a dress shirt, and a blazer, so he looked passable for once. He saw me and waved me over. I took a look at his illusion, and this time he looked like another kid, my age. Making it look like I was meeting up with a friend.

"Hello," I said as I arrived.

"Hey," Mr. Brown said.

"I never did ask. Why the illusions?"

Mr. Brown smiled as he pulled out his wallet. "Oh, that? Well, since Atlantis doesn't know we exist, I don't want them to trace my contact with you to me."

That made sense to me.

"So, I wasn't the only person who joined Atlantis recently. Are you recruiting the others?"

"The others aren't like us."

Should have known he was after me for my power.

"I take it you know a fair bit about being an aberration then?" I asked as I walked down into the golf course. I figured if he wanted to get me to switch schools, he'd better show he knows what he's talking about.

"Not as much as we would like, but yes. Our current theory, and it is still holding strong, is that there are twelve aberrations in total," Mr. Brown said as he lined up his ball and took his first swing.

"We? Twelve?"

Mr. Brown took a putt to get par on the first hole. "I'm one of the leaders of my little organization, and the other five leaders are also aberrations."

"Six more aberrations?" I said without thinking, "And you think there are twelve, total?"

"Yes, one for each school of magic."

"Why do you think that?" I asked.

"Well, let's see, you are the master of time and space, I'm the master of illusions, among the co-leaders of New Asgard we have the masters of fate, the elements, emotions, physical magic, and life and death. There is another, but if I told you much about him, you would never get a good night's sleep again for the rest of your life. Let's just say that if you ever hear the name Alpha, you run."

I think he was trying to hide it, but Mr. Brown was pretty clearly terrified of this Alpha person. He also didn't mention Drake. Does he not know about Drake? Should I tell him?

"So, you know of eight, but are convinced there are twelve?" I said, deciding to keep Drake's identity a secret.

"The odds of there being eight aberrations of different schools is small enough that it makes sense. My best guess is that aberrations are the masters of each of the schools of magic. But that's just an idea."

I think he was playing me there. He knew that I wanted to understand just what it meant to be an aberration and he was using that against me. Knowing that he was playing me didn't stop me from wanting to know, though.

Mr. Brown leaned on his golf club and said, "Teaching moment. I want you to watch that man there, in the ripped jacket. He's going to try and steal that rich man's wallet."

I saw the two he was talking about. The thief's jacket wasn't the only thing that was ripped. He was someone I wouldn't give a second look to, 'cause I wouldn't want to think people like him are around. The rich man was in a fancy suit, talking on his cell phone.

The thief walked close by the rich man, and I watched him reach into the rich man's pocket. But he took nothing out.

"Focus on seeing the illusion."

I did. There was a flicker. It was very slight, but I could see that the man thought he had a wallet in his hand.

I smiled, "He thinks he stole the wallet. That doesn't do much to stop the thief from trying again."

"Perhaps," Mr. Brown replied, "But this might."

The thief's eyes bulged and his hand started grasping, he looked around and on the ground for something.

I leaned on my golf club as Mr. Brown went to take his shot, "You made the illusion go away. He's starting to think he's going crazy."

I shuddered at the thought. Tricking someone into thinking they were crazy. It didn't quite sit well with me.

Mr. Brown took his shot, "That's just a sample. Let's wrap this game up early. As much as I want to beat you, I have other things I want to show you, and these kids in front of us are taking forever."

"I accept your surrender," I joked as we walked back to the mini-golf entrance, dropped off our clubs and balls, and headed out of the mall.

I know, I know, don't go for rides at night with strangers. But I was starting to trust the guy. He had come to my defence, he stopped a man from getting pick-pocketed; he was good as far as I could tell.

Mr. Brown drove us downtown. He had a really nice car, brand new. If he's not supposed to be drawing attention, then he wasn't doing a very good job of it. He parked the car and told me that we would do the rest on foot. It wasn't too far until we were in the bad part of the city. I saw a scantily-clad woman walking the street. She had bruises, like she'd been beaten. I could feel my body tensing up, ready to fight or run if I needed to.

"So, what are we doing?" I asked, keeping an eye out on my surroundings. This is the kind of place my dad always used to warn me about.

"Just watch," Mr. Brown replied.

I did. I watched as people made deals and what was clearly drugs swapped hands. I watched girls younger than me step into the cars of men my father's age. You always know this stuff is going on, but it's almost scary just how easy it is to see it in action just by being in the wrong place at the wrong time. I couldn't stand it.

As we continued, I saw a couple of men with guns go into a building. The guns surprised me more than anything else had. I'd never seen a gun on anyone but a cop before. Okay, maybe hunting rifles back home. But a handgun? Never.

The building looked trashy. It had wood over some of its windows. I'd guess whatever shop this used to be was out of business now.

A shot rang out from inside.

"Shall we deal with this?"

My mind reeled at that idea. Deal with it? What could we do against people with guns?

I didn't have to wait long to find out. Mr. Brown walked up to the door of the building and opened it.

Why would Mr. Brown do that? We should have snuck in a window if we did anything. I know that Mr. Brown said that his group believed in using magic to help people and stop criminals. But I had no training. What could I have done?

Mr. Brown ushered me over to the building. I was terrified. There were people with guns in that building, who clearly did not have an issue with firing them, and Mr. Brown wanted me to look in the front door.

Cringing, I went to the door and took a look in.

I could see them perfectly, some of them were even looking in the same direction as the door. I was sure that they could see me. Mr. Brown was trying to get me killed!

Except . . . they didn't notice me. They were angry about some guy who was there on the floor, bleeding out from a gunshot, but didn't even notice that the door was open.

"What are you doing?" I asked Mr. Brown.

"Look for the magic."

And I did. I saw that, despite the door being open, there appeared to be a door right in front of me. It was fuzzy, and if I wanted to I could see through it. But I could see that this door looked exactly like the one that had been opened.

"An Illusion?" I was tempted to touch it, but it was the only thing between me and some gangsters.

"Yes, now shall we stop this?"

"How?"

"Watch," Mr. Brown said. He started to concentrate, he must have been about to do something big. "Focus on seeing the magic."

I did, and I saw the door smashed down and the boarded windows smashed in. Dozens of police officers surged through the doors, firing.

The criminals fired at the police. The police fired back and the criminals fell.

"How?"

"Their minds have been tricked. They think they've been shot, and will continue to think that until I stop the illusion."

My mind reeled in horror. Illusions could make you believe you'd been shot? They could trick you into feeling pain? Mr. Brown could be nigh unstoppable with that kind of power. I'm glad he was one of the good guys.

Mr. Brown pulled out a phone. "Now we be dutiful citizens, and phone the real cops. Would you care to do the honours?"

Mr. Brown handed me a cell phone. It looked cheap, like those burner phones you see spies use. That set off a few warning bells in my head, but if Mr. Brown's organization was so keen on keeping the world safe, they would have to be secretive.

"What do I say?" I asked, taking the phone.

"Just say you heard what sounded like gunshots at this building."

I dialed nine-one-one and told the police what had happened.

We continued down the street as we heard the sirens of the police approaching the building.

"So, what do you think?" Mr. Brown asked.

I thought it was amazing. Mr. Brown got a couple of

criminals arrested using his powers. And he stopped them from killing someone. The man who was shot would probably live now.

There was one question I had for him though.

"Is your name even Mr. Brown?" the words slipped out of my mouth before I could think about whether it was a good idea to ask.

Mr. Brown paused for a moment. A flare of anger swung across his face for a brief instant, only to be replaced by a smile as he said, "I guess not."

I stopped and glared at him. "You guess not?"

"Is a role you play anything other than part of your person? Any name you take on essentially becomes your own. So, in a way, I am Mr. Brown."

He sounded like those sleazy lawyers on TV, or a politician, trying to get away with not giving a real answer. "Uh huh. So, what is your real name?"

"Ra."

"Ra?" What kind of a name was Ra?

"It's the sun god in Egyptian mythology," Mr. Brown said, noticing my confusion.

"That can't be your real name."

Mr. Brown shrugged, "Then call me Mr. Brown. Now, come on, it's late and a school night, you need to go home."

We started heading back downtown to Mr. Brown's car. After a couple blocks, Mr. Brown stopped walking, held out his arm to stop me, and whispered, "Look."

There were a couple of guys looking at a nice car on the street. One of them nodded, and the other pulled a wrench up and smashed the driver side window and opened the door. The car alarm was blaring, so they were trying to work fast.

"You want this one?" Mr. Brown asked me.

Me? But I couldn't do anything.

"What can I do?"

"Forget what they told you in Atlantis. You're an aberration. Just want your magic to work and focus."

It couldn't really be that easy, could it?

I thought about slowing down time, so that the carjackers

couldn't get away. But nothing happened. In fact, I think they were moving faster. They hot-wired the car and were driving away. All while I stood around doing nothing.

Mr. Brown put his hand on my shoulder and said, "You need to believe you can do it. Without confidence that it will work, magic never works. Think about what you have done before, and try doing it on purpose this time."

I tried. Tried to use my magic for once because I wanted to instead of my instincts deciding it was a good idea.

The car began to slow down. Slower and slower.

My breathing was already a bit heavy as I said, "Okay. I think I've got this."

I thought about teleporting inside the car.

And I was there.

They were too slowed down to notice me before it was too late. I punched each of them in the back of the head. Their heads shot forward and smacked into the wheel and glove compartment, knocking them both unconscious.

The car slid off the road and stopped as it nudged into a mailbox. I teleported out of the car.

"Not bad," Mr. Brown said as the car siren continued blaring, "We should leave though."

I agreed, so we hopped in the car and Mr. Brown took me home.

"I think that was a good first night," Mr. Brown said as I got out of the car about a block from my house so my parents wouldn't my ride. "Take some time and think about my offer, okay? Atlantis won't let you do the kind of things we did tonight, and with your kind of power, you shouldn't be doing nothing. Great power and great responsibility, right?"

11| BLAINE

THE DAY AT SCHOOL WAS A DULL BLUR. THE ONLY THING THAT REALLY stood out was that Grant had decided to start picking on me. I guess the fact that I got away with winning the fight didn't sit well with him.

At lunch, he 'accidentally' slipped and spilled his entire lunch all over me.

I leapt up from my seat, my hands clenched. He was smiling, and I was ready to rearrange his jawline so that he'd never smile again.

"Dude," Jake said, "Settle down."

I looked at Jake, and back at Grant. Grant wanted me to react. He was waiting for it. I hated that doing nothing was the best option, but I sat down. I wish I had teleported away before he had spilled his lunch on me, but it was spaghetti. Nothing hot and dangerous, just messy.

I ended up late to my next class because I was cleaning myself off. The teacher wasn't too impressed with me, and wasn't interested in my excuses.

It felt like a blessing when six o'clock arrived and I was teleported to Atlantis.

I arrived at class about five minutes before nine. Matt was already there, and Sheila and Jasmine were already seated beside him. I went to join the group.

Sheila glared daggers at me as I sat down. Jasmine gave a friendly hello, and Matt gave me a nod. Man of few words, he was. Matt had ditched the military outfit this time. Blue jeans and a black t-shirt instead.

The bell rang for the start of class and Amber walked up to the front of the room, "Good morning, class, glad to see you all back. We're going to continue today with—"

Before she could finish her sentence, the classroom door opened. Drake walked into the room, wearing a backpack, which just looked weird on him.

"I'm here to give Blaine his private lessons."

In the chaos of last night with Mr. Brown I had completely forgotten that I was going to be getting lessons with Drake.

Frank, the middle-aged businessman, looked at Drake and then at me as he said, "Why does he get special lessons?"

I decided to give him a demonstration as to why. I disappeared and reappeared at the front of the classroom.

"That's why," Amber said, gesturing her hand at me. She gave me a nod, and what must count for a worried look from her, as I walked out the door with Drake.

Drake wasn't waiting for me. Amber did the same thing back when she was leading our tour group. I'm starting to feel like no one in Atlantis waits for anyone, you just better hope you can keep up.

"Why you?" I asked as I followed Drake out of the school.

"Because we're the freaks. I know a thing or two about how your magic is different from everyone else."

Drake was largely silent as he led me to what must have been a domed baseball diamond.

The place was completely empty. That wasn't scary at all. You would think a building this big would have a lot more people in it. As I walked out onto the diamond, I saw baseballs, basketballs, and other kinds of balls all over the field. I had to keep my eyes on the ground to make sure I didn't step on anything. When I took a glance at Drake, I saw the balls rolling out of his way, and then back to their normal positions. After almost falling over one I was tempted to shout at him, but I held my tongue.

Drake arrived at the pitcher's mound.

"Batter up," he said as he lifted a basketball telekinetically and tossed it at me. I reached for it instinctively instead of trying to teleport. But when the ball was about to hit me, a blue aura surrounded me and the ball bounced off. I didn't even feel the ball hit me.

Drake arched an eyebrow, but put it back down only to replace it with a huge smirk. "Anything I throw at you telekinetically can't affect you either. How interesting. A thought for another time though. This time, dodge."

Drake tossed another ball at me, faster this time. I willed myself to teleport, and I managed to reappear ten feet away, out of the way of the ball.

"Nicely done," Drake replied, "We're off to a good start. Now let's keep at it."

He tossed ball after ball at me. Even though they couldn't hurt me, I still wanted to dodge them. And dodge them I did. I teleported to the left, to the right, forward, backward, whatever way I needed to in order to dodge the ball. I had to focus on my locations though. Had to watch where I was going, there were balls all over the ground and I couldn't let myself land on one of them.

I was feeling really exhausted after my twelfth teleport, ready to take a nap. I was pretty winded, huffing and puffing for air.

After the sixteenth teleport, I fell to the ground.

I woke up laying on a bench, Drake looking over me.

"Got to earn your Zs, I see," Drake said as I pulled myself upright.

"But I thought that I wouldn't . . . ."

"You earn your Zs any time you try and use more magic than you have left in you," Drake said as he took a seat on the bench next to me, "We aberrations may have a lot more magic than everyone else, but we're not perfect. Just rest for a bit, magic doesn't come back all that fast. Now you're new, and an aberration like me, so I give it two hours until you're back up to full strength."

"Is that why I—"

"Still feel exhausted?" Drake finished for me. I was really beginning to hate that about him. And was surprised that he could do it when he couldn't read my mind, "Yes. It was a good first step, though. I needed to see what you are capable of. We need to get you to practice long range and blind teleports."

"Blind teleports?" I asked, the exhaustion clear in my voice.

A water bottle from across the diamond flew into Drake's hand. He passed it to me. "Drink, it will help." He waited for me to take a sip before he continued, "You're always looking where you want to go. With enough experience, your body will adjust your teleports to make sure you don't teleport into, or onto, anything dangerous."

I think I was managing to keep up with him. Yeah, my head was spinning a little, but I'm pretty sure that was from passing out and not from what he was talking about.

"You know a lot about time and space for someone who can't use it," I said.

"I know a lot about it all," Drake replied. He telekinetically pulled a book out of his bag and moved it over to lie on the bench next to me. "Most people learn that magic is real and they go 'Oh, I want to learn that. I want to cast spells and fly.' Me? When I learned about magic, my first thought was, 'How does it work?'"

I picked up the book, "A Thesis of Magic."

"It's a dense read, but it is the best place to start, unless you want me to throw A Beginner's Guide to Magic at you." He said the words 'A Beginner's Guide to Magic' like it was something filthy and disgusting. I was already getting the impression that Drake wasn't just the master of mental magic, he was really smart overall.

"I can give it a shot," I said, kind of wishing he had passed me the beginner's guide instead; this looked bigger than most of my dad's old university textbooks.

That put a smile on his face. Not his usual smirk—a smile, warm and friendly. Like he was trying to be my friend.

"So, if you know so much about my magic, what will I eventually be able to do?"

Drake laughed, "Short version? In a few years you'll be able to teleport anywhere in the world whenever you want."

Drake stood up and reached his hand across the coliseum, and a couple bags of chips came shooting over at us.

"Where did you—?" I asked.

"The concession," Drake replied.

"You stole them," I said, putting down the bag I had grabbed.

"I'm allowed, part of the agreement when I took on training you. Don't worry. Now eat. Magic recovers slower on an empty stomach."

I opened the bag of chips and had a couple. My mom would kill me if she saw me eating chips before lunchtime.

Drake continued talking as I ate. "If you can't teleport a half dozen people with you before you finish your first year, I will be shocked. In a few years time you'll probably be doing stuff that no one has ever done before. I know that I've done a thing or two that people didn't think was possible."

"Like what?" I asked.

"I can create a telepathic network, keep myself loosely in the heads of hundreds, if not thousands of people all at once, and I can make myself focus on a specific person in an instant if they say or think a keyword that grabs my attention. Recently, I've been working with a mortician to see if I can read the final thoughts of the deceased. Not easy or fun, let me tell you, but it seems to be working."

Drake said it like it was the most casual thing in the world. Like the fact that he could be reading thousands of peoples' minds all at once was no big deal. Or that reading the minds of the dead wasn't downright spooky. It made me even more grateful that he couldn't get into my head. But it also made me curious.

"Any theories about what a more powerful teleporter could do?"

Drake's face lit up like someone who had a great day and gets to talk about it. "Teleporting people or objects alongside you without having to touch them is the most common theory, but some of the more outlandish theories suggest things like being able to teleport people away from you by wishing it . . ."

Teleport people away by wishing it?

I started to think back to that day in the back alley. The people in suits, holding their guns on the man in the trench coat. One of them had noticed me and pointed her gun at me. And then, I remember, the two of them, the two with guns. They reeled like they were in pain, and then they disappeared. Had I done that? Had the man in the trench coat?

". . . or being able to teleport an item or person from anywhere in the world to you as long as you know where they are. There was another one, but it might be too morbid for you, kid."

Somehow, I hadn't missed a word he'd said. I reached into my shirt, clutched the little cross on my necklace, and said, "Tell me."

But Drake was transfixed on something else. He stared at my hand in utter disbelief. "A cross? Really?"

I honestly had no idea what to say to that, other than, "What's wrong with a cross?"

"Well . . . ." Drake began, but then he shook his head, stood up, and said, "Never mind. The theory is that you could teleport only part of something. The theorist, war general might be more accurate, gave the example of being able to teleport the heart out of your enemy's body."

I felt my face go green, my stomach churning at the thought. I held it in though and, thankfully, did not vomit all over the place.

Drake shrugged as he looked at my strained face. "Told you it was morbid."

"Why would . . . why would anyone want that?" I said as I finally became willing to open my mouth again.

Drake smiled and pulled another book out of his backpack and telekinetically placed it on top of the other. It was called, Magic Throughout the Ages: A History of the Great Cities. "It's a more recent book, but it covers all of the important facts."

"How many books are you going to give me?" I asked, looking incredulously at the first two books he had passed me. They were each as long as the Bible itself, if not longer!

"Well, there's this one," Drake said, and on top of the two tomes dropped a book called, Mastery of Time and Space.

"And this one for some light reading," Drake said as he pulled out a fourth book and placed it on top of the other three. This one looked somewhat smaller than the others, but to call it light reading would be like saying The Lord of the Rings trilogy is light reading because it's shorter than the Bible. The title of the book was Theories and Speculations on Time Travel.

"Time Travel is light reading? Also, time travel? Really?"

"No one has ever done it, but there is no reason to believe it is impossible."

But I was going to be the best at it. Would that really mean . . . .

"So, I could change the past, like in Back to the Future?"

Drake looked at me like I was an idiot and said, "Like in what? Mundane world science on how time works suggests that even if time travel was possible, you couldn't change the past. Anything you did in the past would be what was necessary to create the present you came from."

"How do you know all of this?" I asked, getting up from the bench to give my legs a stretch.

"I study the world instead of frivolously seeking entertainment," Drake replied, a bit of a superior tone to his voice, like he looked down on people who didn't study the world as much as him. I hope he didn't think I'd be too much like him.

"No entertainment?"

"None," Drake replied, "I get my entertainment from having a fuller understanding of the world around me and the way it works."

"So when I mentioned Back to the Future?"

"That's a movie, right?"

"You've never . . . ."

Drake shuddered as he said, "The amount that most people need stories instead of studying the world around them baffles me. How could I waste my time reading or watching fiction when the facts of the world are far more interesting?"

I wasn't too sure how I could respond to that. The thought of someone who doesn't watch movies or read novels was baffling to me.

"Enough talk, though," Drake said with a quick smile, "you've probably got enough magic in you for a little more practice and I want you to try your hand at something else."

Drake hovered over to the middle of the field and telekinetically brought all of the baseballs around the field to him. He opened a door with his telekinesis and a pitching machine flew out and landed next to him.

"Just stand right there," Drake said as he pointed at home plate. "I don't want you to dodge the balls. I want you to slow time down enough that you can catch them in your bare hands."

He tossed a ball in the machine and it launched at me. I focused on the ball, slowing it down, slower and slower. But it was still coming in too fast. I reached out my hand to grab it, and I did.

Only to drop the ball as I keeled over, gasping for breath.

Drake hovered over to me and helped me to my feet. "You okay? I guess that was a bit much for you, huh?"

"Yeah, I think so."

"Okay," Drake said, "you're not recovering as fast as I thought you would. I guess even among aberrations there are some differences. Maybe you should just head back to your regular class for the rest of the day."

Before I did, I turned back to Drake, who was cleaning up all of the balls he had tossed all over the place.

"Hey, why are you teaching me?"

"I want to know more about us. Don't you? This seemed like a good way to do it."

I walked away from the coliseum. Drake was right. I did want to know more about us. I was already looking forward to my next lesson. As long as he didn't expect me to have all of these books read for a few months.

12| SHEILA

So we had been learning magic for, like, an entire week now and half the people in the class hadn't even managed to do anything. Jasmine got her first taste a couple days ago when she managed to use light magic, and I got my second taste when I managed to use water. Two different types of magic for the so-called weakling. I was the second one in the class to get two different types of magic. That felt really good.

My sister was outright shocked when I turned out to be good at water magic. Her jaw literally hit the floor. Water magic represents a person who can stand strong, while being fluid.

Of course, using water magic had the delightful result of making me convulse again. My sister was angry about that, and almost demanded that I stop. But I kept showing up for classes, and despite being teacher, she couldn't kick me out if I wanted to be there.

Today was going to be illusions day, after lunch, anyways.

The morning was boring. Blah blah blah, magic is dangerous, blah blah blah, you can kill yourself if you're not careful, blah blah blah.

Afternoon finally came, and in the classroom was a medic and an expert in illusions. I was used to the medic by now; they keep one around in the event anything bad should happen. My sister was probably lying about that and the medic was there just for me. She would do that kind of thing.

The Illusionist was an interesting man. He was hot. Of course, after taking a moment to stop drooling I realized that his appearance was probably an illusion.

Amber strode to the front of the room. "You know the drill, everyone, it's testing time and today is illusions," she said.

"Blaine, would you please come on up?" Amber said, asking him politely, even though she, like the rest of us, knew that it was a waste of time. Farm-boy was so good at that time junk that there was no way he was actually good at any other type of magic.

"Concentrate, Blaine. Think about a time when you had to hide who you truly are."

Farm-boy gave it a shot. And we wasted ten minutes watching him try.

Farm-boy adjusted his ball cap as he walked back to our little group and took a seat.

"Sheila," my sister said.

If all I had to do was concentrate on a time when I had to hide who I was, then this one should be easy. I do it every day. All those popular girls and all the nonsense about makeup and boys and celebrity gossip and all that garbage; caring about any of that bull was a lie.

I've loved cheerleading since I was a little girl. I love the flips, the teamwork, the synchronized moves, all of it. But at high school, being a cheerleader also meant being popular. If I wanted to keep doing what I loved, I had to pretend to be one of those trashy idiots.

So I did. I started wearing more makeup than any sane person should. Started going to parties all the time. Drank a couple times when I couldn't manage to get out of it. That was becoming more and more common.

And then I found myself being a monster towards other people, even when the other cheerleaders weren't around. Being rude to my sister, dating a football player who was a complete jerk, being a nightmare to all those new girls at cheerleading tryouts. The lie had become my face.

I felt my body start to twitch.

It was working. I was good at illusions! No one was going to think I was the weakling. The first in the class to be good at three different schools. I . . . .

The spasming got worse. I could still tell what was going on around me, though, like I could every time.

The medic in the room moved swiftly to me. I felt his hand

on my chest, trying to heal me. I could feel the spasms getting lighter, slowing down.

But then they sped back up, faster and worse than before.

The medic pulled his arm away, "She's dying!"

Dying?

"You have to do something!" Amber shouted as she grabbed the medic and pushed him down beside me.

"I don't know enough," the medic protested, "she needs an expert and she needs them now!"

Farm-boy raced over to me, placing his hand behind my head. "I'll take her. Is she safe to teleport?"

"No," the medic said, "but she's dead if you don't. Go!"

Farm-boy placed his hand on my chest, and in an instant, the surroundings looked completely different. I think it was the Life building. The hospital. Not that I could move my head around to check.

"She's dying. She needs help. Now!" Farm-boy shouted through the hallway.

I couldn't see enough of what was going on, but I felt myself get picked up, Farm-boy carrying me in his arms. He must be getting such a thrill out of this, the creep.

"Doctor Edwin is on the fourth floor," the receptionist said.

"Got it."

We teleported again. I could feel my body shaking worse than before. I honestly don't know how Farm-boy was able to keep a hold on me.

"HELP!" Blaine shouted as he reappeared.

"Oh my god," I heard a woman say, "What happened?"

"She made an illusion, and now—" Psycho stopped. Was he stammering?

Doctor Edwin said, placing her hand on me. "She pushed her magic too hard. Her life is leaking out of her. She's dead in under a minute unless . . . ."

"Unlesswhat," I heard Blaine say, but he said it super fast, I barely understood him.

"Areyou—?"

"Slowingherdown,whatdoyouneed?"

"Sheneedsalifetransfusion."

Life transfusion? What was that? I felt my body convulse again, the room started to go blurry, and my chest hurt, a lot. I would have screamed in pain, if I had been able to scream.

"Doit."

"Ineedsomeonetotakelifefrom."

"Hersisterwillbe here soon," I heard, as time started to come back to normal.

"She has seconds."

"I'll do it," Farmboy said, as if he actually cared about me.

"You're going to lose some of your life. At least six months, maybe as much as twenty years. Are you sure?"

At that moment, I knew I was dead. No way Farm-boy would do that.

"I'm saving someone's life. What other choice is there?" Farm—no, Blaine said, as he placed me on a gurney that a couple of nurses had wheeled into the room.

He would do that for me?

"I need your hand."

Blaine grabbed the doctor's hand, and the doctor grabbed one of my hands with his other.

"This will hurt, a lot," the doctor said.

"Just do it, she's dying!"

I heard a scream, no, two screams. Blaine was screaming . . . and so was I. I stopped seeing the hospital. Images flashed before my eyes. There was a man, bleeding out. And the hospital, and the needles. The locked room.

It hurt, it hurt so much. But I . . . I . . . .

I awoke in a hospital bed, Amber looking down at me.

"What happened?"

Amber almost leapt over and hugged me, but stopped herself short. I then saw the nurse beside my sister, and my sister gave a sheepish grin as she backed away to let the nurse through.

"You gave us quite a scare, little miss, why, if it hadn't been for that boy right there, well, I don't think you would be with us right now."

I glanced over at the other bed in the room. Blaine was lying there, unconscious. Matt and Jasmine were at his bedside.

"Oh my god, is he—?"

Just resting," the nurse replied, "you have a very brave friend."

"Ugh," I heard Blaine say as he moved his hands to rub his eyes.

Amber stepped over and sat down on Blaine's bed, stopping herself short from hugging him, "Thank you. Thank you so much. If she had . . . thank you."

My sister, speechless; you don't see that every day.

The nurse was quick to scoot everyone out of the room. "Alright, they're okay. Now let them rest. Life transfusions are not easy."

Matt left quickly and quietly, Jasmine hesitated, but didn't argue much. My sister? The nurse almost had to push her out of the room.

"Hey there, you okay," Blaine asked as he leaned over to look at me.

"Yeah," I replied. I felt okay. Actually, I felt more than okay, I felt fantastic. What was up with that?

"Why did you do that?" I asked.

"Do what?"

"Save me."

Blaine glanced away from me, looked up at the ceiling, and said, "It was the right thing to do."

I had been completely wrong about Blaine. He was a decent guy.

"Thank you, Blaine," I said, leaning on my pillow so I could look over at him. "And I'm sorry. I think I owe you an apology for the way I treated you. I think I know what you went through."

Blaine's head jerked so fast I thought he might get whiplash. "What?"

"I . . . when you were transferring your life to me . . . I think some memories came in, too."

I don't think I've ever seen Blaine so scared. "Please, don't tell anyone. I don't want to do that to my parents. I don't want to have to move again."

"I won't," I said. And I meant it. Blaine saved my life. I would never do anything to hurt him.

"I just . . . ." I started to say, but paused and then started to whisper, "I just don't really understand what I saw. I caught bits and pieces. A man bleeding in a back alley, being in a hospital, getting injections, stuck in a locked room; what was that?"

Blaine hesitated for a moment, then looked back at the ceiling, unable to meet my eyes. "That's how I got my first taste of magic. I saw that man in the back alley, he was shot by two women in suits. And then the women disappeared, like they teleported or something. The man died and . . . well, when I tried to explain everything I sounded crazy. I went back to school, and got teased by my classmates. I fought a few of them. Got suspended a couple times. My teachers thought the death had bothered me, told my parents I should get tested. Doctors said I had Post-Traumatic Stress Disorder. I spent most of the summer in a psych ward."

I laid there, dumbfounded.

"Happy?"

"Blaine, I'm sorry. I shouldn't have asked."

"It's okay," he said, still not looking at me.

It wasn't until that moment that it clicked in me that Blaine didn't really like me either. But he had still saved my life.

"I haven't been the best person to you," I began, "Can I get a chance to change that?"

Blaine actually looked over at me when I said that, surprise and skepticism on his face. "Are you serious?"

"Yeah," I said, "I mean, you just saved my life. I don't think I can ever really pay that back. But I can be your friend."

Blaine raised an eyebrow, "Really?"

"Yeah, I mean, we learn all this magic together. And it would be great to talk to someone outside of Atlantis about it who isn't my sister," I said with a laugh. "So, friends?"

Blaine smiled, "Sure, friends."

"Good, now maybe you can show off that teleporting thing to me sometime when I'm not dying."

13| SHEILA

IT'S BEEN OVER A MONTH SINCE BLAINE SAVED MY LIFE. IT SOMETIMES feels like I'm wasting the life Blaine gave me when I keep trying to learn magic. But he has been super supportive and has helped me out a ton. I'm going to get out of this Intro to Magic class and move to start taking full-time classes in just a week.

I've learned a lot. I'm okay at phasing, water, and illusions. I've not only stopped convulsing when I use magic, but I can even get off two or three spells in under an hour before I end up earning my Zs! The illusions are the easiest. Illusions are all about hiding who you really are, and I do that on a daily basis.

Grant and I are still together. I'm not going to screw up. Good marks, popular, all that stuff. I'm going to be valedictorian in a few years, just like I always planned, and I'm gonna lead the cheerleaders to nationals, if not higher. I'm technically not the leader of the cheerleaders, that's Natasha, but seriously, I'm the best the squad has.

As I sat down for lunch with the girls, I looked over. Blaine was sitting with a couple of other guys from the school. He and I act like we're not friends outside Atlantis. The cheerleaders don't like him, and Blaine gets that I need them to like me. Or rather, he puts up with it. Blaine was laughing, probably at some joke Jake told him, when Grant walked by and 'slipped.' Grant's tray of food, including hot soup, spilled all over onto Blaine.

Blaine yelped and jumped up. I saw his fists clench, he was tired of Grant and his constant bullying. One day he wouldn't hold back anymore and Grant would get it.

But today was not that day. Blaine unclenched his fists, grabbed a napkin to clean himself off, and that was it.

Blaine could have used his magic there. He could have

used it every damn day for the last two months that Grant has been tormenting him. Stop time, challenge him to a fight and take revenge. Blaine could beat Grant in a fight easy. Maybe even without magic. But instead, Blaine lets Grant and the other jocks bully him. I've tried to get Grant to stop, but he doesn't listen to me.

Fortunately, today was one of the better days, for Blaine, anyways. Mr. Brown was watching, and Mr. Brown looked out for Blaine. "Grant, come with me, now."

Grant ignored Mr. Brown and continued walking. He gave me a smile as he headed to the table.

Mr. Brown put his hand on Grant's shoulder. "I said, come with me."

"Hey, you can't grab me, man," Grant said, turning around.

"I will grab anyone I want when I see them being abusive towards students in this school. Now, as I said, come with me."

Grant yanked Mr. Brown's hand off his shoulder and glared at him. "No way."

It almost looked like Grant was ready to get into a fight with Mr. Brown. I know he doesn't like the guy. Grant thinks Mr. Brown is out to get him.

Mr. Brown's frustration vanished, replaced with a weird calm, "I could always get you suspended, or expelled."

Grant laughed. "I would love to see you try, the principal loves me. I'm the best quarterback this school's ever seen."

Mr. Brown looked more dangerous than I thought he could, a small smile on his lips as he said, "Apologize. Last warning."

Grant laughed, turned his back to Mr. Brown, and said, "Good luck, geezer."

Grant grabbed me from the table I was sitting at, lifted me up, and said, "Hey, babe."

Mr. Brown walked away and pulled out his cell phone.

"Man, can you believe that douche?" Grant said.

I smiled that smile no one knew was fake. "Oh, totally, and he, like, plays total favourites."

"Yeah," Grant said, "I'd sure love to take him down a peg."

Somehow, I knew that if Mr. Brown and Grant were to fight, that Mr. Brown would come out on top.

When cheerleading practice ended after school, Natasha bolted over to my locker. "Make him happy."

She passed me a key. A motel room key.

No. Oh, god no. Not this.

It was an unwritten thing in the cheerleaders. After a big loss, or any problems with a member of the team, the cheerleaders rent a motel room and have sex with their boyfriend to cheer them up.

Grant and I had never done it. I know he's wanted to, but I've managed to get him off my back about it. I'm just lucky Grant would rather have a rich girlfriend than one who puts out. I pay for everything, and sex has always been off the table. I wouldn't be surprised if he was cheating on me. I don't ask. I don't want to know. I'm only dating him because he's popular.

"What happened?" I asked, trying to keep the fear out of my voice. Not an easy thing when Natasha can smell fear like a shark smells blood.

Fortunately, she didn't notice. I have no idea how she missed it. "Grant's suspended. Make him happy." She said the last part painfully slow and aggressively.

I wanted to shove that key in her face and tell her to go screw herself. But I couldn't do that. If I wanted to remain on the cheerleaders, if I wanted to keep my popular boyfriend and one day become prom queen and valedictorian, then I needed to keep up appearances. Even if that meant doing the stuff that my sister says 'No self-respecting woman would ever do.'

"Grant knows. He's grabbing his car. Go." Natasha grabbed my books and bag, shoved them back into my locker, and slammed it shut.

I headed out, still in my cheerleading uniform. I pulled out my phone, and sent a quick text to Blaine. 'Grab my stuff?'

Blaine responded quickly. 'Okay.' Not K or OK, the, like, proper-spelled version and all. He never shortens words in his texts or anything, it's, like, proper grammar and stuff all the time. I've bugged him about it so much.

Grant was waiting with his car right at the entrance, where

the buses are supposed to park. In fact, there was a bus waiting for him to move. The bus driver was honking the horn at him and demanding he move.

But of course he wouldn't. So I had to fix it. I dashed to the car, hopped in, and we headed off.

Grant was unusually quiet. That was not good. He was one of those quiet-fury types. If he was fully and truly angry, he just stopped talking, like, totally and completely.

Grant drove aggressively. He was going way too fast, darting and shooting in between lanes so that he didn't have to slow down. We almost got in an accident six times in as many blocks.

"Um, Grant, maybe just, like, calm down, you know?"

Wrong thing to say, Sheila. Absolutely wrong thing to say.

Grant got insulted and accelerated harder. We were now going over eighty in a fifty zone.

I didn't say another word. We raced out of town in complete silence.

It didn't take long before we arrived at the motel. I walked into the room, terrified. I wasn't one of those prudes who wanted to wait until marriage, but this didn't seem like the way my first time should go.

Grant started kissing me. I usually enjoy that. But today it felt all wrong. His lips felt slimy and sweaty, his tongue like a worm. His hand went underneath my skirt less than a minute after we had started.

I put my hand on his, "No."

He ignored me. His hand started to reach for the shorts I wear under my cheerleader skirt.

I grasped his hand and pulled it away.

Grant was not expecting that. His other hand came around, and held my arm down while he reached for my shorts.

"No! Stop!" I shouted at him, panicking.

Grant looked at me and said calmly and firmly, "No. You stop."

"Stop it! I don't want this."

"You've made me wait for over a year. And today, on the worst day of my life, you won't do this for me? How selfish can you be?"

I tried to get out from under him. But I couldn't. He was too strong.

"Please, don't," I said, tears streaming from my eyes.

"What are you doing? Stop crying!"

I wanted out. I needed out. I couldn't breathe. I was gasping, choking.

"I said, stop crying," Grant shouted. He slapped me in the face. I felt my lips crack, and in a couple seconds I could taste my own blood in my mouth.

I screamed.

"Stupid bitch."

He pulled my shorts off and started to reach for my panties. He was too strong. There was nothing I could do.

Except . . . .

I phased. His body went right through mine and I slid off the bed and onto my feet.

"What the—" Grant shouted. "Get back here!"

Grant beat me to the door.

"You had the key. This was your idea!"

I kept as far from him as I could. My breath was short. I had a month of training in me, but it still exhausted me to do that level of magic.

Grant lunged. I phased again and he went right through me, slamming his head on the nightstand by the bed.

I ran out of the motel room while still out of phase.

Grant burst out of the door after me, "Get back here!"

I saw him bleeding from his forehead as he ran after me.

I ran, trying to get somewhere, the front desk of the motel. There had to be someone there. But Grant was faster than me. He grabbed my arm. I tried to pull away from him, but his grip was too strong.

"Oh no, you're not getting away this time. You've been teasing me for the last year. Today, today I get what I want."

"N-N-No," I said, still struggling in his grasp.

Grant shoved me into a puddle. He reached down to grab me, by my hair.

I didn't know what to do. I had no way out. I wasn't strong enough to hurt him. I needed something to hit him with. Something to stop him. But there was nothing. Just the road and a damn puddle of water.

Water!

I was tired, weak. But I needed my magic to work. I needed to cast one more spell without passing out.

I focused on the water, not on Grant standing above me.

I focused on the water, on the memories of all the times I had gone with the flow, and shattered those memories with a time I went against the flow.

I focused on right now, on my fear, standing strong despite it.

The water rose up from the puddle. It forged into a ball. And I hurled that ball right at Grant.

The ball hit him square in the chest and sent him crashing to the ground. I could hear him moaning in pain.

I raced behind a car, out of view, and I pulled my watch to my face, "I need a mind-wiper now. Someone saw magic."

It took less than ten seconds before there was a portal, and that General guy, Cab something, came out, along with, like, a dozen other people.

"No Blaine?"

I shook my head. No Blaine? Why was he asking about—

"Put up a Time Stop," the General replied.

Oh.

"What happened?" the General asked.

"He was trying to . . . to . . . ." I stuttered.

The General grabbed me in his arms and gave me a hug. I don't know why he did that, but it felt safe. I needed safe.

"I understand," he said calmly, releasing me from the hug. His hands were on my shoulders as he looked me in the eyes. "You're safe now. He can't hurt you. What would you like us to do?"

I didn't know. I just wanted out.

"Do you want to forget this?"

A mind-wipe? On me?

I just started crying. I couldn't stop. The General held me in his arms as he said, "Shh, shh, it's okay. He will never hurt you again."

"B-b-but he's my . . . ."

"I know. Take a few minutes, cry, get it out of your system." The General let me go, and had me sit down as he walked over to his men.

I just sat there as two of the soldiers with the General held Grant down, and a third reached over and put his hand on Grant's forehead.

"He won't remember the magic. What else you want him to forget is up to you."

The words hung in my head for what felt like forever. They were offering to alter Grant's memories around however I wanted. I couldn't process it, but eventually it finally clicked in my mind. Stealing his memories, changing them, that would have been as bad as what he tried to do to me.

"No, don't do anything," I wiped away my tears and got to my feet, still trembling. From fear or nearly passing out from using too much magic, I'm not sure. Probably both.

I thought about what was going to happen tomorrow. I had turned down Grant, star of the football team. If he remembered, he would break up with me. Natasha would find out, and I would be off the cheerleaders so fast it would make my head spin, quite possibly because they'd hurt me to get me off of the team.

I could have taken it all back. Have them erase any memory Grant had of me resisting. I could go back into that room, sleep with him, and keep everything the way it was. Remain a cheerleader, remain the girlfriend of the most popular guy in school, remain popular. I could have it all, and it would only cost my dignity.

But no. I couldn't do that. I wouldn't let him use me.

I was done with that. Atlantis had shown me that I didn't need that. I had friends there. Real friends who would stand by my side. Friends like Jasmine and Matt.

And Blaine.

I stood up, wiped the tears from my eyes and said, "I'll deal. Do what you have to and nothing else."

One of the soldiers looked at the General, "The boy has a cracked rib, sir."

General Cabrera looked at me and said, "We can heal it if you want."

I thought about that. Thought about it long and hard.

"No," I replied, "he needs the injury. He tried to rape me, I cracked his rib. He needs something to show him that he can't just keep doing whatever he wants."

The General had his time and space master come over. "He will take you home. We will deal with the rest."

"Thank you," I said to the General.

The man teleported me home. It's funny, but after all of that I wasn't thinking about how scared I was, or how much I hated Grant and the cheerleaders. It seemed like a distant blur, like something ages ago in the past; because, although I shared her looks and memories, I was nothing like the girl who stepped into that car with Grant just an hour before.

14| BLAINE

SHEILA HAD NEVER MISSED A LESSON BEFORE, AND WE WERE IN THE LAST couple days of class. Matt, Jasmine and I were wondering about her.

We'd become kind of tight over the course of our Intro class. Sometimes it felt like the three of them were the reason I kept coming back to Atlantis.

I've been working with Mr. Brown. Mostly just here or there in the evenings. It's usually two lessons a week, maybe three. Mr. Brown had been helping me a lot with mastering my aberration. Drake tries, but he can't compete with Mr. Brown's knowledge.

I've stopped a few crimes. Nothing too big, mostly pickpocketing and theft. It's not like I live in a place where I could expect a murder every day.

Class was kind of boring. Amber had even pointed out that anyone who made it this far was pretty much guaranteed to pass the class. Hard to believe that after only a couple months magic can seem dull, but studying up on what all the different schools of magic can do isn't as exciting as actually doing the magic. At the end of the day I asked Amber where Sheila was. Her reply? "Leave her alone."

Which really just meant doing the usual outside Atlantis.

I got my first hint of the problem during first period. Sheila came in and took her usual seat. The other cheerleaders sat around her, but didn't seem to be talking to her. They were talking around her.

Okay, I got it, Sheila had done something to tick off the other cheerleaders, and now she wanted back in.

I prayed that there would be partner work in second period so that Sheila and I could talk, but luck wasn't with me then.

It took forever for lunch to arrive. The clock felt like it was draining away every second so slowly. I needed to talk to Sheila, see if she was okay, but there was no way to ask. I grabbed my lunch and hung out with Jake and the guys. Sheila wouldn't want me to break our standing relationship, even if she was having an awful day. I took a glance over at the cheerleader table, where Sheila was standing with her food, but no one was making room for her.

The place was loud, what cafeteria isn't, but I could still hear her.

"Is this how it's going to be?"

I could hear Natasha respond, "You know what you did."

Sheila's voice spewed the venom that I remember being directed at me only weeks ago, "Oh, I'm sorry. I didn't realize NOT sleeping with my boyfriend was a crime."

"You cracked his rib. We're gonna lose today's game 'cause of you."

The few tables next to the cheerleaders went quiet. Jake whispered to me, "Cat fight incoming."

I would have laughed, if Sheila wasn't involved.

"You act like just 'cause he's the quarterback, I'm supposed to lie down and take it. Well, I'm sorry, but unlike the rest of you, I have a little something called integrity," Sheila said, as she forcibly put her tray down on the table, on top of the meals of some of the other cheerleaders.

Natasha's scowl could have been declared a lethal weapon as she replied, "Integrity? You sound like all of those losers who call us whores behind our backs. They have to tell themselves that to get by every day knowing they don't matter."

Sheila, hands on her hips, defiance on her face, said, "Here's how much I think you matter," she began, emphasizing the 'you', "One, you can tell Grant yourself that things are over between me and him, just in case he's thick enough to think otherwise. Two, you can say goodbye to that week-long trip out of the country that the cheerleaders were going to take during finals week in January, the one that had us writing our exams a week AFTER everyone else."

"You can't do that, you don't . . . ." Natasha stammered,

fear mixing in with her anger.

"Over half the cheerleading budget comes from my dad. If I leave, you're broke. Oh, don't try to apologize now. None of you came rushing to my defence. None of you are really my friends, so you can all go screw yourselves. Or go screw your boyfriends, that seems to be all you think you're good for."

There was a lot of whooping and hollering from the other tables. Sheila smiled, put up one of her hands, asking for silence, as she walked through her audience. "And three..."

Sheila pulled me to my feet and kissed me, in front of the entire school!

My eyes bulged. Suddenly, instead of there being loud noise and cheering, it was dead silent.

Sheila smiled, "You didn't need to stop time."

It took looking around the frozen and silent room to realize that I had indeed stopped time.

"That good, was it?" Sheila said, as she leaned her forehead into mine.

"I'm not even sure I like you that way," I said, taking a small step back.

Sheila laughed, "Right, time stopped because you weren't enjoying yourself."

I felt my skin turn red. Do you know how embarrassing that is, to literally feel your skin changing colour?

"Can we talk about this later?" I asked, desperate to change the topic.

"Sure, but it'll look weird if we aren't still kissing when your time stop ends. Ready to keep the show going?"

I nodded.

She kissed me again, and I managed to not stop time.

The school was cheering like it was one of those old cheesy movies: when the popular girl ends up with the everyday ordinary kid.

Which is exactly what it was. Still, I could get used to this.

15| BLAINE

I COULD FEEL MY PALMS GETTING SWEATY AS I WAITED FOR SHEILA AT the restaurant. Mom had dropped me off, not saying much of anything, but grinning like mad the entire time. The dress shirt I was wearing wasn't comfortable in the slightest, and I kind of wanted out of it.

After an eternity of anticipation, fearing that she wasn't going to show up, I saw Sheila coming towards the doors, so I stepped outside to greet her. She was wearing a somewhat short black miniskirt with a deep blue top. She looked great.

"Hey," I said.

Sheila looked at me, a little surprised. "Flowers? On a first date?"

I looked at the bouquet of roses in my hand, then back at her. "Bad idea?"

"No," she said, though I think she might have been lying. She took the flowers and smelled them. "It's sweet."

I blushed. She smiled and said, "This isn't your first date, is it?"

"No . . . ." I lied very unconvincingly.

Sheila nodded, seeing through it in an instant. "Well then, Casanova, let me ask you an honest question: we're going to a movie after dinner, where am I going to keep the flowers?"

I looked at the ground, unable to look at her face. I could not believe how awkward this was. How on earth do people go on dates, they're the most nerve-wracking thing ever.

Sheila grabbed my tie and smiled. "Come on, I'm hungry."

She tugged on my tie and I followed, gliding my hand down the tie to grab hers. I held her hand as we walked back into the restaurant.

The waiter got us a table for two, off in the corner of the restaurant. It wasn't near any windows, and it was a bit away from most of the other guests.

Sheila whispered something about them "not trusting teenagers." I just nodded, trying to swallow the frogs in my throat.

After the waiter got our drink order, Sheila asked, "Okay, how did you know this was my favourite restaurant?"

"I, uh, Amber . . . ." I mumbled.

"Wait, did you . . . did you call my sister for tips on dating me?"

Busted.

"Is that bad?" I asked.

Sheila took a sip of her water. "Naw, it's just . . . weird, I guess. You're trying to do everything you can to impress me. Flowers, great restaurant . . . what movie were you thinking of going to?"

"Well, you said Toy Story was your favourite movie before, so I figured a Pixar film, or as close to a Pixar film as I can get would be a good idea."

"Oh, you mean that new one with the . . . ."

"Yeah."

"I've wanted to see that since the first trailer came out like a year ago!"

"Well tonight's your chance," I laughed as the waiter arrived with our drinks.

"Have you decided on your meals for tonight?" the waiter asked.

I prompted Sheila to go first.

"I want the biggest steak I can get, medium-rare," Sheila quipped, almost salivating as she said it.

"I'll have a steak too, medium," I said, passing my menu to the waiter.

The waiter took the menus and walked away.

Sheila took a sip of her drink. "God, you have no idea how amazing it is to actually drink a coke while on a date."

"Huh?" was the only thing that managed to escape my lips.

"Uh," Sheila began, "I mean, it's been so long since I've had a coke. I forgot how good they are."

"You just had a coke yesterday in Atlantis," I said, because I am clearly terrible at picking up on cues.

Sheila seemed to be a master of conversation steering though, and she said, "Speaking of Atlantis, how are your lessons with Amber's psycho ex-boyfriend?"

"Drake? They're pretty good actually. He's not such a bad guy."

"If your ex wants to light you on fire, you're a bad guy," Sheila replied firmly.

"Okay, you have a point there," I replied. "I just think he's never felt like he could relate to anyone before he met me. I mean, he's had his powers since birth, from what he's told me. Just imagine, spending your entire life always able to read the thoughts of everyone around you, and then for the first time ever, finding someone whose mind you can't read. He has no idea how to have fun, though. I'm surprised he and Amber ever dated."

"But you're actually learning from him? Like, you're getting better?" Sheila replied, steering the conversation again.

"Yeah," I said, "I've actually learned how to teleport somewhere without seeing it. You know, as long as it's not too far away. I suck at anything long."

Sheila giggled.

"What?"

"Just think about what you said."

I did. I could feel my face scrunching up as I thought about it. I didn't get it.

"Really?" Sheila said, looking at my confused face. "You don't get it? Oh my god. You have got to have one of the cleanest minds ever."

And then I got it. If there had been a mirror around, I'm pretty sure my face could have been reasonably compared to ketchup.

Sheila was laughing so hard that there was a person or two in the restaurant looking over at us.

"Okay," I said, trying to speak with confidence despite my red face, "it wasn't that funny."

Sheila calmed down after a few seconds. "No, it *was* that funny. I can't wait for your next slip up."

"So, that's what I am to you?" I replied, mock-angrily, "a source of amusement?"

Sheila's leg glided up mine under the table as she replied, "Yes, but in more ways than one."

And the red returned to my face.

Sheila laughed again as she said, "Okay, this blushing is hilarious, but it is going to get old really fast."

"Okay?"

Sheila continued to run her foot along my leg. I almost started shaking, I was so nervous. God, I've dealt with car thieves and criminals. I've helped Mr. Brown get people with guns arrested. Why on earth was I so afraid of Sheila?

"I'm not stopping until you stop blushing," Sheila said matter-of-factly, her leg running up and down my own.

I needed a way out. And I needed it now.

So I stopped time.

I took a sip of water, and stood up, looking at Sheila, frozen in time. I'd never looked at her that way before. God, she's beautiful.

But it wasn't helping me calm down, not enough, anyways.

I sat back down and time resumed.

I looked at her and said with as much confidence as I could muster, "You done trying to embarrass me?"

"Never," Sheila replied, "though I guess I can do you a favour and take a break. Besides, our food is here."

Sheila was grinning as she cut into her steak and took her first bite. "Mmm, this is delicious. I never could have had a steak with Gra—" She stopped herself short. I guess this wasn't so easy on her either.

"It's okay," I said, "You don't have to hide that you've dated other people."

"Just him," Sheila mumbled, loud enough that I'm not sure I should have heard it, but I did.

"Oh, um . . . ."

"Sorry, I shouldn't have—it just kind of slipped out," Sheila said, not able to look at me.

"Don't worry," I replied. "So we're both not that good at this."

"Well, at least I'm better than you," Sheila joked, "Mr. Tomato Face."

She slid her foot along my leg again, trying to get a reaction from me. I didn't let her. It took a lot of focus, thinking about everything other than her, but I did not feel my face go red.

She continued, a smile on her face. "You're getting better."

As the meal finished, the waiter returned with the bill. Sheila reached for it, but I grabbed it first.

"What are you doing?" I asked as I took a look at the bill.

"Paying for the meal," Sheila said.

"I asked you out," I replied. "Why on earth would you pay for anything?"

"I guess I'm just kind of used to paying," Sheila responded awkwardly.

It hadn't even occured to me that Grant might have made her pay. I know Sheila's family is rich, but that's no excuse to be a jerk instead of a gentleman.

"Well, maybe I'm a bit traditional, but I believe that since I asked you out on the date, I should pay," I said as I pulled out the cash to pay for the meal, leaving a generous tip.

"Does that mean the movie too?" Sheila asked.

"Yes."

"And popcorn?"

"And drinks," I replied before she could ask about that too.

"You can afford all of that?" she asked.

"Hey, I'm not broke," I said as I stood up.

"But your parents . . . ." Sheila took my hand.

"Have both found jobs in the city since I told you they were unemployed," I replied as Sheila and I walked out of the restaurant holding hands.

"Oh, what do they do?"

"My mom works as a receptionist."

"And your dad?"

I felt a little awkward answering this question. Sheila squeezed my hand and said, "It's okay, I promise I won't laugh or make fun of it."

I sighed inwardly. "Somehow, I doubt that."

"Come on, just tell me."

I couldn't even look at her as I muttered, "He actually does sell farm equipment now."

Sheila tried. I could see it in her face, she was trying not to laugh. But it wasn't very easy for her.

"Okay, you can laugh."

And she did. She burst into an uproar of laughter. When she finally stopped laughing she wiped the tears from her eyes. "Oh man, I'm not even sure I should see that movie tonight, it's not going to seem as funny after all of this."

I gave her hand a gentle squeeze and said, "Whatever you want."

Sheila paused, contemplating what she wanted to do. Eventually, she asked, "How far can you teleport?"

"A couple blocks, at best, why?"

Sheila pointed at a building and said, "I think that's the highest point in the city, you could look down on the entire city from there."

I smiled. "Do you want to go up there?"

Sheila nodded.

"Hold on tight."

Sheila squeezed my hand and I thought about what I wanted, being on top of that building. I kept thinking about it, and then, I was up there, Sheila holding my hand.

I looked over at her. Her eyes were closed. I whispered in her ear, "We're here."

Sheila smiled as she looked out at the city. She leaned her head against me and said, "This is better than the movie."

I leaned in and said, "May I?"

Sheila nodded, and puckered her lips.

I kissed her, on top of the entire city.

She leaned back in to me as the kiss was done and said, "I wish every night could be like this."

I whispered in her ear, "Give me a few months, I'll become good enough to take you away for a day in Paris anytime you want."

Sheila nuzzled her head against my chest as she said, "I don't need to go anywhere. I just need you to be there."

16| BLAINE

"SO, YOU'VE HAD AN EVENTFUL WEEK," MR. BROWN SAID.

Mr. Brown and I met at the mall again, by the mini-golf. We always played a round before going out. He'd settled on an illusion that kind of looked like an older brother for me. Helped it to make sense why he was always paying.

"Yeah, it's great, I mean, now she's not hiding that she knows me."

"You had previous interactions with her?" Mr. Brown asked.

"Well, we're both learning magic . . . ."

Maybe I shouldn't have said that. But I liked Mr. Brown. He's actually doing stuff with his magic. Saving lives, helping people, it's what magic should be used for.

Mr. Brown scored a hole in one. Lucky shot.

"Shall we cut this short? I have somewhere we should go."

"You're just saying that because you're finally ahead," I replied.

"You can be so competitive," Mr. Brown replied.

"And you're not?" I asked.

He looked at me with a mischievous smirk, "Come on. I think I found a meth lab in someone's house. You know you want to take down something that big."

"Meth lab?"

"Yeah, all the windows cardboarded up. Probably some kind of drug making at least. So we're gonna go in and take a look. You know the drill?"

I did: teleport in and time stop to take a look around.

I'm not going to lie. Dealing with drug dealers was scary the first couple of times. But with some time stops, I could stop them without being seen.

We walked up to the house. Mr. Brown was hiding himself with illusions, I was acting like a kid out for a walk late at night. Suspicious, maybe, but not necessarily a troublemaker.

I checked my surroundings like Mr. Brown was always telling me to. There was a cop car across the street from the house with two cops inside it.

"Hold up," I said to Mr. Brown, who was standing beside me, although no one else could see that.

"What is it?"

"It looks like the cops already have this man under surveillance."

Mr. Brown glanced over at the cop car. "They can't go in without a warrant; or probable cause. Let's give them some."

"I want to check it out first," I replied.

"It's locked, windows are blocked. And you're still not that good at blind teleports."

"Good time for some practice," I replied.

I pulled up a time stop and teleported inside the house. I focused on wanting to get inside, to the front entrance, and it worked.

I raced up the stairs and took a look around the main floor. Nothing in the kitchen or living room. I dashed around and opened bedroom and bathroom doors. Nothing.

I raced to the basement. Had to hurry, my time stop wouldn't last much longer. There it was. This was drug central. There was a man standing over a table, trying to make the drugs, I was guessing. I ripped a piece of cardboard off of the window. Seeing outside would make this easier for me—not seeing where I was going when I teleported was exhausting.

I teleported out of the house with only four seconds to spare before my time stop ended. Time returned to normal, and I was on the street, walking away, Mr. Brown hiding under an illusion at my side.

"Hey, you, what are you doing?" I heard a voice shout as one of the cops got out of the car.

Mr. Brown vanished.

The cop ran at me and grabbed me by the arm. "What did

123

you do?"

I tried to stop time, but his grip remained firm. It didn't make any sense. Had he managed to be in my time stop?

"You're Blaine" the cop said, "Amber mentioned you."

If I wasn't panicking before, I was certainly panicking then. If Amber had mentioned me to this cop, then he must be a mage too.

I felt the wind blow on my cheek. The wind wouldn't be blowing if I had stopped time. The cop knew anti-magic.

"I'm Dwayne. What are you doing here? Did you go in there?"

"I..."

"Idiot kid. You thought your magic meant you could play vigilante, didn't you?"

I did what any kid who thinks they are in trouble would do. I ran. Or rather, I tried to.

I know, brilliant plan, but hey, I can stop time and teleport, I thought that I could get away. But nothing happened.

Dwayne's grip tightened. "Kid, I hate that I have to do this, but you know Atlantis' rules."

I felt like I had been punched in the gut. He was talking about putting me through a mind-wipe. I couldn't let that happen.

"Please, you don't have to do this. I'm sorry, I won't do it again, I promise."

He let his free hand crackle with lightning for a brief moment, "Kid, if I thought it was okay to use magic against criminals, I'd shut off the power to any house or device I wanted. But that's not how we work."

He ignored my pleading and pulled his watch to his face, "This is Dwayne Cooper, I have a Code Blue involving Blaine Allan. Requesting an escort team."

They couldn't teleport in if I didn't let them, so I focused on preventing anyone from teleporting.

Dwayne tightened his grip on me, "I've known magic for ten years. You're not good enough to break through my anti-magic."

Within five seconds, a team of two dozen people in the military suits of Atlantis appeared. General Cabrera himself was with them. He brought a pair of handcuffs over and slapped them on me. I could feel magic from those cuffs coursing through me, cutting off my own magic.

There was a look of disappointment on his face, as though Cabrera was sad that he had to do this to me.

Still, it didn't stop him from performing his duty.

"Blaine Allan, you are under arrest for vigilantism and illegal use of magic."

17| BLAINE

I WAS TAKEN TO A HOLDING CELL. IT FELT LIKE A PRISON, BUT WAY TOO clean and shiny to actually be one. The walls were white tile, as was the floor and ceiling. It was perfectly square, and there was nothing in it. If gravity were to disappear in this room, you would not be able to tell which way you came in, even the door disappeared as they locked it behind me. It kind of felt like . . . being back in the psych ward. I started to shake. No, I was better. I knew that I wasn't crazy. But that man, and the guns, and the blood . . . .

I stopped thinking about it.

After being stuck in the cell for what felt like forever, someone finally came to talk to me. Someone wearing a nice suit. They told me to not worry about my family finding out. I noticed a squad of a dozen men in yellow outside my door when my lawyer, or whatever he was, left the room. They all had the three-headed dog Cerberus emblazoned on the backs of their uniforms. Masters of Protection. They were hoping that a dozen people focusing anti-magic on me would prevent me from using any.

Getting a trial seemed downright weird. I'd only been in Atlantis for a month or so, but I hadn't seen or heard of a trial happening before.

After another eternity, I was finally summoned.

The dozen guards in yellow marched me to the chambers, my hands and legs in chains. Chains similar to the handcuffs they had put me in before. But stronger, much stronger.

I entered one of the city's coliseums. And it was packed. I was taken to the centre, where there were seven people seated on a raised platform.

General Cabrera was there, left of centre, and Amber was on the far right. In the middle was a woman I had seen images of, but had never met: President Mbanefo, head of the entire city of Atlantis. She kept her hair particularly short, and her black hair was almost the same shade as her skin. She looked like a proper and regal person, nice suit, professional hair and make-up. Though she was overdoing it with the jewelry: she had at least a dozen rings between all of her fingers. All of the rings had gems that looked almost identical to Amber's necklace. The President must really hate having people get in her head. Or it was a safety thing. The President needed a mind that couldn't be influenced. I guess then the better question would be, why doesn't anyone else have some level of protection?

Speaking of the others, I recognized a couple of them from times in my Intro to Magic classroom. The one seated beside Amber was Doctor Edwin, the one who saved Sheila's life. On the far left was Master Tantalo. He taught us about aberration magic on our first day of classes. And between the Master and General Cabrera was a man who had stepped in on my Intro class a couple of times. The Teacher Folstad, head of the school. I had no clue who the woman seated next to the President was though. But I could take a guess. Amber mentioned in our Intro to Magic class before that there were six leaders in Atlantis: the President, the General, the Doctor, the Teacher, the Master, and the Lawyer. The last one must be Lawyer Sagoung.

What was Amber doing with them?

"The council of six rises, and acknowledges Amber Bennett, warden over Blaine Allan, as the seventh in this trial."

The president stood, a level of calm on her face. "We come together today to deal with a very serious issue. The charged, Blaine Allan, has been accused of illegal use of magic in the real world for the purposes of vigilantism."

There was murmuring from the crowd, but when the President spoke, all other noise stopped immediately. "Would Dwayne Cooper please speak."

Dwayne came forward, stood on a platform and began to speak, all noise save his voice vanished, "I'm a cop. My partner and I were watching the house of a suspected drug dealer when

I saw Blaine Allan. He had disappeared and reappeared. At the same time, a covered window of the house became uncovered. I can only ascertain that Blaine utilized teleportation and time stopping magic to enter and exit the house."

"Objection," I tried shouting, but no sound came out.

The President noticed that I tried to speak and said, "Would you like to say something?"

"Yeah," I began, staring them down. Not an easy thing to do when their platform had them easily ten feet above me. "You can't say I'm guilty just 'cause I happened to be near a certain place."

"Dwayne Cooper's partner is not a mage, and was present to witness what you did. You are being charged with either using magic to be a vigilante, or with reckless use of magic in mundane populated areas. Either one warrants the same charge: banishment."

Maybe a trial is what happens when people get banished, but certainly not with this much fanfare. Not with an audience. I would have heard about that. "And where is my jury? All I see are seven judges."

"Amber's appointment is the closest you will get. Amber is your warden, you are her responsibility. As such, she is entitled to the seventh seat at this trial," the Master said.

"Sounds like you have alrea—" I was cut off again before I could finish.

"You will be given permission to speak," the President said, "when it is your turn."

I stood there, furious at my voice having been cut off. The President seemed to have some sort of silence field working. I saw a remote at her seat, probably to mute the crowd, or me, or whatever.

"Blaine, why were you at the house in question?" Lawyer Sagoung asked.

I didn't know what to say. To not be banished, I would have to lie. And I didn't want to get stuck in a cycle of lies again, like it took me to get out of the psych ward.

Fortunately, I was given a reprieve when a man walked into the coliseum and marched straight to the counsel.

Drake.

"I have an objection to make," Drake shouted.

"You will contain yourself," The President shouted as Drake approached.

"No," Drake replied. I could see some sweat on his brow. He was concentrating on something. I don't know what, but unlike me, they weren't silencing him.

"What do you want?" Master Tantalo demanded.

"I have been personally training Blaine. Why was I not informed that he was on trial?" Drake said, fury seething from his voice.

"His trial is none of your—" the President began. Several guards started to approach Drake. He hovered above them and pushed them away with ease.

"That wasn't very nice," Drake said.

"What do you want?" the Master demanded.

"Your job," Drake replied, looking the Master square in the eyes.

If the crowd hadn't been utterly silent already, they sure were then.

"I beg your pardon?" The Master said, but you could tell he was more nervous than anything.

"The Master is supposed to be the most powerful mage in the city. I'm the most powerful. And all of you know that."

The president looked furious. Master Tantalo looked terrified. He was scared. The most powerful mage in the city, and he was scared. Now that said a lot about just how strong Drake was.

"Drake, now is not the time nor pl—" The President began.

Drake interrupted as a book telekinetically floated up to the stand where the President sat, "Actually, it is. The case of Wilhelm v. Kathri of 1942, stated that a challenge to the Master's status as the best mage can be made at any time. So I will fight for the right to take my position on this council before any votes are cast."

The President stepped down from the platform and whispered to Drake. I could hear it, but I doubt anyone else could. "You will become a member of this council over my dead body."

The audience gasped.

Drake laughed, "Poor choice of words—I have my mind linked to everyone in the audience. Anything I hear, they hear."

The President smiled at Drake, "They're not gasping at your mental message, they're screened from magic. They're gasping because illusionists made it look like you just hit me."

The President stepped back. "Guards!"

At least fifty soldiers charged towards Drake, all wearing the Cerberus symbol of those specialized in protection and anti-magic.

Drake tried to push them away, and succeeded with about half, but the other half got through and restrained him. They tossed chains on him. Just like the ones I had.

The President calmly responded, "Drake, you have attempted to disrupt our lawful courtroom and assaulted the President. I find you in contempt of court. You will be placed into a jail cell for the remainder of your days, forever locked away in Atlantis. Council of six, please raise your hand if you support a sentence of life in prison for Drake."

Master Tantalo, Lawyer Sagoung, Teacher Folstad, and the President all raised their hands.

"Four to two," Lawyer Sagoung said, "The motion carries."

The guards dragged Drake away.

"Shall we proceed with the charges?" The Lawyer asked before Drake was even out of sight, "How do you plead, Blaine Allan?"

I hadn't done anything wrong. I was taking down a drug dealer. I wasn't the villain.

"I was doing what you should be doing," I said.

The words came out before I realized just what I was saying.

"I beg your pardon, Blaine?" Lawyer Sagoung said. "But it sounds like you just admitted to committing the crime that we have accused you of."

I glared at her. "I committed no crime. I did what was right. Using magic to help people, stopping criminals. Where were you during the holocaust, or 9/11?"

The President looked at me and responded, "And pray tell,

130

Blaine, whose side should we take? How can we intervene when we have citizens from every single nation? Do we tell some people we have chosen to side against them? Then what? Do we banish them? Jail them? Let them stay and risk civil war? No. We do not interfere in the affairs of the mundanes. We remain neutral. Not because we do not recognize how horrendous these actions are, rather because we will not take actions that will divide our people. Atlantis is a safe haven from the rest of the world. Their concerns are not ours."

I could not believe what I was hearing. I mean, you look back at history, the Nazis were wrong. They were evil. Why couldn't we intervene then? And the 9/11 terrorists? They weren't attached to any nation. They were a terrorist organization. They were the bad guys.

Mr. Brown was right about Atlantis. How did that old saying go? All it takes for evil to win is for good men to do nothing. Well, Atlantis certainly was doing nothing.

"We could save the world. We can actually cure cancer. Why aren't we doing that? I can teleport anyone out of danger just by touching them. What about our seers? They could tell us when tragedies are going to happen so that we could stop them. We could be saving lives, stopping bloodshed, and making the lives of every person on the planet better. Why aren't we?"

"You would have us reveal ourselves to the outside world?" Teacher Folstad asked, "And how do you think that will go? How do you think people will feel when they find out that their neighbours have the power to start fires with their minds? Do you think they will welcome us? No, they will fear us. And that will make them do something about us. Declare war, or make us register with our mundane governments. And those who don't fear us will be trying to use us for their own benefit. What will the armies do with the soldiers that have magic?"

"Sounds like excuses to do nothing while the world suffers."

"Enough!" The President shouted. I looked out at the crowd, some of them seemed to be cheering me on. I wasn't completely wrong. Some of them did agree with me. Maybe not enough. But I wasn't alone.

"We will proceed with the charges," the President said. She

was trying to speed things up. I had started to win the crowd over, and she couldn't allow that. Not if she wanted to remain the dictator that she was.

"Blaine Allan, you are accused of magical vigilantism. Do you deny those charges?"

"No," I said. I wasn't going to be intimidated by them. I would stand strong. Maybe others would follow my example and Atlantis would change someday.

"Are you repentant of your actions?"

"I did what was right. I won't apologize for that."

I didn't want to stay there. Not if it meant sitting idly by when I could help the world. I was doing the right thing. And they responded by putting me on trial. I was done with them.

I looked into the crowd. It wasn't until that moment that I thought about who might be hearing what I was saying. I saw Sheila in tears. Could I do this to her? If they wiped my mind, would I still care about her?

"The Council will vote to approve a mind-wipe for Blaine Allan. All in favour, raise your hand."

The President, Lawyer, Master, and Teacher all raised their hands. Amber, the Doctor, and General Cabrera did not.

"If I may," Amber said, standing up.

"The council recognizes the seventh."

Amber looked at them and said, "We need a better solution. Mind-wipes are harmful—"

"Mind-wipes are perfectly safe," Doctor Edwin interrupted, "and I will not allow this farce of a trial to descend into a platform for pseudo-scientific bull."

"Farce?" the President replied.

"This trial is ridiculous and you know it," the Doctor replied. "Yes, he broke the rules, and arguably should be banished; but we haven't done a trial like this in over a decade. Why all this fanfare?"

"Are you changing your vote, Doctor?" the President asked, outright ignoring the Doctor's concerns.

"I have seen this boy sacrifice himself to save another. I do not want to banish a good man for wanting to do more good. I also do not want to allow vagrant lies to be spread as truth, or for anyone to think that I agree with this idiocy of a trial."

"Vagrant lies?" Amber shouted.

"You will contain yourself during these proceedings, Miss Bennett. Your position as the seventh in this case can be revoked," the president reminded Amber.

Amber calmly sat down, trying to restrain herself, "Doctor, please allow me to finish my comments. Mind-wipes are harmful in the best of circumstances. I would argue that we should not be doing them until such time as we have carefully examined them. Doing a mind-wipe on Blaine, over such a minor and easily fixable offence is ridiculous. Now, perhaps we put him under surveillance, because of his recklessness, but I don't think we need to erase his memory."

"Minor offense? He has been engaging in vigilantism!" the President responded.

"So did I, once, President. And all I got was a slap on the wrist," Amber replied coolly, "Though I guess that was before you took office. Should I be banished too?"

"That is enough. This is not a platform for you to question the authority of the council. One more word from you and I will have your position as Warden revoked," the President replied.

The General took the moment of silence between the two to stand up. "If given proper training and time to grow, Blaine could become a welcomed and desirable member of our society, perhaps even a skilled member of our security force. He would be an invaluable asset, and we should not be throwing away that asset over such a minor offense."

The President replied, "Your objections have been noted. Has this argument swayed the vote of any of the other councilors?"

None of the other councillors raised their hands.

"Blaine, you will be banished and have your mind wiped. Any last words?"

I wanted to think of something. Something brilliant that would make them let me stay, and put all of them in their place.

"I did what was right."

Several people dressed in purple moved over to me. One touched their hand to my forehead. I screamed, louder than I have ever screamed before. My body jerked and buckled. I tried to use magic, but it was being cancelled, being countered. I could feel them reaching into my mind, taking the memories and pulling them out. The girl who wore the yellow shirt, who wanted to be a healing mage more than anything else. What was her name? It started with a J, didn't it? And that guy in the military uniform, he's important. Isn't he? And that man in black, the one who said we had a lot in common . . . what was his name? I needed to remember his name. I needed to remember his name. I needed to . . . whose name was I even trying to remember?

There was some figure, it was hazy, but I didn't . . . I didn't remember. There was something I was supposed to remember, wasn't there?

Did I forget my homework?

18| BLAINE

MY HEAD THROBBED AS MY EYES CAME INTO FOCUS. THE ROOM around me was very black, but I could see some of what was in it. I was on a bed, and there was someone standing overtop of me.

"Feeling better?" Mr. Brown asked.

Where was I?

I got up out of the bed and stretched. "Yeah, and I remember everything. Didn't they wipe me?"

"They did" Mr. Brown replied, "but, we've been ready for that."

A half dozen other people appeared in the room. All of them looked pretty buff and fit, and a quick glance showed me that one of them had been casting an illusion.

"You didn't think we were alone all those times, did you?" Mr. Brown asked, that confident smirk of his on his face. "I had a team backing us up. My friend here is passable at illusions, and we had another friend here, an expert in mental magic, who has been mind-locking your every encounter with me."

"Mind-locking?" I asked as I took a look at the group of people surrounding me. Mr. Brown noticed my apprehension. He snapped his fingers and his team walked out of the room. I'm pretty sure of it, I tried to make sure they weren't just showing me an illusion.

"It's a technique we developed," Mr. Brown commented, answering my question after his men had left the room. "No one in Atlantis has heard of it. We can lock away certain memories so that they don't show up during a mind scan. They couldn't find any memories of me in your brain. But when they brushed up against our locks, we knew that we needed to get you and bring you someplace safe."

Safe? Where was safe? Wait, locks in my heads?

"You were in my head? And you were using illusions to hide your men from me this whole time?"

If Mr. Brown wanted me to trust him, he had just shown that he was doing a terrible job at it.

"I am a leaders here. Do you really think I go anywhere without an armed escort?" Mr. Brown said it as though he felt I shouldn't be angry. But he had lied to me.

"You didn't have to hide them from me."

Mr. Brown put his arm around my shoulder and sat me down on the bed. "If you had known there were other people with us, people more qualified than you, would you have done half the things you did?"

All of it was a lesson? He had people who could help stay back just so that I would get experience?

"If you can help people, you shouldn't be holding back."

"Then how would you learn?" Mr. Brown replied.

He had a point. I wouldn't have had the nerve to help people without his push, his guidance.

"By the way," Mr. Brown said, changing the topic, "I hope your room is to your liking."

I hadn't even bothered to look around the room yet. When I did, I had to admit that it was really nice. There was a fifty inch television on the wall with several video game systems hooked up, a computer in the corner, and a bookshelf that included every single book I had read in the last four years.

"We figured you would like a few amenities."

Mr. Brown stood up and walked to the door, "Do you need a minute? I'll give you the tour whenever you are ready."

"Where am I?" I asked as I explored the room. It had everything I would want all in one room. Well, everything I would want in a bedroom. I had to wonder if they looked for what I would like when they put the mind-locks in.

"Our base," Mr. Brown said, "New Asgard."

"New Asgard? Was there an old Asgard?" I asked. I thought I had heard of Asgard before, maybe something Amber mentioned when talking history of Atlantis.

"A tale for another time," Mr. Brown said, "and far better explained by our leader than by me."

"Your leader?" I had never heard him talk about a leader before.

"Yeah. Just don't go telling any of the others I said that."

"Oh?" I was starting to feel like I didn't know anywhere near as much about Mr. Brown as I should. Was I in an entirely separate magic city? Just who else did Mr. Brown work for? I'd been so busy doing the right thing—fighting crime, helping people—that I don't think I ever really learned much about his organization. I knew he wasn't the only aberration, and that they believed in using magic instead of hiding it from the world, but beyond that, I didn't know a thing.

Mr. Brown shrugged as he checked himself in the mirror, "Some of the other council members think we are a council of six, now seven, equals. We're really not."

"Now seven?"

Mr. Brown turned around in the mirror, fussing about his appearance even though he wasn't doing much to change it. Perhaps he was adjusting his illusions, I took a moment to try and see them. Yep, he was trying on different faces.

Mr. Brown continued as he turned back to me after finding a face he liked. "Aberrations lead here. You're an aberration."

That was certainly some promotion. Go from being the banished vigilante mage from Atlantis to being one of the seven leaders of New Asgard?

"Isn't that a bit, um . . . I mean, I'm only fifteen. Do you really think people will listen to me?"

"Don't worry, you'll be fine," Mr. Brown said, waving his hand in the air as if to dismiss my concerns. "Besides, we'll do our best to try and fit the big, important meetings into your schedule."

My mind tried to process why they would have to arrange meetings around me. And then it hit me. I looked around the room for a clock.

"Six-ten? I would have left Atlantis less than ten minutes ago," I said, "Your city isn't in a time stop and cut off from the rest of the world like Atlantis is.

137

"Yes. The one piece of Atlantis technology we have struggled to duplicate," Mr. Brown replied, "Perhaps with the master of Time and Space on our side, we might be able to figure it out."

"So, now what?" I asked.

"Whatever you want. No pressure. Relax if you want. But, if you are up to it, the other abberations would like to meet you."

The video games and books were tempting. But I had too many questions right now, and they needed to be answered.

"Take me to your leaders," I said, in my best robotic voice.

Mr. Brown chuckled, "Okay. Just be careful."

I raised an eyebrow. "Why?"

"Well . . . ."

I got the message. The other leaders were not the caring-and-easy-to-get-along-with types that Mr. Brown was.

Mr. Brown and I headed through the corridors. A couple of people flew by us in the hallway, racing each other through the air, wearing helmets and padding as they rammed into walls during their race.

"Looks like fun."

"Well, all work and no play is no way to live," Mr. Brown responded.

The place was pretty incredible. Solid black stones polished to gleam like black gems made up the walls, and torches adorned all of the walls instead of lightbulbs. It had this really medieval feel to it. Which was kind of cool if you ask me.

As we continued along we came across a long hallway with a red carpet going down it.

"Let me guess, that leads to our meeting room."

"Ishtar's request," Mr. Brown said, "when it's something this small, it's best to just let her have her way."

"Ishtar, is she one of the . . . ."

"Yes," Mr. Brown replied, a mild look of frustration on his face. Not from my question, though, but rather that he didn't like Ishtar.

"And your name was . . . Ra?"

"Yes," he said this one more matter of fact.

"What is up with that?"

Mr. Brown didn't even break stride, "We aberrations name ourselves after deities, a reflection of our power. You know my name, but we also have Ishtar, Babylonian Goddess of fertility, love, and sex; Ares, Greek god of war; Lempo, a Finnish fiend, considered a deity of the bad parts of love such as the insanity it brings on; Loa is a spirit of Haitian Vodou, kind of the middleman between humans and god; Finally, Odin is our leader, a god associated with war, victory, wisdom and a bunch of other stuff."

"So what will my name be?" I asked.

"Choose one for yourself. That's what the rest of us have done," Mr. Brown said as he pushed open the door at the end of the red carpet. The door was gold, with carvings of some of the mythical beasts associated with the schools of magic emblazoned on the gold plates. Six were completed though a carving had begun on a seventh. Mine, I'd guess.

The room beyond looked like a throne room, albeit a fairly empty one. There was a throne in the room made of gold and adorned with jewels, with an elderly man seated upon it, a man and woman seated at either side of it in chairs that were a bit more humble.

The old man had an eyepatch over his left eye. I'd guess that was Odin. I mean, if movies had shown me anything, it was that Odin has only one eye.

The man beside him was in a fancy suit that looked somewhere between basic and navy-blue. He had large framed glasses on his head, and short, professional hair. He looked like he was in one of those lawyer shows or something.

The lady to the right had to be Ishtar. She even dressed like she should be walking down the red carpet. Short, red, cocktail dress, fancy hair, makeup, and all that stuff girls do to look pretty. She had olive skin, but whether it was natural or from tanning, I couldn't say.

Odin stood up and descended the steps from the throne. "It is a pleasure to finally meet you, Blaine." I heard Odin's bones popping as he took every single step. It sounded brutally painful. I held myself back from cringing at the sound. His skin was ridiculously wrinkled and old looking. I mean, I don't think I've ever seen anyone who looked that old outside of movies and TV.

Odin reached for my hand and shook it.

"Thank you, sir," I said, shaking back carefully. I felt like I could break him if I shook too hard.

"Please, no 'sirs'," Odin replied, a smile on his face.

"Okay, I'm still taking it all in I guess. It's really amazing."

"Not quite what you were expecting?" Odin said with a laugh that reminded me a bit of my grandpa.

"No, I suppose not. I mean, I expected some kind of military ops since you claim that you work to try and help the world."

Loa looked at me, then at Mr. Brown, before saying, "I see you brought him directly here."

Mr. Brown shrugged. "It's what he wanted. Any chance Ares and Lempo will be showing up?"

"Don't tell me we're waiting for those two?" Ishtar said, angrily.

Odin said, "This meeting is Blaine's introduction to us. I would prefer to wait for the others."

Ishtar sighed. "I suppose I can give the kid an autograph while we wait."

The dumbfounded look on my face was clearly not doing the trick at conveying my confusion.

"Should I know you?"

The look on Mr. Brown's face made me feel like I might have just unleashed the apocalypse. And a quick glance at Ishtar's told me that he just might be right.

She was downright furious, and started marching towards me.

She didn't get far before Loa had his arm on her shoulder and said, "No."

"You'll have to forgive Ishtar. She sometimes forgets that being famous does not mean everyone knows who she is," Odin commented.

Ishtar pulled Loa's hand off of her and retook her seat. I saw Mr. Brown breathe a sigh of relief. Odin flashed me a quick smile.

"Yo, my homeboys. What's rockin' the joint tonight?" A

man walked into the room. He was wearing . . . I don't even know how to describe it. It looked like the forbidden love child of Tarzan, Superman, and a Teletubby. He was wearing only a loincloth and a cape and had used duct tape to strap a flatscreen TV to his chest.

"Nice to see you, too, Lempo," Odin said.

"Whoa!" Lempo ripped the TV off of his chest, tossed it to the side where it cracked, and ran to me, "we gots a youngling with us. Hiya, I'm Lempo." Lempo reached over and grabbed my hand and started shaking it furiously. "We're gonna be bestest-best-bestingly buddies. We'll do our hair up in pigtails and have sleepovers and talk about girls and watch Spider-Man cartoons."

I took a step back. What the heck was . . . why would they let him be in charge? He's crazy. And I should know!

A couple seconds later a man came shooting through the door. He was wearing a tank top and shorts, and had muscles that would make most men jealous.

"Sorry for running late. My watch broke."

"AGAIN?" Mr. Brown shouted in disbelief.

"They're cheap and easily breakable," the man said defensively.

"Ares, I'd like you to meet our newest member," Odin said.

"Oh, hey, the kid's joining us. Cool. Maybe I'll finally have someone who will join me at the gym."

"Loa goes to the gym all the time," Mr. Brown replied.

"Loa doesn't count. Oh, if the kid's here, did someone get a bigger table?"

Loa stepped up and said, "Yes. You need not worry about such trivialities."

"The day that Loa hasn't thought of everything is the day we're all in trouble," Odin said with a laugh.

I moved to the table to sit down with them. It felt kind of weird. Like that feeling you get during the holidays the first time you get to sit at the grownup table. Weird, but good.

"First order of business?" Loa asked. He was seated at one of the two ends of the table. I felt like I was looking at the man who, if he wasn't in charge today, would be in charge tomorrow.

"Have appropriate measures been taken to ensure that Blaine's disappearance can be explained?" Odin asked.

"I got it covered, Odin," Mr. Brown replied.

"Good, but I would feel safer if I could give them my blessing. Please bring them up on screen."

A huge theatre screen descended from the roof. It started to project, and it showed me, sitting in my bedroom at home.

"Magic scan on," Loa said.

And suddenly, there were a half dozen people in the room. Okay, that was pretty impressive.

"Leave the visual up. I will focus upon them as we continue," Odin replied, a shortness to his breath and sweat beading down his face as he said so, "Second order of business?"

"All is quiet on the Alpha front," Ishtar replied.

"Alpha?" I asked. Mr. Brown had mentioned that name before. Who was Alpha?

Odin hesitated, "Not one of the first things I would want to discuss with a newcomer, but important enough to deserve to be. In short, Alpha is a threat. His organization is the closest thing to a third magic city in the world. Where Atlantis believes in non-interference and we use magic to help people, Alpha wants power by any means necessary. You will have access to all of our files if you wish to investigate further. For now, I would prefer that we move on with this meeting."

We continued the meeting by discussing various operations going on. It kind of made my head spin. Everything from problems in the Middle-East, to foiling terrorists' plots, to solving murders. I wanted to help people, but listening to all of it made me feel like the weight of the world was on my shoulders.

At the end of the meeting, after Ishtar, Ares, Lempo, and Loa had left, Odin said to me, "So, Blaine, I hope we didn't intimidate you too much."

"No, sir," I replied.

"What have I said about calling me sir?" Odin said with a laugh.

"Right. Sorry. I should probably get home."

"Yes. Do make sure that you take some time to figure out a name for yourself."

"Okay . . . ." I was about to head for the door when I said, "How am I getting home?"

Mr. Brown tossed me a box that he had pulled out of his pocket. Inside of it was a watch. Very similar to the ones that they have in Atlantis.

"Works the same as Atlantis?" I asked.

"Yes," Odin replied.

"I'm off then. Thanks. This was a lot to take in, but I'm glad to be here."

I pushed the button and went home.

The troops there backed out, and oddly, gave me a salute before leaving. I guess I will have to get used to that.

I went to my computer. What god did I want to name myself after? It needed to be something good. And fitting.

I went to my computer and typed in 'gods of time.' I didn't want to go Chronos, too obvious. No way I'm going to be called Father Time. I kind of like Aion. Saturn didn't sound too bad either, but he wasn't always associated with time. Maybe I'd just present both names to the others and see what they think. Well, maybe Mr. Brown, Loa, and Odin. The others were a bit crazy.

Hmm, Aion or Saturn.

Aion.

19| RA

SPENDING THE LAST MONTH UNDERCOVER AS A TEACHER AND TRAINING the kid a couple nights a week was ruining my social life. So I conjured up a few illusions, made myself ruggedly handsome and filthy rich, and headed out to a club. One of my favourites, where the women were hot and loose.

I bought champagne from the bartender and slipped him an extra hundred (or so he thought). "You know the drill," I said with a smile.

I took a moment to gaze around the bar to see if I could find what I was looking for.

Bingo, table of four hotties. I glided over to them.

"Hello, ladies, you look like you could use some drinks." I popped open the champagne and smiled a big hollywood smile.

And they were mine. I loved this bar.

We drank, we danced. One of them made out with me. This was the kind of night that makes life worth living.

And then my phone rang. The important phone.

"Yeah."

"I'll wait." It was Loa. He was able to tell in an instant that I was at a club and waited until I could hear him better.

"Ladies, gotta split for a minute."

I walked out of the club and used an illusion to pass the bouncer a couple hundreds so he'd know to let me back in.

"Okay, I can talk," I said, already cringing at what was about to happen.

"Can we meet?"

"Uh, sure," I replied, cursing on the inside, but knowing that Loa would never call for something stupid. "What's going on?"

"I would like to talk about our new friend."

"I'll be right there."

I looked back at the club. I was half-tempted to go back in and tell the ladies I needed to leave. But it didn't matter. I could go to almost any club and find four girls just as hot and easy.

I teleported to headquarters. It was quiet for a Friday evening. Usually someone tried to have a party of some sort. Not that I stick around for those. Mages know to check for illusions, and that just ruins the night.

I headed to Loa's office, far off in one of the corners of the castle. He liked his privacy; there's nothing but empty rooms down the hallway before his office. I knocked on the door and opened it a crack.

"Hey, Loa, you wanted to talk?"

Loa nodded, so I stepped into the room and took a seat. I felt like I was seated in the study of a college dean. Ridiculously classy room with a library's worth of books. The room was well kept, as always. I wouldn't be surprised if Loa cleaned the room himself every hour. It was just downright immaculate. I felt kind of bad sitting there in a pair of sweatpants and a t-shirt.

"What are your thoughts on Blaine?" Loa asked as he stood up from behind his desk and started to pace around the room.

I sighed. "This is going to take a while, isn't it?"

"Possibly."

"May I?" I went over to behind his desk and reached for a bottle of fine scotch that he keeps on the shelf. I'm not sure why he keeps it, I've never seen him drink. Though it wouldn't surprise me if he keeps it specifically for meetings like this. Loa is always prepared.

Loa nodded as I poured myself a glass. I took a sip. "Man, I forgot how good this scotch is. Almost worth losing a night out for scotch this good. Sorry, to answer your question, the boy's nice. Probably a bit naïve, but he's a good kid."

"Any problems you can see?" Loa asked.

I had to think about that. Not a whole lot came to mind. There was Sheila. His girlfriend. And his childish thoughts on right and wrong.

"He has a strong opinion on what is right and wrong. He'll turn on you in an instant if he thinks you're not good."

Loa took a seat at his desk again. "So, he could be dangerous if he thinks we are in the wrong?"

"Not sure I'd go so far as dangerous, but yeah, there could be problems. He's a very black and white type."

Loa wrote down what I was saying in a journal. There were a few pages in it already, but it was mostly empty. Details on Blaine? I wondered if he had journals like that on the rest of us. That was a stupid question though—of course he did. A better question would be why I didn't.

"Elaborate," he said, pen still on paper.

I took a swig of scotch before continuing, holding the glass in my hand, "He has a massive hero complex, he needs to help people. He also has a very strong and unchangeable opinion on right and wrong. It's what made it so easy to get him to our side. Far as I can tell, his greatest problem would be trying to figure out who is good, 'cause he's also naïve enough to think that one side must be good. I know he doesn't like Atlantis for not interfering in the mundane world. He actually sees them as villains because of it. So, in return, he thinks of us as the heroes."

Loa stood and looked out a window, out into the blue sky and the clouds below. "I find it hard to believe that anyone could see us as heroes."

"No argument from me there," I said, holding up my glass in a mock toast before taking a sip, "Freedom Fighters, maybe, vigilantes, sure. But heroes? I doubt it. But the kid thinks we are."

Loa looked at me with his cold gaze. Not dark or scary, just eerily calculating and lacking in any emotion. "Will we need to hold off on our plans?"

I had to think about that one for a minute.

"I dunno. He has no love for Atlantis. But he is dating a girl who goes there."

"Sheila. Your reports mention her," Loa said, flipping back to one of the earlier pages of the journal. Yep, definitely notes on Blaine. "Will she be a problem? You are the one who said we needed to get Blaine out of Atlantis and part of our council before he fell in love with her."

"I don't know. Were she gone, I'd say we would have him completely."

Loa closed the journal, and with a look of tranquil fury said, "We are not going to kill the girl."

I almost dropped my glass of scotch. "Wait, what?"

"You were implying that it would be easier to guarantee that Blaine was on our side if the girl were no longer a factor."

"Yeah, but I didn't mean that we should kill her," I said, backpedalling like mad. Loa is the last person in the world I would ever want to make angry.

"Good, I would not have liked that," Loa said, his calm returning. He reopened the journal to a blank page and picked up the pen that had fallen to the floor.

"You've killed children before," I said, because apparently I sometimes have a death wish, "I've watched the recordings. Never had a problem with it."

"Child militias and high school cheerleaders are different things."

"I know, I'm just—" I started before Loa interrupted me.

His voice so calm that most people would not realize how much strength was going into each word he said. "That I do not express my feelings should not constitute belief that I do not possess them. I am not a heartless monster. I would not kill a child without proper justification. And the possibility that the girl's death could turn the boy further to our side is nothing more than speculation. I will not kill a child solely on conjecture and untested hypotheses."

I took a sip of scotch to calm my nerves before replying. "I never said you would. I was just pointing out how important the girl is."

Loa nodded his understanding, "We should delay our plans for now then, until we are confident the boy is on our side."

Loa sat back at his desk.

I finished my glass of scotch, put it down on Loa's desk, and was almost out the door and back to a night of partying, when my conscience came up. Or rather, my brains.

"I don't think we can afford to wait."

I could hear the quiet in the room. I turned back to look at Loa. He was seated, pondering what I said. He reached up behind him, grabbed the bottle of scotch, refilled my cup, and gestured for me to take a seat again. "Elaborate."

"Look, you know I love the man, but Odin is not going to be with us much longer."

Loa's eyebrows lowered, almost glaring.

"Loa, I know," I started, "You've been with him the longest; you pretty much think of him as your dad, or perhaps your grandpa, but the point doesn't change."

I didn't know it was possible to look so angry and so calm at the same time, but Loa pulled it off. "We are not discussing Odin's mortality. He is the master of fate. He is the luckiest man alive. He will be fine."

I was tempted to lie. To take it back. But I know Loa. No matter how much he hates the truth, he hates a lie even more. He is the only person in the world that I would never lie to or trick. I'd lie to Odin before I'd lie to Loa. So I told the truth, which I have to admit, I'm not all that good at. "Yeah, Odin is the luckiest man alive. And he's also over one hundred and twenty-five. He fought in World War I in his mid-twenties! I don't care how lucky he is, his age is showing. The older he gets, the more he has to focus on using his luck magic to keep himself alive and healthy. Or haven't you noticed that it's been getting harder to keep his attention, to keep him focused at our meetings? He was gasping and sweaty just from focusing on giving his luck blessing to the people maintaining the Blaine illusion. Being lucky is not going to keep him going forever, and we need to be prepared for that."

The room started to get ridiculously hot. From a comfortable twenty celsius to over forty in under a second. Then the heat left the room just as quickly. "You are right. My apologies. But although his death would be tragic, the rest of us would pull through it. The council would be fine."

"The council would be without its leader," I replied.

"Odin is not our—"

"Can it, Loa," I said, taking a seat and grabbing the scotch. "Odin is the boss, and you know it. He tries to make it seem like we're equals, but let's be honest, he's in charge. The others don't see it. We do. And we need to be ready so that we don't collapse inward when he bites the big one."

Loa nodded. "I suppose this is the part where you ask me to support your bid for leadership?"

I laughed. Me? The leader? That had to be the most ridiculous thing I had ever heard.

"Not on your life. I'm saying it has to be you."

Loa raised an eyebrow. He took a sip from his mug. Coffee, I'd wager. "Why me?"

"Ares is a dumb jock, Ishtar is a conceited drama-queen, Lempo is crazy, and I'm a fat, lazy pervert," I said, because self-deprecation is one of the greatest strengths a person can have. "You're the only one of the five of us who could be considered leader material. I mean, sure, Ares and Ishtar would both want to be, but if they can't, the only person they would tolerate is you."

"You are forgetting Blaine," Loa commented. From his tone I could tell that he was covering all his bases rather than bringing up a legitimate argument. But when Loa asks a question, you give him an honest and accurate answer.

"Blaine is so new and young there is no chance the others would ever think of him as a leader."

Loa scrutinized his mug for a moment, not that I bought for an instant that he was actually inspecting it. He was taking his time, contemplating what to say before responding. "You intend to have these conversations with the others? You will become everyone's confidant. Everyone thinks they are in charge, but you end up as the one truly running things."

"That would be a brilliant plan if Ares and Ishtar didn't hate my guts and I actually wanted to lead," I responded. Seriously, did Loa think I was capable of that level of manipulation? Okay, fine, I am. But I'm also too lazy to run things when someone else will do a decent job. "Come on, Loa, I'm the guy who uses his magic to get laid. I never work hard. And you think I want to be in charge? I've got my PhD; I'm done working hard. I'm on your side. Join the side with the biggest guns, as they say."

"I do not know if anyone says that," Loa responded, and then after a brief pause, "biggest guns?"

I was starting to get frustrated at his questions. Loa's need for clarity could be tiring. "You control the elements. Hurricane Katrina happened less than a week after the last time you cried, and personally, I don't think it was a coincidence."

Loa paused. "That is pure speculation, but your point is made. As is your assessment that I am better suited for dealing with the madness of the others than anyone else."

"Good." I was about to finish off my second glass of scotch when I paused. I figured that if I was discussing my concerns with Loa that I may as well toss another one his way. "One other thing."

"I am listening," Loa replied.

I stood up, and reached for the scotch again, refilling my cup as I continued. "We have no idea what happens to an aberration when they die."

"True," Loa began, "but how could we find out? None of us are going to die, and a confrontation with Alpha is not in our best interest."

"So what options does that leave us?" I asked, downing my glass of scotch before continuing. "Wait patiently until Odin dies? We have no idea what will happen. For all we know, he could explode and take us with him." I'm not afraid to admit the alcohol might have been talking by this point.

Loa took my glass and controlled all of the alcohol in it, raising it up into the air magically and pouring it back into the bottle. "You are drunk. We will continue when you are sober."

I had the door open when Loa shared his parting comment with me, "But you are right. We cannot wait much longer."

20| BLAINE

I HAD BEEN OUT OF ATLANTIS FOR A COUPLE OF WEEKS, AND I HONESTLY could not believe how well things were going between Sheila and I. The movie nights, the walks in the park, she had just met my parents last night and they loved her.

Honestly, I'm surprised she decided to stay with me when it meant having to keep so many secrets. It was this weird and complicated thing where she thought I didn't remember magic, and I had to let her think that I didn't remember magic. And yet, we were working. We were great together, despite everything.

I'd been working with Mr. Brown and the others of New Asgard pretty often. Not as many meetings as I would have expected, but I kind of liked that. Even if it seemed like they weren't letting me do anything serious. The training had been great. I was better in a fight than ever before.

This day was a bit different. I was meeting up with Mr. Brown before school. He had something that he needed to tell me and it couldn't wait.

He shut his classroom door after checking to make sure no one else was in the hallway. "Hello, Aion, glad you could make it."

"No problem, what's so important?"

"You're not an idiot, Blaine. You know we've been hiding something from you," he said. "Today you learn the truth."

That felt really ominous. I was terrified. What truth could they have to tell me? It couldn't be anything that bad though. I mean, they were the ones who were actually helping people.

Ra reached for his watch. I nodded and reached for my own.

I reappeared in New Asgard in my private quarters. I

walked out the door and started towards the throne room. Ra was just down the hall. He called down, "Odin is waiting for us. He knows the story better than anyone. He lived it."

I followed him to the throne room.

Odin was seated on his throne, reflecting on something or barely clinging to life, I wasn't too sure. Sometimes it felt like you could mistake him for being dead. Other times he seemed like a wise and brilliant leader, benevolent in his gold and bejewelled throne. I had never understood how Ishtar and Ares had missed the fact that Odin was the leader when he kept sitting on a throne.

"Good morning, Aion, sorry to ask you here so early," Odin said.

"It's okay," I replied, "so what am I here to learn about?"

Odin adjusted in his chair and invited me to take a seat right before the steps up to the throne. "As you can tell, I was around for the wars." He gestured towards all of the medals on his uniform. "World War I and II, among many others."

Odin paused to take a deep breath. He sounded worse than my grandpa did when he was in the hospital and dying. I sometimes worried that he was going to die on us. And he seemed so stubborn; he never had nurses or healers or anyone around to help him.

There was the oddest look in Odin's eye as he began to talk, like he was remembering the past and wasn't sure if he liked it or not. "Atlantis has always believed in never intervening in the world, never interfering. There have been times when they failed before, but only one time when they outright broke that rule. And that one time was me."

Odin paused in his story, his breathing heavy, but after a moment and a quick glow that looked like magic, he was fine. "Before I was even born, there was a prophecy. Some mage in one of the magic cities, for there were over a dozen magic cities back then, had looked into the future further than anyone had ever looked before. And he saw the end of the world."

The end of the world? But magic was still around. How far into the future had the person looked? Odin was old, way old. Over one hundred, or so I was told. I'd never heard of anyone being able to look more than five years into the future, and yet someone had looked over a hundred years?

"As I am sure you know, fate magic is not perfect. It can only show possibilities. But more and more mages who looked learned to do what this one mage had done. They looked far into the future, to verify what had been seen. And they all saw the same thing."

The world would end? Is that what New Asgard was preparing for? Is that the secret that they seemed to be keeping from me?

"But some of them started to see more. They saw that there was one man. A man whose actions would lead to the end of the world. If that man were to die, they theorized, the world would be saved. And so, in order to save the world, they were determined to find this person . . . and kill him."

So, in the past Atlantis had used their powers to interfere, when they felt that they were at risk. Typical, looking out for their own interests and only helping the world if it would help them.

"The first time they tried to kill me, I was twenty-five years old," Odin continued.

I tried to hide my shock when he said that, but I couldn't. "You? They thought that you would end the world?"

Odin continued, "Yes, and they were ready to kill me for it.

"I had never even heard of magic before that day. I was a soldier, pretty much on the front lines of the Great War. I was sitting in a trench, grateful that the day had been relatively quiet and I hadn't needed to fire my gun. That's when they appeared. About a dozen of them teleported in. I thought it was some new German technology. I shot and shot and shot. Trying to kill them before they could kill my entire company. I didn't know that they only wanted me dead. And neither did the friends that I had at my side. Alexander shot and killed at least five of them on his own. Mark, Peter, and I got the rest."

Odin, his fists shaking, tried to stand up. His legs were wobbly as he tried to take a step. He tripped.

I caught him before he hit the ground.

"Thank you, Aion."

Odin brought himself to his feet, but needed my help to get back to the throne, which he slumped into. Odin started coughing, and as he did so, some blood came up.

"Odin, are you okay?" Ra asked.

Odin smiled, the same smile my grandpa gave me on the day he died. "I will be fine, Ra, don't worry. Now, I should continue."

"We didn't know what had just happened, but Alexander was the first to examine the bodies. He was kind of the leader of our little band of four. Gone through everything from basic training onward with those guys. And if they hadn't been by my side, I would have been killed a dozen times over, if not more. More and more mages came after me. While the world was in the middle of World War One, I was in the middle of my own war against some kind of strange enemy that wanted me, and just me, dead."

He coughed again before resuming, "There were times when I wanted to give up. They didn't want anyone dead except me. But Alexander wouldn't let me give up. He didn't believe I was going to end the world like one of the prisoners he had interrogated said. He said that I had a right to life, and he would help me fight for it whenever they came my way."

Odin coughed again. Blood dribbled onto the floor, almost invisible on the red carpet. I was about to speak, to beg Odin to go and get some help, but he just continued on. "I slowly began to realize how I had managed to survive all of those incidents. I had magic of my own, an aberration. It's also why it took them years in between each time they came after me. If I didn't stay in one place, they had no way to find me."

Odin paused. A tear slid down his cheek. He started to tremble as he said, "I gathered up more and more people, trying to teach them magic. Not all of them could learn, but some did, and they helped me to fight back, to defend myself against what had happened."

"But then one day we were almost destroyed. Peter was taken captive by the mages, and they forced their way into his brain and stole all of our secrets. I lost Peter that day. Mark too, along with almost all of my troops. Alexander and I, along with barely a handful of my army, were all that was left to fight after that devastation. But we learned.

"We created the mind-locks. A way to safeguard our minds from any kind of mental intrusion. Mind traps that would attack or even kill the person trying to read the mind. But doing that was a mistake."

The mind-locks were a mistake? But they had done the same thing to me.

"When they realized they couldn't read our minds without it hurting them, they stopped taking any of my people prisoner."

Odin paused, his breath getting heavy. A few sparks came out of his hand, back into his body, and his breathing eased.

"Fifty years ago, my team fell apart. There were almost no survivors." Odin paused for several seconds before he continued, "Atlantis believes I am dead. That's why we are so secretive. Atlantis doesn't tolerate magic they don't control. I know, I spent fifty years on the run from them, fighting them."

I didn't know what to think. I knew Atlantis was trouble, that they were wrong for not helping the rest of the world, but I had never thought it would be that bad. I never thought that Atlantis would kill people who didn't agree with them.

It took me a few seconds to find my voice. "I'm sorry, Odin."

"It is okay, Aion, it happened long ago. But it is time that Atlantis did more for the world. We want to make sure of that."

"Blaine," Odin began, "We plan to attack Atlantis."

"What?" I couldn't have been hearing him right. Atlantis had done some terrible things, but there were innocent people there. People like Sheila, Amber, Matt, and Jasmine.

"Why?"

The door to the throne room opened and Loa walked in before I could get an answer from Odin. "My apologies for being late, Odin, Ra, Aion. I was ensuring that the troops were ready."

"The troops? You're doing this today?" I practically shouted at them, "I thought you were keeping something from me, but you didn't trust me at all!"

"We were concerned that your . . . girlfriend might complicate the issue for you," Odin responded, though I could tell that he wasn't convinced by what he was saying.

"So you didn't tell me?"

"We didn't want to force you into such a difficult decision,"

Ra began, "We've been planning this since before we met you. We were considering going ahead with the mission without telling you."

"What changed your mind?" I demanded, fury rising in my voice.

"How will you ever trust us if we don't trust you?"

I didn't agree with that. Trusting me would have been telling me the truth from the start. But I just crossed my arms and glared. "So, what is this plan?"

Loa began, "We are targeting their military complexes. With the Atlantis military crippled, we will be able to use magic openly. I have assembled a retrieval team if you wish to ensure your girlfriend remains safe through this attack."

I think my eyes nearly jumped out of my head. They were supposed to be the good guys. Good guys find a way where no one gets hurt. We had to find a way.

"But won't that hurt a lot of people?" I said, scared.

"I'm afraid so," Odin said, putting his hand on my shoulder.

What about Amber? She was a warden. She was pretty much a part of the military because of her responsibilities. She could definitely become a casualty. Sheila would never forgive me if her sister got hurt and I could have done something to stop it.

"Won't you end up hurting innocent people? People who are learning magic in Atlantis 'cause they don't know of any other option."

Ra put his hand on my other shoulder. "Look, kid, I know it's not pleasant. But we gotta do this. And yeah, some people are gonna get hurt. But we can't wait. Just think about how many lives we could save by being able to protect the world without having to worry about Atlantis. I know we shouldn't try and make it a numbers game, but sometimes that's what you have to do to get yourself to do something unpleasant but necessary."

No. I could not agree with that. There were too many people who could get hurt because they were just in the wrong place at the wrong time. There had to be something that I could do about this.

"There has to be a way to do this safely," I said.

"If you can think of it, be my guest. But I don't see how we can do this without hurting someone," Ra said, starting to get a little impatient.

"But you're the good guys."

The three of them looked at me with a mixture of pity and apprehension.

"Maybe we are the good guys. But if we are, then you can't see that the villains are running everything. We need to stop them. And sometimes that means doing ugly but necessary things," Odin said.

"No, killing people is wrong. It's always wrong."

I realized the truth in that moment. The reason why I had always been uncomfortable and nervous here. Why I had never fully trusted them.

These people weren't good.

But Atlantis wasn't good either.

My mind was reeling at the thought. I had been certain that one of the sides had to be good. But what if that was wrong? What if there was no good organization that used magic? Just some good people working for one or another evil empire.

"I'm sorry you don't agree, Blaine. But we are going through with our plan," Odin said.

"No," I teleported across the room, keeping my distance as I shouted at them, "I won't let you hurt Atlantis. If you're strong enough to take their military, then you're strong enough that you can talk with them and make them listen. We can come up with a better solution."

Odin's fatherly demeanour was gone, frustration written all over his face. His voice rose louder than I had ever heard from him before. "If there was another option, don't you think that I would have pursued it in the last hundred years? There is no other option. To think that you can find one is nothing but the arrogance of youth."

I felt a pair of hands on my shoulders. Loa had snuck behind me while I had focused my attention on Odin and Ra.

"What did you mean when you said that you won't let us?"

His voice was calm, but the grip on my shoulders was firm.

I tried to push Loa off. But I couldn't. I tried to teleport or freeze time, but neither would work.

Loa tightened his grip on me even more. "You should know your magic cannot affect me."

"What are you going to do to me?"

"Lock him up," Odin said. "We can't have him interfering."

I struggled to get out of Loa's grip, but it accomplished absolutely nothing.

I couldn't escape. I couldn't use my magic around them, and if I couldn't use my magic, then . . . .

But.

They hadn't taken my watch.

In a movement as swift as I could manage, I reached for my watch and pressed the teleport button that would return me to where I had been, at school, in the classroom.

"NO!" I heard Odin and Ra shout as I dematerialized.

I focused on my aberration, focused on making sure that no one except me could teleport anywhere near me. I had no idea what my range was, but I hoped it was large enough to give me some time.

They would be moving fast. I had no time to waste.

Sheila would be at school. I had to find her. Had to get her to take me to Atlantis.

I had to warn them, or they could die!

21| BLAINE

I RAN THROUGH THE HALLWAYS AS FAST AS I COULD, STOPPING TIME TO give myself as much of it as possible.

I ran past the library, past the cafeteria, and sprinted downstairs. I needed to find Sheila, and nowadays, that was where she went before school started.

I checked my watch. 8:35. She would be here by now.

My time stop ended. I was about to start another one when my shirt was yanked and I stumbled to the ground.

Ra and at least a half dozen men were standing around me. It was Ra's team, the team he had hidden when he was training me. I could see them, but no one else seemed to; illusions. Ra was wearing a huge trench coat, a much different look for him.

"Don't tell me you thought you could outrun us," Ra said with a laugh. "I know you're the master of time and space. But you're not that good. I've had this team ready since the day we found you."

I struggled against the grip of two of Ra's men. I tried to use my magic, but it wasn't working. Anti-magic. I could feel the hands of the two holding me, they tingled on my shoulders. Pushing their anti-magic into me. "What are you going to do, kill me?"

Ra smiled and leaned his face much too close to mine. "I'm sure you've heard all the rumours about mind-wipes. That people who go through a wipe might end up crazy."

I nodded. I could feel a cold sweat on the back of my neck. My hairs on end. Was he going to wipe my mind? Screw me up mentally?

"It's bull," Ra said, looking away from me and out at all my

159

classmates. "Mind-wipes do nothing but erase memories. It's just something people believe 'cause of word of mouth and one or two so-called experts. Kind of like how some people believe we faked the moon landing or vaccines are dangerous, that kind of quackery."

"What are you talking about?" I struggled against the two men holding me, but it was no use.

Ra took a quick glance back at me before continuing to watch the students walking by, "Sometimes the quackery can be used to your advantage. Wouldn't it be easier to control Atlantis if we could get the people on our side? The military implements the mind-wipes. If we make people think we are fighting against mind-wipes, if we can convince people that mind-wipes are harmful, they will cheer when we fight the military. We're going to be the heroes."

"No one will believe that."

Ra laughed, "Of course they will. Anyone will believe a lie as long as you keep it believable. Kind of like how I lied to you from day one."

My body shook. Lied to me . . . what was he . . . .

"Do you really think Odin would risk either of us fighting common street crime?"

I stopped struggling for a moment, out of pure shock. I couldn't believe that. It couldn't be true, "You can't lie to me, Ra, I can see through your illusions!"

"And only my illusions," Ra said, almost laughing. "It never even occurred to you that there could be a second illusionist, creating every single problem that we solved. Kind of sick when you think about all of the things that we did. You were ready to believe all of it because you wanted to play hero so badly."

"You're lying," I said, continuing to struggle against the grip of his mages. I was shouting as loud as I could. The louder I was, the harder it was to hide the noise. I could maybe break through that way—maybe have someone hear me. "What about Dwayne Cooper? The cop who spotted us, who got me banished from Atlantis."

"Dwayne works for me."

It had all been a lie. The criminals I stopped; being found

out and banished; all of it was because they wanted me to leave Atlantis?

Ra read the confusion on my face, "We knew you would have to choose Atlantis or us one day. I was sure you would choose us. But then you and that girl hooked up. And we knew it would tie you to Atlantis. So we had to get you out of there. Of course, you still managed to keep dating the stupid whore. So we had to prepare for your betrayal."

"You won't get away with this. People will find out," I shouted.

"Maybe eventually. But if there is one thing that stops people from questioning, it's fear."

Fear?

Ra pointed at Jake as he turned the corner and walked towards us, oblivious to us being there at all, "That's your friend Jake over there, isn't it?"

I yelled at Jake, shouted at him to run. But it was a futile gesture. No one could hear me.

Ra glanced at one of the men with him, "Do it!"

An illusion was put up over Ra.

He looked like me. Exactly like me.

Ra shouted, "Hey, Jake!"

Jake turned around. "Hey Blaine, what's up?"

Ra smiled and said, "Not much . . ."

Time stopped without magic as Ra opened his trenchcoat. My jaw hit the floor, my eyes bulging in terror. I tried to scream, but I was too shocked to get anything out.

There were guns. A half dozen at least.

I watched as the first gun was pulled from its holster. Watched as Ra drew a bead to Jake's chest. Watched the briefest moment of terror flare up in Jake's eyes.

I heard the gun fire, and at the same time saw an explosion of dark red come out of Jake's chest. He slumped to the floor. He wasn't moving. He was . . . he was dead!

". . . you?" Ra finished.

There was screaming in the hallways as Ra started firing, shot after shot after shot.

I was screaming. "No no no no no no no nooooo!"

Students scrambled, barricading themselves in classrooms.

But, dear God, there were already several bodies. Natasha, Sheila's old friend lay on the ground, spasming, blood coming up through her mouth and the two bullet wounds in her stomach.

"STOP!" I shouted at Ra, but he just dropped his first gun and reached for the second.

"Congratulations, Blaine. You're going to be our lie. How we convince Atlantis that mind-wipes are bad. Today is the day you snapped."

22| SHEILA

I SWEAR, SHE NEVER LISTENS TO ME. I TOLD AMBER THAT I WAS MEETING Blaine before classes at 8:30 like always, and that I was going to be late if she didn't hurry up, but did she actually get me there on time? Nope.

As I walked into the school, I heard shouting. People ran past me, heading for the doors.

What on earth was going on? More people ran out the door behind me, running for the streets, screaming.

I tried to ask what was going on, but everyone just kept racing past me. And then I was alone.

There wasn't a single person in the hallway.

Probably something done by the drama department; they always liked to sensationalize everything. Weren't they doing some kind of zombie apocalypse show in a few weeks? That must have been it. I was certain that if I kept walking through the hallways I'd see a zombie.

I headed upstairs to my locker and grabbed my books for first period, thinking that the building was oddly quiet.

And then I heard it.

Just this loud, pop-pop-pop, explosive noise.

Coming from downstairs.

It sounded unreal. I wasn't even sure what it could be until the very idea made me sick to my stomach.

Someone had a gun in the school.

I dropped my books and ran. The noise had come from downstairs. I had to find somewhere to hide. I ran to the nearest classroom.

It was locked. I fidgeted with the lock for forever before

running to another room.

I kept running down the hallway. Saw light coming from one room. The door was still open. Another student and I ran for it.

"What's going on?" I whispered as the door was shut behind me and the lights were turned off.

Mrs. Bates directed us to the corner, away from the door and windows, "Everyone, please be quiet. Phones on silent and text or call 911. Does anyone know what's going on?"

The guy who just got in with me said, "There's this guy, he's got a gun. I think he's alone, and I think he's a student, but I don't know."

I pulled out my phone and texted my sister. 'Gun in school. Not joking.'

Come on, sis, answer.

I looked at the time on my watch.

My watch.

But I'm not supposed to reveal . . . .

Screw it, there was no way they could get angry at me for this.

I pushed the button on my watch to contact Atlantis.

Nothing happened.

I pushed it again, and again, and again.

Come on, work, you stupid thing!

I heard a flat voice in my head, telepathy. "Atlantis cannot be contacted right now. Please remove yourself from the presence of mundane humans and try again."

I pushed the button again.

Same message.

I mashed the button a dozen times.

"You have attempted to contact Atlantis twenty times while in the presence of mundanes. Your watch will be turned off. Contact your warden to regain admittance to Atlantis."

Terror overtook my body. I could barely think straight. Atlantis had to help me . . . they had to. They couldn't just leave me . . . .

Tears were streaming down my face.

They weren't coming.

I started pleading with the universe. Where were you, Amber? You're always nagging me that people shouldn't answer their phones while driving, but please. Just this once. Please check your phone while driving. PLEASE!

There had to be something, someone, who could save us. Blaine! Blaine was here. He was probably getting people to safety, I was sure of it. He could teleport people out. Or even better, use his time-stop magic to go and get the weapons away from whoever was doing this.

I sent a text to Blaine. 'U here? What do I do?'

Yeah. Everything would be okay. Blaine could do this. He's really good at magic.

Except he doesn't remember magic.

Stupid, Sheila!

Okay, Blaine wasn't answering. What if he's sick, or if that psycho with the gun comes here first? Or what if . . . what if he already got Blaine?

No. He couldn't be dead. I'd know.

There was fidgeting at the door. The handle was moving. Someone was trying to get in.

They banged on the door, shouting, "Come on, let me in!"

It was Grant.

"Please! Let me in!" he shouted.

He was being too loud! I wanted to shout, tell him to be quiet. But I couldn't. I couldn't do it. Couldn't let anyone know that there were people in here.

"Oh no, oh no . . . ple—"

There was an explosion from the hallway. Followed by a thump, like the sound your body makes on the floor when you trip.

Oh god. Grant was . . . oh god.

There was more fidgeting with the door handle.

Another explosion of noise. The glass around the window shattered and a hand reached into the room and unlocked the door.

Someone had to do something. I had to do something. But what could I do? I barely knew any magic. But I guess that was probably better than anyone else.

I could try maybe drawing the guy's fire. I could phase. Or maybe there was some water that I could use to hit him. No, there was no water. At least, none that I could see.

What could I do?

I could put up an illusion.

But I'd never been able to make an illusion last for more than about twenty seconds. And I hadn't been able to use an illusion in weeks. Not since I kissed Blaine. But I had to try. It had to work. I had to make this psycho believe that there was no one in the room.

The door opened and I started my illusion.

But it wasn't working. My illusion wouldn't go up. I couldn't do it. We were going to die, and all because my magic wouldn't work.

The shooter entered the room.

BLAINE?

I thanked the heavens for bringing him to save me. I knew he was alright. I knew he would protect me.

But . . . but he had a gun in his hand.

NO. No no no no no no.

It couldn't be. Blaine wouldn't do this. He couldn't hurt anybody.

I stood up. I don't know what compelled me to do it. It was totally and completely crazy.

"Blaine . . . what's going on? This isn't you. You wouldn't do this." Blaine just smiled and raised the gun, pointing it straight at me.

No . . . he wouldn't do this. He wouldn't shoot me. I love him. I love—

It wasn't him!

The illusion faded. I could see it all. There was a fat man in a trenchcoat holding the gun, and there were a half dozen other people with him, two of them holding Blaine back as he screamed hoarsely, "Sheila, run!"

It wasn't Blaine!

It wasn't . . . .

23| BLAINE

"NOOOOOOO!"

Sheila's body fell to the ground. I tried to break free, but those men still had a solid grip on me. Blood pooled from her chest. I couldn't breath, could barely think.

"No . . . ." I muttered again, fighting to stop myself from crying. I would not give Ra that. I would not give him the satisfaction of seeing me cry.

Sheila. If I hadn't run—if I had pretended I was okay with it, maybe you would still be alive.

You and everyone else in here . . . .

Ra aimed his gun and fired at the group huddling in the corner. I could hear them crying, and screaming.

One of them stood up and tried to charge Ra, tried to fight back. But Ra's speedster dashed in front and hit the guy back down. Ra shot the "hero", and continued with the rest. It took only a few shots before they were all dead. Their bodies bleeding onto the ground. So much blood. So red.

I shuddered. "Please . . . stop," I begged, trying to hold back the tears, trying to keep from crying, but failing miserably. "Why keep killing? Why?"

Ra unloaded the gun's magazine clip and put another one in, as calm as if this were a walk in the park. "Every death makes this more traumatic."

"How can you do this? How can you be so calm?"

His calm through all of this just added fuel to my anger. He was making it easier to focus on hating him instead of crying over the deaths. I needed that anger—wanting to hurt him was the only thing keeping me trying to fight back.

"We all wear illusions," Ra said, "We like to think we're

one person. But we're not. There's nothing but the personality we choose to show at a given time. We are all capable of murder without remorse. And once the killing is done, we change into an illusion where we claim that such actions are wrong and that we are a good person. But I'm waxing poetic now. Best make good use of these bullets."

I shouted at one of my guards, "Aren't you bothered by this? How can you help while he murders innocent people?"

"Part of the mission," one of the guards said, his grip on me tightening.

"And you're okay with that?"

"Collateral damage."

"You will pay for this, Ra," I promised, my body trembling, but from fear, anger, or sadness, I couldn't say.

The red and blue lights of cop cars were around the building. I could see the light coming in from the windows. Ra glanced out the window and smiled. "Look at that, the cops are here. Oh, and so is the media! I guess it's time for the grand finale."

Ra left the room, a gun in each hand, and walked towards the stairs.

"Freeze!" a voice shouted from behind. A pair of cops had their guns in their hands, aimed at Ra's chest.

Ra turned, raised his guns, and shot both of them. They fired back, but the bullets went right through us.

"Ah, goodie," Ra said, almost laughing. "I was hoping I could make this worse."

As the entrance to the school came into sight, another pair of officers were coming in. Ra fired and they fell, dead, their bodies clearly visible to anyone outside.

"Perfect," Ra said with a smile.

With a smug swagger, Ra and his troop left the building.

There were dozens of cop cars, dozens of officers with their guns drawn, car doors open so they had some cover.

Ra dropped his guns, raised his hands above his head, dropped to his knees, and shouted, "I surrender!"

Ra stood, and immediately the men holding me pushed me down onto my knees where Ra had been.

The cops came up and grabbed me, tossing cuffs on my wrists.

"You are under arrest!" the cops said as they picked me up and started to drag me into a prisoner van.

I heard a shout. A quick glance of my head told me that it was a woman with a microphone, someone from the media. "Why did you do it?"

I heard in my own voice, "Because it was fun."

Ra's man was still putting up illusions.

As I was shoved into one of those huge police bandwagons, Ra, the two anti-magic mages, and Ra's accomplice illusionist walked into the back of the truck with me. It got really cramped in the back of this car when four cops also stepped in.

As the van started to drive away I could see one of the cops shaking, his face was red, he was furious. "You monster. Hiding behind a gun. They didn't appreciate you so they deserve to die. Is that it? Well, you're not so tough now."

"Are you really trying to rile him up?" the clearly youngest one of the four said.

"Cut it out, you two," the oldest one, their superior, said. "You just want him to fight back so you can hit him. Knock it off."

"This asshole deserves it, and worse," the first man said, gesturing his arms in the confined space.

I couldn't believe he didn't brush up against Ra's men.

"Of course he does. But not acting on that is what makes us different from him," the senior officer responded.

The angry cop looked like he wanted to say something, but he thought better of it. His shaking was starting to go away, but his eyes would not leave my body for even a second.

Ra started talking to me, the illusions hiding his voice from them. "This is what everyone is going to think about you forever. Having fun?"

I tried to head-butt him, best I could do with my arms cuffed behind my back. I stumbled and almost fell over.

The angry cop picked me up and slammed me into the wall of the truck. "Don't even move, you disgusting piece of shit."

"Settle down," his superior barked.

He let go of me.

"You can talk to me," Ra said, "they're not gonna see it. So, come on, spit that venom. Not good to keep all of that hate bottled up."

I wanted to kill him. I wanted to just reach over and grab him and start strangling him. No, I can't. Killing is wrong. But he deserved it.

Ra pat me on the back, "Say, buddy, do you know what would be worse than being responsible for the worst school shooting in history?"

"What?"

"Escaping police custody."

Ra and his three associates each pulled out a gun and killed one of the four cops.

"Now then," Ra said as he opened the back door of the truck while we were still driving, "Run along."

I didn't move. I wasn't going to play their game anymore.

"I'm not going anywhere."

One of Ra's men pointed his gun at my head. "You still haven't beaten that instinct to teleport when your life is in danger, have you?" Ra asked.

I heard the gun fire, and then I was outside the vehicle, on the street, and the cuffs were off me.

I was a few blocks away from the school already. Nothing huge, but enough distance to make a run for it if I wanted to. But should I?

What could I do? Sheila was dead. Ra and his people had framed me for it. They were going to attack Atlantis, and no one would believe me. What could I do? Where could I go?

I heard the sounds of a police car coming after me.

There was one thing I did know. I had to run, even if it was what Ra wanted me to do. I was no good to anyone in jail.

I wondered how long it would be before Atlantis realized what was going on and sent someone to try and—

"Freeze, Blaine!"

I took a look behind me. It was Dwayne. Ra's double agent.

I ignored him. I tried to teleport away, but it was a struggle. Dwayne's anti-magic was strong.

Dwayne fired a shot at me. I teleported a few feet to the side on pure instinct. At least that part of my magic was too strong for him to stop.

"What are you doing? I thought Ra wanted me to escape?"

But Dwayne didn't say anything. He fired another shot at me.

I teleported so that my fist would line up with his face and punched him.

He fell to the ground, his nose bleeding, I might have broken it.

He reached for his watch. He was trying to call Atlantis. But why? If he was working for Ra, why would he want Atlantis to catch me?

It didn't matter. I couldn't let Atlantis catch me. I needed to stop Ra, Odin, and all the others. I just needed a plan.

I froze time, it was hard, but I did it. I raced at Dwayne, ripped the watch off his wrist, and started to run. My time stop ended and Dwayne reacted. "Get back here!"

He started to give chase, but he wasn't moving fast. Suddenly I saw a flash of light to my right side, crooked and jagged, like a miniature bolt of lightning.

Great.

There were buildings around, nothing too high, all one-story structures. Easy enough to get on top of. I teleported and ran along the length of the roof, then teleported to another roof.

I did that for several blocks. Dwayne was long gone. Either I lost him, or he wasn't bothering to chase me. Regardless, it meant I had a break.

But a break to do what?

I tried to press a button on the watch. Maybe I could contact someone I could trust, like Jasmine or Matt or Amber.

"Not Dwayne Cooper. Authorization denied."

Idiot. The watches only respond to their owner. It was of no use to me.

I tossed the watch to the ground and was about to teleport away when I heard noise come from the watch again.

"DNA recognized . . . Blaine Allan. Not authorized. Emergency. Red Alert. All military personnel to be notified."

NO!

I smashed it to pieces. I had to run fast. The people from Atlantis couldn't keep up with me, and they couldn't detect me. I focused hard, focused on forbidding anyone from teleporting or stopping time anywhere near me. That should give me some time.

But time to do what? What could I do now?

Amber! She's in the city. I needed to talk to her, convince her I was framed, that she could trust me, that Atlantis was in danger. She knew me. She'd give me a chance. She'd hear me out. I needed to find Amber. Before anyone else found me.

24| AMBER

MY PHONE BEEPED AS I DROVE TO SCHOOL. SHEILA, I'D BET, I COULD see some of her makeup in the backseat. Probably texting me to turn around and bring it to her because she can't go an entire day without it. Not a chance.

I made it to the university and parked. I got out of the car and sighed as I pulled out my phone to see just what the text was. Sheila's name popped up. Boy, could I call them or—

I dropped my phone.

I scrambled to pick it back up. I had to read the message again.

'Gun in school. Not joking.'

No. No no no no.

I looked at the time of the text. It had taken me fifteen minutes to read it.

Fifteen whole minutes.

And she hadn't sent another text. She couldn't be . . . I couldn't let myself believe that.

I texted, 'U ok?'

I didn't wait for a reply.

I jumped back in my car and peeled out of there. I weaved in and out of traffic, plenty of cars honking at me. I didn't care— I drove right through a red light and just kept going.

I checked my phone. Still nothing. What else could I do? Who else could I call?

Blaine!

I started to text him as I drove through the streets, twisting and weaving. Going into one lane, flying back into the one I was in. I was so close to getting in an accident so many times that I would probably lose my license.

The cops saw me and started to take chase. I didn't care, they'd be following me to where they were needed.

I ignored the cops and kept driving towards the school. I turned off towards it, and the cop turned his lights off as he followed me. He understood. He knew what was going on. The cops were there. My sister would be fine.

But then why hadn't she called me?

I parked in the nearest spot I could see, over a block away from the school. There were dozens of cars already there.

I ran to a gathered crowd of parents, and teens.

One of the cops came out to the crowd, standing at the edge of the police 'do not cross' line, "Quiet, quiet down, everyone. Please. We are still looking around the school. It's not safe yet."

"But haven't you made an arrest?" One woman in the crowd shouted.

"Yes, we have the guilty party."

Another cop came up to the one at the barricade, he whispered into the cop's ear.

The jaw dropped on the officer who had been talking to us.

"You can't be serious," he whispered, but I heard him. I was trying to hear everything important.

The officer looked at the crowd and said, "Attention everyone. The guilty party has escaped from police custody and is currently on the run. He is believed to be armed and dangerous. His name is Blaine Allan, and he was last seen wearing a red plaid shirt, blue jeans, and a black ball-cap."

Blaine?

Did Blaine . . . .

No, I told myself, Blaine wouldn't do this. He was a good guy, there was no reason he would do this.

Except . . . he had his mind wiped.

I knew wipes were dangerous. This is exactly what we feared would happen.

My panic returned as I realized just what it would mean if Blaine was the shooter.

I pushed my way to the front, "Excuse me, did you find a girl, she'd have blonde hair, looks kind of like me. Sheila Bennett."

The officer looked at me and said, "I have an officer over there, he's been working with the principal. All the students who made it out of the building have been giving us their names. You can go see if she has been accounted for."

There were lots of other people in the line too. Parents mostly. I could just imagine what they're all thinking. If we haven't seen them already, then . . . they are probably . . . .

I couldn't think about it. She'd be fine—she had to be.

I waited in the line, and waited, and waited. All these people, moms, dads, brothers, sisters . . . .

Mom and Dad. They didn't know.

I pulled out my cell phone and called Dad.

It rang.

And rang.

And rang.

The phone came close to finding out fast and far I could throw it. Come on Dad, I thought, for once in your life pick up the damn phone!

"You've reached Sebastian Bennett, leave a message and I will try and get back to you."

I shut down my phone. I'm not leaving him a stupid message about Sheila.

I made it to the front of the line.

"Name?"

"Sh–Sheila Bennett," I stammered.

The man looked at the records, I could see him going through it. Names highlighted in yellow, others in red, others not checked off.

He came to Sheila's name. It was in red.

"I'm so sorry, miss, at present we believe that she is among the deceased."

I couldn't breath. An officer had to escort me out of the line. I managed to get some control again, and the officer went back to helping the line.

There was a garbage can nearby. I leaned onto it and

threw up, heaving my guts out. A glimpse into the trashcan told me I wasn't the only one who had done so today.

Sheila was gone. I didn't know how to process it.

I tried calling Dad again.

This time the phone was answered on the third ring.

"What is it, Amber? I'm in the middle of an important meeting."

"Dad . . . ." I choked out.

"If this is another one of your calls to protect the Amazon rain-forests or some other stupid hippie thing, then I'm hanging up right now."

"No!" I started crying, and held my forehead with my left hand. How do people do this? ". . . Dad, it's Sheila."

"She has you calling for her stupid boy problems now?" Dad said, his voice clearly letting everyone know that I was giving him a headache.

"No, Dad, just . . . just listen. There . . . there was a guy in her school, with a gun. Sheila's . . . she's dead, Dad."

There was a long pause on the line. For a second I thought that we had disconnected or that he had hung up on me.

I then heard shouting from the other side of the phone. He was yelling for someone to turn on a TV.

"And you're sure she was . . . ."

"I dropped her off myself. I've talked to the officers on sight, they have her listed under the dead."

"Have you called your mother yet?"

"No, I . . . ."

"I'll call her. Find out for sure." His voice was cold, colder than usual. But that's dad. His voice gets cold and harsh when he is trying to hide how he is really feeling.

"Okay, Dad, I can . . . I can do that."

"I'll be there as soon as I can, even if I have to buy a plane to get me there."

He hung up.

I went over to an officer at the scene. "When . . . when will we be able to identify the bodies?"

"I have no idea," The officer said, shaking a little himself.

176

"It's a mess in there. We're going to be going through the place for a long time. I think we have some coffee I could get you, and some volunteers are coming to provide food for everyone."

I walked away.

I needed to do something. Anything . . . .

Magic. I could use some magic. My detection magic wasn't the best, but I could do this, feel around, see if I could find Sheila.

I focused, focused on the school in front of me.

I went through the walls, detecting desks, and chalkboards, book bags and lockers, and . . . lumps . . . of clothing and flesh on the ground . . . .

Dear God.

They didn't even detect as human, as alive . . . they're just . . . they're just bodies.

There were so many of them.

I stopped, gasping, and threw up. I didn't even make it to the garbage this time. Just spat up all over my clothes and everything.

I took a quick glance around.

Was anyone looking at me?

No, they weren't. Everyone was like me, too wrapped in their own tragedy to notice anything going on more than a couple inches from their face.

I used some fire magic. Burning off the vomit without even the slightest singe on my clothes. It took a lot more to concentrate than usual. I could feel the sweat on my brow.

I tried again. I looked through the entire school. What was Sheila wearing today? I had to remember.

I searched the school, the main floor, nothing. Upstairs. The music room? No, Sheila didn't take any music classes. The biology room? No, Sheila didn't take Bio, dissections freaked her out, all that blood and guts and . . . .

I threw up again.

I ignored it. I tried to concentrate on the building, but I went weak at the knees and fell down into my own vomit. I was dizzy. I hadn't been practicing my detection magic enough. It was exhausting me. Not that I wasn't already exhausted.

I took a minute to pull myself together.

I looked through the rest of the building. There was a room with a broken window on the door. I went into that room. There were bodies, eight of them. And one of them . . . was Sheila.

She was dead!

I couldn't breathe. It was . . . it was too much. I looked at my watch and realized that I was already late for my test.

My test. Like any professor would refuse me a rewrite after this.

It was so stupid. Why was I even thinking about that when Sheila was gone?

Because thinking about anything other than Sheila was the only thing actually keeping me going. I could feel the tension in my face, my knees shaking, my body wanting to collapse in on itself.

I fell to my knees in the grass, and just . . . I just let it out.

Tears streamed down my face. I sobbed uncontrollably into the grass, pounding it with my fists as if the grass and dirt were responsible, or could bring her back to me.

Sheila was gone. And she probably thought I hated her. No . . . worse than that . . . she died hoping I would save her.

I pulled out my phone. I looked at the text again. The text had come in five minutes after I dropped her off. Five minutes. If I had just done something, she wouldn't be dead. I could have been there. I could have answered my phone just this once while I was driving. I could have stormed in there with my fire and burned that gun-waving madman to the ground.

I could have saved her. I could have . . . .

And so could Atlantis.

I pressed the button on my watch to contact them. It didn't connect. I looked around. Too many people who could see it working. I had to go somewhere else.

I walked about a block away, went down a back alley. Now there was no one around. I pressed the button again.

"This is Amber. Did Sheila Bennett try and make contact today?"

The operator took a moment before responding, "Yes, we have a log of her trying to use her watch earlier today."

"And you didn't send help?"

The operator looked nervous as he said, "She was in the presence of mundanes; the watch would not connect her to us."

"She's dead because of you!"

I could see the colour leaving his face.

"I'm . . . I'm sorry . . . I really am. But you're . . . you're a warden; you know what the rules are. We don't interfere, no matter what."

I screamed.

"We interfere when it's one of ours, don't we?" I said angrily.

"Your sister was—"

"I don't mean my sister. Get me General Cabrera, now!"

It took a couple of minutes, but General Cabrera finally appeared on screen.

"What is going on, Amber?" Cabrera said. He looked concerned.

"My sister is dead because you wouldn't help her!"

"I know you're angry. I know what happened. But you know we don't interfere in mundane events. Even to save our own," General Cabrera responded calmly, as if he was losing his patience with me. It wouldn't be the first time.

"Yeah, well, maybe you should check closer into just what the problem is. 'cause Blaine killed her!"

For the first time in my life, I saw General Cabrera surprised.

"No . . . impossible. The mind scans would have picked up if he was mentally unstable."

"General, it's like I've been saying for years," I almost shouted, "the mind-wipes are not safe. All the proof you need is my sister, today!"

"Are you saying this is our fault?" Cabrera responded.

"My sister would be alive were it not for your stupid rules and your accursed mind-wipes. Blaine wouldn't have been banished and wiped. And right now Blaine is on the run, who knows where he is?"

Suddenly my watch went off—

At the bottom of the screen, under the visual from the General, was text. 'Dwayne Cooper Watch: DNA recognized...Blaine Allan. Not authorized. Emergency. Red Alert. All military personnel to be notified.'

It had a location. I knew where the watch was.

Blaine was going to pay for what he did to my sister. And it was going to be me who made him pay. Not those corrupt bureaucrats in Atlantis.

"General, I'm going after Blaine."

"Amber, we will be there immediately," Cabrera responded.

"No, you won't. Blaine can stop teleports. I'll get to him first."

I stood up and looked up into the sky.

"Amber, what are you doing? There are hundreds of people near enough to see you. Do you have any idea what you are doing?"

"Send more mind-wipers then—if you can convince anyone to do them after what happened to Blaine. I'm not letting him get away." I started to hover. I focused on getting my fire ready.

"You'll destroy all of our secrets. The world will—"

I ripped my watch off and shot straight up into the sky.

I was going to avenge my sister. I was going to make Blaine pay.

25| ALPHA

THE COFFEE ON MY DESK SMELLED WONDERFUL. I LIFTED THE MUG TO my mouth and took a moment to enjoy the scent. I contemplated taking a sip. Letting myself enjoy the coffee. Letting the memories of a time long gone past overwhelm me in that single taste of such a simple liquid.

But no. It would not be the same. The taste might be there, but the sensation would not. The alertness the coffee used to provide, nothing but a distant memory. This coffee, nothing but a reminder of what I once was.

I poured the cup of coffee into the trash, wiped off the mug so that no stains would end up on my desk, and returned to my papers.

Why did I do this? Every morning it was the same thing. Smell the coffee, reminisce, but never drink.

There was a knock on my office door. Who would disturb me this early in the morning?

"Enter."

A young man practically raced into the room. "Sir! There is something that you may wish to see."

It was one of the interns. New to the job. I could go for the impatient leader route, but by now everyone knew exactly what was important enough to be worth bothering me in my office over, and if he didn't, then he'd just have to learn the hard way. "Go on."

"Um, if you'll just . . . uh . . . turn on the news," the intern said, realizing he was being unprofessional around his boss. He learned faster than some who worked for me, I'd give him that.

I turned on the television.

"Channel?"

He was nervous. Most of the interns are, though. Good. I'd rather have them scared of me than like me.

"Um, channel 210; you'll want to turn on your magic scanner."

I snapped my fingers, turning on the device that detected magic, even in the video shown on camera. The words at the bottom of the screen told me the story quicker than any media person could. A school shooting.

"I fail to see why I would care about this," I said as I placed the remote back on my desk and returned to my seat.

"Um, just . . . just wait, sir, there was a—"

He didn't finish his sentence, what he wanted me to see had just appeared on the screen.

I leaned forward in my chair as I watched the screen. "That boy, there are people around him that no one else notices."

"Yes, sir," the intern replied.

"Hmm, so someone in the magical community is trying to frame this boy for murder. Interesting. Not really Atlantis's style," I began pondering, before a closer visual told me the truth, "That's Ra."

I couldn't help but smile. Ra and his friends: Lempo, Ares, and my dear Loa and Odin. So they were behind this. Well now, that ought to be interesting.

"Yes, sir. Which is why the mundanes can't see him or his team."

I smiled. The intern was so naïve.

"Ra isn't the one casting the illusions," I said as I pointed at the screen, at the man who was actually doing the magical heavy lifting.

"I don't understand."

"You are new and can be forgiven for your minor imperfections, but if you look hard enough you can tell who is casting the illusion. And it's not Ra," I said, my behaviour returning to that of the teacher, the educator, I once was. Though my days of teaching students, or my troops, were long gone.

"But Ra is the most powerful illusionist in the world. Why have someone else cast?"

"What would happen if Ra tried to use his illusions on me?"

The conversation with this intern was surprisingly refreshing. Perhaps a more personal hand with my troops was just the thing I needed in my life.

The intern's eyes widened. It pleased me to see he wasn't an idiot. Not a complete one anyways.

"They wouldn't work sir, because you're an aberration. Which means that the boy . . . ."

"Exactly," I said, cutting him off and feeling the pride that a teacher gets when an incompetent student manages to get a question right. "Do we know what happened to the boy? Do you have him?"

"He escaped police custody, sir, he is currently on the run."

I stood up from my desk, a smile on my face. The kind of smile that I haven't had in years. "Get a team ready. Recall Gamma, Epsilon, Zeta, and all the other top agents. I'm taking my best for this. It's been so long since I last worked with a fellow aberration. I think he needs to know there is a home waiting for him."

The intern looked uncomfortable at that. "The planes are ready to have us there within the hour. All efforts to teleport in have failed."

A slow smile crept over my face. Omega, you sly bastard, "So, we found him, the heir to time and space. We can't just teleport in and take him."

I wanted him. This child, he was going to serve me, and someday, become my new lieutenant.

"I will be joining the mission," I said as I adjusted my tie.

"You, sir?" the intern replied, taken aback. I can forgive that level of surprise; most agents have not been here long enough to recall a time when I went on a mission myself. But something this important required a personal touch. Maybe I was getting a bit nostalgic, but I was looking forward to doing the work that I often had others do for me.

"Excuse me, I didn't catch your name," I said, as I turned back to the intern.

"It's Shawn, sir, Shawn—"

"Last name is unnecessary, Shawn," I said, maintaining my charming smile, "Thank you for bringing me this information.

Could I get you to fill up my coffee mug. The machine is right there in the corner. And grab yourself a cup too."

Shawn was quick to oblige and filled my mug with coffee. He was about to start filling his own, "Stop, Shawn. Please, drink from your mug."

"There's nothing in it, sir," Shawn replied.

"Look again."

There was now liquid in the cup.

"What is it, sir?"

"Poison."

Nothing is ever so exquisite as the look on a man's face when he knows you are going to kill him. That look of absolute terror. If I live a hundred lifetimes I will never get sick of it.

"Sir? Please, no. Please, don't make me drink it."

I turned away from him and looked out the window, it was a magnificent view of the city out there. "As part of your internship you had your entire memory scanned, correct?"

"Ye–yes."

I stared at his reflection in the glass of the window as I continued, "Then you know that if you do not drink the poison we will kill anyone and everyone on the face of the planet who could look at your picture and name you. Everyone who knows your name will be killed, unless you drink that cup of poison in your hand."

He was trembling. Some of the poison spilled out of the cup, but disappeared before it could touch the ground.

"Sir . . . what did I? What did I do wrong? I thought I had done a good job."

Pleading. So annoying. I hated it when they couldn't take their death with some dignity. But I suppose most are cowards in the face of death.

"You did, which is why I am granting you such a quick death," I replied, "but if you must know, look at the entrance."

I watched his eyes drift to the entrance to my office. A gasp escaped his lips before he could contain himself.

He looked down at his shoes, covered in mud, and how he had tracked mud all over the carpet in my office.

"Sir, please, I'll hire someone, I'll get it cleaned. You can take it out of my paycheque."

I turned back to him and slowly shook my head before replying, "If there is an afterlife, tell whoever is in charge that you are in it because you do not know how to be neat and tidy. Hopefully, the lesson will sink in. It has been nice, Shawn. I enjoyed talking with you. Please drink the poison, give me my cup of coffee, and excuse yourself from the room while you still have the strength. If you manage to do it correctly then your sister will live. If not, well, sacrifices must be made to maintain discipline around here. I trust that you understand."

Shawn looked down at the cup. He trembled as he pulled it to his lips and drank, gulp after gulp until it was empty.

Shawn struggled, but managed to stay on his feet as he gave me my cup of coffee. He continued to walk towards the door to my office. But he fell to his knees. He continued crawling, trying to get out of the room, but before he could, he fell down dead, one foot still in my office.

I walked over to my phone, picked it up and pushed a button. The phone was answered on the first ring.

"Xi. I have a job for you. That new intern, Shawn. Kill his sister. Thank you, I appreciate all the hard work you do for me, Xi."

I glanced at Shawn's body and then at the cup of coffee in my hand. I debated over whether or not to drink the coffee. I smelled it, the rich aroma. Wonderful smell. I put the cup to my lips and took a sip.

I was wrong. Some days, coffee just tastes fantastic.

26| DRAKE

I THOUGHT PRISON WOULD BE BORING.

But when you're a telepath, being alone with your thoughts is never truly that much of a problem.

True, I was in an anti-magic field. They were trying to stop me from using any magic. But the problem with magic is that, just like anything else, there is always a loophole. And to find a loophole, you must start at the beginning: how does magic work?

It's all in our blood, and our brains.

But then the question becomes how does having magic in your blood and brain do anything?

Simple, magic runs on memories. I still remember my initial reaction was to say that made no sense. But if looking at someone you find attractive can trigger chemical responses in your brain, then having the chemical reactions from thinking about your memories result in magic is at least plausible.

And those memories are where we find the loopholes.

Take anti-magic. It's a very restrictive thing. You are denying someone else the ability to do something that is as much a part of them as breathing. Very authoritarian. Which is why the memories that work best for it are thinking of times you were in control.

The theory for breaking through anti-magic most people had was simple—and stupid: force as much magic as they can at the person to break through. The problem is that it comes down to whose willpower is the strongest. Even if you win, you'll probably be exhausted.

Some people think the trick is to focus on two memories at the same time: A memory that connects to whatever type of magic you are doing and a memory about a time when you disobeyed the rules. But, since your focus is split, it's even less effective than brute force.

They are on the right track though. Their problem is that it's not enough to think about a time you broke the rules. You have to focus on a memory of a time where you broke the rules and no one even noticed.

That's why I haven't been bored in jail. I've been reaching out, sliding my way into people's memories to see what was going on in the outside world.

I heard some people actually defend me. They said things like 'as much as I hate him, Drake is right, he is the best, and he deserves his spot on the council.'

That was good. I wanted people to think I was unjustly imprisoned. I could wait. The people seemed to be on the rise in my support. I mean, maybe I twisted a few thoughts to make people think better of me. But really, that was just to get the ball rolling. Public opinion was slowly moving to my side. They'd have to let me out of the cell sooner or later.

Then a day came where things seemed different. The military was in a panic. Something about mind-wipes not working and a school shooting. That was just stupid. Mind-wipes work just fine. I should know—I'm the master of them.

A thought came in that took me out of my relaxed stupor. They were saying that Blaine had killed people. Blaine! Of all the outlandish things a person could say, suggesting that Blaine had the capacity to kill anyone is one of the most ridiculous.

I put aside my emotions. I had to think about why this would happen. With magic, it certainly would be possible to frame Blaine. Though why anyone would do it, I didn't know. And I hated not knowing. My plans to wait and gain sympathy so that I could become the Master would have to wait, or be sacrificed. Blaine was the only other aberration I knew of, I couldn't risk anything bad happening to him. If he was just mind-wiped it wasn't a threat, I could get him back after my plans to become the Master were complete. But if Blaine was being accused of crimes, if they would have to arrest him, or kill him, then I couldn't stand by.

I had to break out of jail.

I thought about the guards outside my cell. Four anti-magic specialists to support the anti-magic energy infused into the room.

Nowhere near enough to stop me.

I reached into their minds. Slithered into the deepest recesses unnoticed, and then surged forward, to take control of every single synapse. Their bodies mine to control.

I could see the world through their eyes. See the looks on their faces as they looked at each other. Saw the camera in the corner of the room. Guess I'd be putting on a show. They utilized their passwords, opened the door, and I stepped out of my cell.

"I'd say thank you," I said as the four men stood at attention and saluted me, "But really, it's me doing all of this."

I mock inspected the four as I said, "Now, I want the four of you to lock this door and remain on guard duty for the next several minutes. When I leave your minds, you will have no memory of this. Goodbye. Prison has been nice; I would happily do it again sometime. But unfortunately, I have a friend in need. Did you get all that?" I said the last line to the camera that was no doubt recording my every word. I knew they were watching, and that they were getting ready to do something about this.

I started towards the door out of my cell block but it opened from the other side before I reached it. Two guards, with guns in hand, stood there.

"On your knees," one of them shouted at me.

"How foolish of me. I was able to take complete control of four guards with no effort, but two more is simply too much," I said, using telekinesis and entering their brains, forcing them into temporary comas.

I exited my cellblock, focusing my telepathy outward. If any sentient being got too close to me, I would be in their head before they could do anything to stop me. Of course, it had to be sentient beings, and I wasn't sure soldiers qualify.

A group of four more guards came at me, and to my delight, they were rookies. Not a one of them had more than two years of training in them. Bravery before self-preservation, it would seem.

One of them looked familiar though. Dark-skinned male,

early twenties like me. I remembered him now. That one was Blaine's friend.

I dropped the other three into temporary comas. I looked at the military man, pointing a gun at me.

"Hello," I began.

He fired a shot at me.

Had my telekinesis not stopped it, that bullet would have hit me right in the heart. The man had some uses, I suppose; that was a good shot.

"Let's not try that aga—"

He fired off multiple shots. I stopped the bullets, but it wasn't easy.

I ripped the gun from his hands and entered his mind before he could reach for his spare. Because a man like him always has a spare.

In his head we could talk at the speed of thought. Much faster than verbal communication.

"You heard what happened to Blaine?" I asked.

"They say he's a killer. I don't buy it." The thoughts left him and entered my head instantly.

"I'm escaping to prove Blaine's innocence. Are you still going to stop me?" I asked.

"Could I?" The sound in his thoughts said he was doing his duty, that he didn't really think he could do anything against me, but that he would fulfill that duty.

"No."

"Why talk to me? You knocked out everyone else." I could sense the tension in him. He knew I could sense everything he was thinking. He couldn't do it back and he hated that I had an advantage over him.

"People who will vouch for Blaine have value," I responded.

His mind was ready to accept what I had to do as he thought, "My word about Blaine has no value if I help a prisoner escape."

So I dropped him into a coma alongside his allies. I found myself surprised to admit that this military man, Matt, had kind of impressed me.

The building was not as occupied as I would have

expected. I dropped several more people into temporary comas, and made it out the front door.

As I entered the courtyard, I could sense the minds of over twenty people, all with guns pointed at me. All between me and the exit.

Well...they would be, if I was aiming for the door.

I used my telekinesis to raise myself off the ground and into the sky.

There was a dome overhead surrounding the entire prison, but that wasn't going to be a problem. I used my telekinesis to push against it, and eventually, it cracked.

I soared through the hole. The guards started to chase me. A couple flew after me, several others racing to grab hover packs.

"Stand down, Drake. You will return to your cell or suffer the full force of Atlantis's might."

The sky itself seemed fake. No surprise there. Just like Atlantis, the prison was in its own separate pocket dimension. Except that the prison existed in real-time with Earth so they could actually keep me prisoner indefinitely. There were a dozen guards outside of the dome not including the guards who had flown up to try and stop me. And I had thought it would be too easy.

"I know about Blaine. And that situation is a bigger problem than me escaping," I shouted at the leader of the group.

The flying agent was nervous. I didn't need to read minds to know that I had called his bluff. He knew he couldn't stop me.

He tried anyways, and a barrage of bullets from all of the guards came surging at me.

I used my telekinesis to stop them. Felt the bullets pushing against my mind's power to resist them. Each bullet felt like it was getting closer. Maybe just a millimetre or two closer, but they were getting closer.

And then I felt something that I hadn't felt in ages.

I felt myself get short of breath after using magic.

I tried to focus on the guns all around me, tried to get them to stop shooting, to rip the guns from their hands. But there were thirty of them, each with a gun, each of them firing at me. I couldn't stop the bullets and try to get the guns out of their hands at the same time. I couldn't—

They couldn't defeat me. I wouldn't let them. I was stronger than them.

A bullet broke through my barrier and nicked my shoulder.

I tried to hold it in, but I screamed at the pain.

The bullets kept coming. I felt one hit my hand, and another hit my leg.

I had to get out of there.

I flew at the closest soldier, grabbed him, and reached for his watch. I focused my telekinesis. Focused on his arm and his hand. I made him reach over and press the teleport button on his watch while I was hanging on.

We teleported. I had no idea where we were. But at least we were on land. The fields were bare. Few trees or anything. Not a promising place to be, but at least it wasn't prison.

Cement roads, lined. A passing car was travelling on the right side of the road.

North America? Reasonable chance.

The soldier tried to fire a bullet at me. I deflected it and pulled the gun to my own hand.

"Just stop. You can't stop me alone. Now tell me where we are."

I was hoping he wouldn't call my bluff. Using magic through an anti-magic barrier, deflecting a couple hundred bullets, I had spent too much power. I could feel it. I might have been able to stop him, but I honestly couldn't say for sure.

I didn't get a chance for an answer from him. A dozen other teleport windows opened.

I let go of the soldier and ran. But where to, I didn't know.

. . . Or did I?

I knew the Blaine situation was serious. They would want every available agent on that. Their watches were probably set to get them to Saskatoon, where Blaine lives. Or as close as they could get if Blaine is denying teleports.

I was close, but had no idea which way to go.

I saw a dozen other teleport circles open. They were coming, and I couldn't win that fight, as painful as it was to admit it to myself.

There was a car driving by. I reached into the mind of its driver, looking for directions, to know where I was.

I went into his head too violently. No subtlety. I wasn't focusing properly. The pain and exhaustion was getting to me far more than I thought. The driver screamed and rammed his car into the brush by the side of the road.

He was bleeding, his forehead had slammed into the steering wheel. He could die.

I couldn't save him. They'd catch me if I wasted that kind of time. It was their job to fix problems caused by mages anyway. They could save him; I had what I needed. The directions were in his head. This road would take me where I needed to be.

I knew Blaine couldn't have done it. He couldn't have killed anyone. He was a good man. Better than I would ever be. Blaine and I were the strongest in the world. Together, we could take them all down. If we had to.

27| AMBER

I HAD TO FIND BLAINE, BUT MY MAGIC WAS NOT WORKING LIKE IT should. I focused hard on not letting my flames out, but I was still sparking. It was hard to focus on flying. I stumbled a few times, my thoughts going back to Sheila.

I don't think I will ever understand how people manage to use magic when their lives have been horrible. How could anyone focus enough on that one memory they use to get their magic working after going through something like the death of a loved one?

I almost fell to the ground from two hundred feet up as I thought about that. I caught myself with less than ten feet to the ground. Good thing no one was around to see me. It was stupid. I knew how to keep my focus better than that.

I still couldn't believe Blaine would kill my sister. But he had been mind-wiped. I'd been telling people wipes were a problem for years. Still, he'd had supper with our parents a few times, and I caught nothing off of him. No sign he was crazy. No sign he would kill my sister. But he had.

I turned on my flames as I arrived at his location, only to see a broken watch on the rooftop. I turned off my flames and landed on the roof, trying to look for some hint of him. I tried switching to my detection magic, scanning the area. Not for him, even with his mind wiped, he still didn't show up when I scanned the area, but I was learning how to search an area for the kind of disturbance he would leave behind.

He was gone. But, he didn't have more than a five-minute head start. I arrived too fast for him to have anything more than that. He could have been in the building, but it was several stories high, no way of knowing where in the building he was, or if he had made it to the ground already.

I saw something moving out of the corner of my eye. I turned and there was someone running across the length of a rooftop several buildings away. Plaid shirt and a ball cap.

"BLAINE!" I shouted, my flames lighting up as I took to the sky again.

Blaine looked at me, and a smile lit up his face.

He was smiling?

He raced towards me.

"Amber, thank God you're here. Listen, I—"

The murderer didn't get a chance to finish his sentence. My flames headed straight for him.

He ran, and the fireball missed, by a lot. I had to focus, get it together. I rubbed my eyes, getting the tears out.

"Amber, please! I didn't kill Sheila. You have to believe me!" Blaine shouted.

I tossed another fireball.

It was a direct hit. I couldn't see him anymore.

"Amber!"

Blaine was on a building behind me. There was no way he should have been able to do that.

"Amber! I didn't do anything. Please, just let me explain," Blaine teleported to the building he had been on before and shouted, "Come on down, Amber, we need to talk. I need someone to help me explain to Atlantis."

Blaine had teleported. And he remembered Atlantis!

He still knew magic. My mind reeled at the possibilities. He was an aberration. Did the mind-wipe not work on him? Was he a monster all on his own? I just didn't know.

The better question was, could I beat him? He could be anywhere he wanted to be. Stop time, slow it down, speed it up. If he wanted to win the fight, he would.

But I couldn't think that. Couldn't be weak. I could stop him. Kill him if necessary, but I could stop him.

I hurled streams of fire at Blaine. Not balls, streams, the fire pouring out of me almost out of control. The flames hit the top of the building and swept across it like a wave, the entire top of the building a sea of flames.

It did nothing. He teleported onto another building and ran.

I chased him down, flying to the next building and burning it with streams of flame, but he kept running. And teleporting. Every time my flames were about to burn him, he would disappear on me.

Of course, I could fly faster than any human can run. I got right up in his face and shot a blast of flames.

Another teleport.

"Amber, please. Just hear me out," I heard Blaine's voice from behind me, "I don't want to fight you."

I turned to shoot flames at him, only for him to disappear again.

"You know me. Would I ever hurt Sheila?" behind me, again. This trick was getting old.

I turned to fire a burst of flame at him . . . and raised my hand behind my back to blast him when he reappeared.

I spun around, expecting to see a charred body. But there was nothing. I saw Blaine on another building across the street. How could I stop him when he could teleport wherever he wanted fast enough to dodge any attack?

"Amber, I never forgot! There are people out there who know magic. People who want Atlantis to fall!"

He was lying. He'd say anything. The mind-wipe didn't work right; he must have remembered things, but in some kind of twisted and distorted way. The mind-wipe messed him up. I was sure of it.

I should have been focusing on the fight instead of what he said. In that brief second, Blaine was gone.

I had to find him. Before he could hurt anyone else.

But some things were bothering me. Like, if he was a killer, why was I still alive? If he could stop time, he could also slow it down, increasing the speed and power of his own punches by doing so. If he's become good enough, his fist could hit with the speed of a bullet.

There was no reason for him to have left me alive if he actually was a killer. Could he have been telling the truth? I needed to find out.

I flew around, looking through the back alleys. Blaine had dropped down to ground level, I'd wager. I certainly couldn't see him on any rooftops before making the descent.

I lowered myself to the ground.

"Blaine! Where are you?"

Before any answer could arrive, I was rammed against a wall.

It didn't feel like anyone had grabbed me, or thrown me.

Telekinesis.

"I'm not letting you hurt Blaine."

Drake stepped out, blood soaking his left arm, rips covering his otherwise dressy clothes.

I pushed myself off of the wall, breaking through his telekinesis. I'd fought him before, back when we were younger. I couldn't break through his telekinesis this easily. Not normally. He was weak. Still, he was the most powerful mage in the world. Even if he was weakened, I wasn't sure I could take him.

Drake tried to slam me into the wall again with his telekinesis.

I pushed back against his magic with my own, my flames pushing against the mental force he was sending at me. But it was a futile gesture. We joined Atlantis at the same time, but he was an aberration. He may as well be thirty or forty years my senior in magic experience.

But I was holding him back somehow. I could feel my power fading though. And fading fast.

And yet...I was winning. He stumbled, and my flames pushed closer to him.

Drake was angry, "Any other time I'd be happy for the challenge. But right now I need you to get out of the way."

He pushed more, his telekinesis pushing my flames away. I pushed back, but I was weakening. I couldn't keep this up. I was exhausted. He was going to win.

He was breathing heavily. Maybe he didn't know how close I was to my breaking point. Maybe he was worried he might lose, too. I needed to take a chance. He said that he didn't want to hurt Blaine.

"I don't . . . want . . . to hurt Blaine," I shouted.

I stopped my magic in that instant, cringing at the upcoming impact, but nothing happened.

"You'd better not," Drake replied, trying to sound tough, but I could see the relief in his eyes. He had dropped his guard. That's all I could ask for.

"Truce?" I said, struggling to stay on my feet.

Drake nodded, "Truce. Why were you attacking Blaine?"

Well, this could be a very short truce.

"I was . . . angry . . . the attack on the school . . . ."

"Yeah, pretty terrible. But I don't care what anyone else says, Blaine would not do that."

"Well, he could have been—"

Drake shot me a look of pure disgust, "Really? You're still one of those idiots who think mind-wipes screw people up mentally. Get it through your thick skull: the only study to ever suggest a link between mind-wipes and mental instability has never had its results duplicated. The mind-wipe did nothing to make Blaine crazy."

I clenched my fist and felt a few sparks, but I calmed myself down. "I disagree, but I will hear Blaine out."

Drake looked at me, an odd look on his face. It looked like concern, but I knew that couldn't be right. "Your flames seem different today. More powerful, but also erratic. Like you're not in control. What happened?"

"Sheila," I muttered. "She's . . . she's . . . ."

Drake put his hand on my shoulder. "She's dead . . . isn't she?"

I couldn't help myself. The tears came and I started sobbing into his shoulder. I don't even like the guy anymore. In fact, I couldn't stand him. But he was here and . . . .

"Amber," Drake said, a bit startled.

"Find Blaine," I said, "we find him and hear what he has to say. You're right about one thing. Blaine would never do this. Not willingly."

Drake wiped off my tears with the non-bloody sleeve of his shirt, "Been a while since I've done that."

"Don't drudge up the past now," I said, pushing him away, "I don't have the time to think about it."

"Okay," Drake replied, being oddly willing to just do what I asked for the first time ever. Did it really take my sister's death for him to treat me with some decency?

We walked out into the street. Drake hobbling a little.

"You've lost a lot of blood," I said to him.

"I'll be fine," he argued as he hobbled forward.

"Let me help," I said.

"Let you what? You don't know how to heal," Drake looked over at my hand, a fireball in it, ". . . you're joking, right? You want to cauterize the wound?"

"It would stop the bleeding."

"I'm fine," Drake replied. I tried to grab him, he was being unreasonable. My hand stopped about half an inch from his skin.

"Holding yourself together with telekinesis is not fine!"

"And I suppose cauterizing the wound is?" Drake said as he hobbled along, his eyes darting around.

I saw a few people, their face's twitched quickly and then went back to normal.

"What are you doing?"

"Scanning memories to see if they saw anyone with Blaine's face."

"Okay, and?" I asked.

"They all have . . . because of that."

There were several stores on the street, and all of them had news reports on them about the shooting, with Blaine's picture.

Word was travelling fast. Blaine's face was everywhere.

"He can't be in public then," I said, "anybody would recognize him."

"Why couldn't one of them have seen him?" Drake cursed.

And it hit me.

"Maybe they have," I murmured, racing over to a woman who looked visibly shaken.

"Miss, miss, are you okay?"

"That boy . . . that boy on the TV, the one who did that awful . . . he was here. He was right here."

"Which way did he go?" I asked.

"Dear, you can't, you're so young. Don't go after him," the

woman replied.

"We're cops," I said, giving a glance to Drake, "We need to find that boy before he hurts anyone else."

Drake got the message. I watched the woman's face as she acknowledged what I said as true without hesitation. Drake had gone in to influence her memory, maybe make her see a badge or something, I don't really know. I don't really want to know. I felt dirty for getting Drake to do this to an innocent old woman.

The woman gave me directions. Blaine had run down a back alley, but he couldn't be too far away. Oh, who was I kidding, with his powers, of course he could be. I started to run, Drake right behind me, his telekinesis holding him together and helping him keep pace.

"What just happened? Why couldn't I see Blaine when I looked in her mind?" Drake said, increasing his pace to match mine. Probably using telekinesis to push himself forward a bit, he couldn't keep up with me without magic.

"Aberrations are undetectable by magic," I began, "and one aberration's magic cannot affect another."

"So I can't even see memories of Blaine?" Drake asked, a sound of astonishment coming from him, though whether it was because the idea was brilliant or he was surprised I came up with it, I didn't know.

"You have a better explanation?"

Drake just laughed. "Why did I ever break up with you?"

"I broke up with you. And we are not talking about that now," I said, not even turning to look back at him.

We raced down into the back alley. The odds of Blaine actually being here were slim, but I had to try.

"Blaine!" I shouted, "We believe you. Please come out."

Blaine appeared right in front of us, his speech fast as he said, "Areyoureallyonmyside?"

I struggled to understand what he said, "You can slow down."

Blaine slowed, but he was still tense, ready to run or fight at a moment's notice "What changed? And why is Drake here?"

Drake stepped in, "You needed help."

He said it like it was the most natural and obvious thing in the world. As if he was the type of person who was always there when someone needed help.

Blaine started talking. He talked about how, since the day he went to Atlantis, he had also been taking lessons in magic from a man named Ra, who worked with an organization that used magic in the real world. When he was banished from Atlantis, he continued to work for them and train under them until today. They had countered the mind-wipe that Atlantis had done on him.

"They plan to attack Atlantis. We have to stop them," Blaine concluded.

"How?" I asked, "Who would believe us? They think you're a murderer, Drake just escaped from prison, and I used magic in view of dozens if not hundreds of humans. We're not exactly people anyone will trust."

Drake had that look on his face that he gets when he has what he thinks is a good idea—even though they rarely are. "How heavily guarded is the school?"

I cringed instinctively. There was no way one his plans would turn out well.

"How heavily guarded is the school?" Drake repeated, after Blaine and I had spent a couple seconds too surprised by his question to respond. "How many cops?"

"A fair amount, but not as many as you might think . . . . Most of them left the school grounds after Blaine escaped custody. Probably ten to twenty."

Drake smiled. I hate that smile. "I think we need to get back there. I have an idea."

Somehow, I knew I was going to hate his idea.

28| BLAINE

"OKAY, EXPLAIN TO ME AGAIN HOW THIS IS GOING TO WORK?" AMBER asked as she finished wrapping Drake up with the first aid kit she had stolen from a parked police car.

"With enough prodding, the synapses in a dead brain can still function. If they do, then I can gain access to all the memories that brain has. I can use Sheila's memories to prove Blaine's innocence. That will make everyone listen to us, at least." Drake replied, protesting with Amber the entire time she tried to wrap the wound.

"Why would my sister's memories prove Blaine's innocence" Amber asked, choking up a little at the word sister. I had to fight back some tears too.

"Someone used illusions to make it seem like you were doing the shooting, right?"

"Sheila knew magic, and she knew how to cast illusions," Drake said, "If her disbelief that Blaine would hurt her was strong enough, she would see through any illusion trying to convince her otherwise."

I could feel Amber shuddering with me at Drake's talk. He had no idea what Amber and I were going through. I would have given anything to be able to just stop forever and cry myself to death. But I couldn't. Not with what was at stake.

"I don't like this," I said.

Drake just replied, "Better ideas always welcome. We all know this isn't a great one."

We left the back alley, being careful to make sure nobody spotted me. There were some people around on the streets, but not too many.

The school zone was still crowded with cops and families.

Many families huddling together, just crying. The cops had given up on getting families to stay off the streets.

There must have been a couple hundred people around the school. Ra was . . . ruthless. There were so many dead.

So many . . . .

I froze. I thought back to the first time I saw someone die. Back in my hometown. Back before I had magic. That man, he was shot down. And he told me to run . . . to run away. Why did—

"Earth to Blaine," Drake said, "we're here."

I snapped back to reality.

"Okay," Amber said, "how are we getting in with Blaine?"

Drake snapped his fingers. "I've got this."

Everyone started looking in one direction. There was some screaming. And suddenly pretty much all of the cops started running away from the building, and from us. And all of the people started running for their cars, or into the nearby buildings, where the local neighbours had their doors open to let people in.

"What just happened?" I asked Drake.

Drake smirked at his own cleverness as he pointed down the street. "Imagination is a powerful thing. I made everyone think they heard gun shots coming from that direction."

"And they'll all assume . . . ."

"That it's you," Drake said with a smile.

"Clever," Amber said, "can we go in now?"

"I'll open a window for myself. Blaine, you can just teleport Amber in with you, right?"

"Yeah."

I wasn't the best at teleporting multiple people yet, but I definitely could do it. I didn't do it often though. Sheila and I had fun with it before, back when I was in Atlantis. But that was mostly it. I honestly hoped I never had to try and do a large group, I wasn't good enough for that yet.

"I'll check to see if there is anyone around before we teleport in," Amber said.

Her eyes rolled back into her head. I'd seen this before; it was what happened when a person focused on their detection magic. She was looking around everywhere. I had to keep an eye out for her while she did this, she was probably so focused on the school that she wouldn't even know what was happening a couple inches from her face. Her eyes rolled back to normal and she almost fell over. "All clear."

"You're in rough shape," I said.

"We all are. Just go."

I teleported the two of us into an empty room. I didn't want to relive what Ra had put me through.

Amber and I walked up the stairs to the second floor. The mural on the wall about love, respect, and community seemed more like a mocking joke today as a splatter of blood was spread onto and around the words. There was someone on the stairwell, their dead body soaked in their own blood. I didn't even know who it was. Older than me, a senior. I think it was one of Grant's friends.

I couldn't stand to keep looking at him. This was all my fault. If I had just been smarter, faster, maybe they would have been safe. Maybe Sheila would be alive. Maybe I would have stopped Ra before he killed anyone.

But I was just kidding myself. I had never saved anyone. It was all lies, created by Ra to make me think I was doing well. I was manipulated from the start. But I knew I would make them pay for that.

We made it to the top of the stairs and looked through the hallways. There was a doorway with a dead student in front of it. Grant. That was the room.

I almost hurled, trembling as I walked towards the room. I think the only reason I didn't hurl was because I hadn't eaten today. Not that I was going to be able to.

Drake opened a classroom door and came out to join us, "All empty on my side."

Drake took a look at Grant and said, "Is that where we need to go?"

I nodded. Drake moved forward and was about to enter the room when someone came out.

Amber shoved me into the men's washroom. I understood. We couldn't have anyone see me.

Drake said, "We're from CSIS. We have reason to suspect

that this incident has more to it than a simple school shooting. May we see the bodies?"

The man seemed a bit flabbergasted. He shouted, "Boss, there's some people from CSIS here."

I heard someone step out, and they said, "CSIS? Really?"

I recognized that voice. It was Ra!

I jumped out of the men's washroom immediately, and Ra's squad of a half dozen stepped out of the classroom Sheila was in.

Ra reached for his guns, and I performed a time stop, focusing on letting Amber and Drake in.

I soon realized, it wasn't working. I couldn't put up a time stop because I can't stop Drake and Ra. Ra's gang moved in swiftly.

Drake pushed out with his mind, trying to get into the minds of all six of Ra's followers.

"Drake," I said as I ran through the hallway to join the fight, "He's got a pair of anti-mages."

Amber used her flames to put up a wall of fire between us and them.

But it didn't stop them. A pair of them ran right through and ran us over.

"Amber," I shouted as I teleported out of the way of the speedster, "Keep your detecting magic up as best you can, we've got two illusionists here and they're going to try and trip you up, if not all of us."

The speedster came at me again. I focused on fast-forwarding myself. I could feel the strain, the difficulty. Those anti-mages were working me hard. But I did manage it. Not as well as I would have liked. But the speedster didn't seem so fast anymore. I swung a punch and hit him square in the jaw. His head cocked back.

The delay was all I needed. This was not a fight we could win. We needed to get out of here.

Drake didn't seem to think so though. And I realized why. Ra didn't know who Drake was, I never told him. Ra thought I was the biggest threat, so his anti-mages were focused on me.

Drake was ready to prove that wrong. I heard one of the

anti-mages scream, and suddenly he was on the ground, passed out, his nose bleeding.

Amber was dealing with the speedster and the phase man. She put a ring of flames around herself, but the speedster and phaser worked together to go through the flames and hit her. She flew back into the lockers and fell to the ground, stumbling to get back up. But when she did, she lit herself on fire, and the speedster decided that hitting her at super-speed was a bad idea.

"Focus, Blaine," Drake shouted. But he should have been taking his own advice, 'cause the speedster spun around and hit him in the stomach.

Focus? Well, there was one of Ra's men holding a gun and just standing back, waiting for a clear shot. He must be Ra's teleporter. That meant he was nothing but a normal guy with a gun as long as I was around.

I teleported behind him, with myself in fast forward, and I put him on slow. My punch sent him flying into the wall. He fell down, unconscious, but not dead. I hoped.

Drake was having trouble with the phase man, who had just reached his hand into Drake's chest.

"Surrender, or I rip his heart out," the man said.

Drake was in pain. I raised my hands. Ra fired a gunshot, and Amber's flames stopped, bleeding coming from her right shoulder.

Drake focused hard and growled, "Get your hand out of me."

The phase man slowly pulled his hand out of Drake, the glazed look in his eyes showing that Drake was in his head. Drake turned around and kneed the man in the groin, then punched the man in the face. Drake shook his hand for a moment after that, clearly not used to how much punching someone hurts your hand.

Ra had his gun focused on Amber and was ready to fire again. I ran, tried using my magic to save her, but it wouldn't work. I pushed her down and out of the way of the bullet.

Amber reached out one hand and focused on her flames. They hit Ra in the back, setting his trenchcoat on fire. Steam came from his hand, and he screamed as he dropped the gun, a burn mark on his palm.

"Heating metal is easy," Amber muttered, before drooping in my arms. She snapped back in under a second, but she wasn't in good shape. Another spell or two and she would be down and out.

Drake used a mental push and forced himself past all of Ra's men, running for the room that Sheila's body was in. He was still trying to get the memories he thought might be there. Couldn't he see that we needed to get Amber out of here?

The speedster came at me again and grabbed Amber, pulling her to her feet and putting her in a chokehold.

"Okay, kiddo, you're gonna want to surrender. Or I snap the pretty little lady's neck."

Amber flashed me a small grin, before being engulfed in flames.

The speedster immediately let go of her, screaming in agony as the flames lit up his clothes and scorched his skin.

The anti-mage looked at Amber, focusing on her, and her flames went away.

But that meant he wasn't focused on me.

I teleported behind the anti-mage and punched him in the back of the head with my body sped up and his slowed down. It was a lot of magic, but it was worth it.

His head snapped forward, and he tumbled over onto the ground. He was out for the count.

Ra had thrown off his trenchcoat. But he wasn't doing anything else. He had an illusion up, probably to save himself from Amber, but I could still see him pretty clearly.

The speedster was back on his feet. Burned, but still moving. And he moved at Amber, who lit herself on fire.

But the speedster was smart this time and started running rings around her. I moved to try and stop him, but the phase man came and reached his hand into my head.

"NO!" Ra shouted to the phase man, "We have no idea what will happen if an aberration dies."

The soldier was obedient, and he pulled out of my head.

"Okay," Ra said, "You've done pretty well so far. But you know you can't win. After all, where do you think my spare illusionist has been this entire time?"

I knew this couldn't be good. "Where is he?"

"Calling Odin for backup, of course. It is taking them some time to get here. Your anti-teleport focus has become quite large. But rest assured, they are on their way. So I suggest you surrender. You'll get to live and be healed up, because we don't want you dead. Which is a pretty good offer right now."

Drake stepped out of the classroom, telekinetically lifted up a set of lockers and said, "Surrender? We may be injured, but we're winning."

Drake tossed the lockers at Ra. They bounced off completely, not a scratch on Ra, he didn't even budge. It was like it hadn't even hit him.

Ra turned to Drake, a look of curiousity on his face. "Well now, I can't believe we never found out about you before. I guess we'll be taking you, too."

"My support will be here any second, and I'd wager Atlantis has troops well on their way," Ra continued, loving the sound of his own voice. "So, what's it going to be? Surrender to me or to the people who think you're a murderer?"

I heard footsteps coming up the staircase, dress shoes, the kind that made a light click. Ra laughed, convinced his back-up had arrived.

The look on his face changed when he saw who was coming through the door.

A man in an FBI-style suit, glasses, and slicked black hair stepped into view alongside a half dozen other people in suits. All of them were holding guns. One had their gun pressed into the head of Ra's illusionist, who was marching in front of him. The man in charge smiled. "May I offer a third choice?"

29| BLAINE

IF I LIVE TO BE ONE HUNDRED, I DON'T THINK I WILL EVER SEE SOMEONE as scared as Ra was in that moment. His eyes went wide, he got down on his knees in front of me and begged, "Blaine, please. Let us teleport. We need to get out of here! Now!"

"So dramatic," the man said with a chuckle as he walked towards Ra. "But then again, that has always been your style. Hasn't it, king of illusions?"

"Blaine, please . . . we need to get out of here," Ra said. He tried to grasp at my shirt but I backed away. He was a good liar; I wasn't going to fall for some kind of scheme. If I dropped my teleport barrier then he could bring in dozens if not hundreds of other people to take me down.

The man, possibly an illusion, glanced over at me. I tried to see through it, but nothing was working.

"Blaine, correct?" the man with glasses asked. He looked directly at me with a level of calm that unsettled me.

"Yeah," I said nervously. There was something off about these people. But it wasn't an illusion, not as far as I could tell, anyways.

"The injured girl and the young man are with you?" The man with glasses asked, gesturing briefly to Amber and Drake.

I nodded.

"And the others are with Ra?"

I nodded again. Unsure what this agent, because in his clothes he sure looked like an agent, actually wanted.

"Blaine, Ra, and those two are to be unharmed," the man said as he gestured to Amber and Drake and stepped behind his agents.

Two of the agents pulled Ra away from me and held him

down. Then the agents fired. The first shot hit Ra's illusionist in the forehead. He slumped to the ground, blood splattering everywhere. They went to the ones that were unconscious, and put a bullet into each of their heads. After just six deafening shots, all of Ra's men were dead.

I leaned over, gasping for air. I couldn't . . . I couldn't handle it. There was so much blood. So many bodies . . . .

I saw him again. That man. The one who died in front of me. Saw him shout at me, "Get out of here, kid!" Saw the shots fired.

I fell to my knees. I couldn't breathe. Couldn't . . . .

I closed my eyes—I had to block it out. Block out the gunshots, the bodies, all the blood. Look up. Look straight at him, at this madman in a suit. There was no blood on him. I just had to focus on him.

I was shaking, but I got back up to my feet.

"What are you doing?" I shouted at him. He knew who I was and he had told his men not to shoot me or my friends. To his twisted mind, he must have thought that was a kind gesture. He wanted me on his side.

"Eliminating potential threats," the agent replied calmly, "Ra gets a reprieve since he is a prisoner of value."

"They surrendered!" I shouted at him, struggling to my feet. "Several of them were unconscious."

The man walked between his agents, avoiding the blood and bodies without even looking at them. As he got closer to me he started to reach out his hand, as if to put it on my shoulder. When he caught the look in my eyes, he was quick to realize it was the wrong move and he pulled his hand back, not bothering to be suave about it or pretend he was trying to do something else with his hand. With his hands in his pockets, he said, "Any one of them would oppose me if they could find an opportunity. I killed them before they could."

"Who are you?" Drake asked. He was trying to sound tough, but he was scared. I could tell. The fight had taken a lot out of all of us. Not that Drake would admit that he couldn't handle this.

"You may call me Alpha," the man replied.

Alpha? Ra mentioned him before. They never let me see a picture of him. Just spoke in hushed tones like he was the boogeyman or something. Five minutes around him was enough for me to understand.

"Why are you here?" I demanded.

The man paused, as though he was surprised that I had not figured out exactly what he was going to do. There was almost a sound of disappointment in his voice as he replied, "I want you to join me, Blaine."

I almost vomited from the mere thought. He wanted me to join him? I was not going to side with a killer. Not again. Never again. I'd had enough of working for psychopaths.

"Why would I join you?" I said, hoping that I sounded strong, confident, and defiant.

Alpha pulled out his gun and shot Drake in the knee. Drake crumbled to the ground, but did not scream in pain, though from the look on his face it was taking a lot of strength to keep it in.

"You will join me because your friend still has a working knee," Alpha replied calmly as he aimed the gun at Drake's other knee.

"I could run . . . ." I said, trying to stall for time, to think of something. Anything would be better than working for a monster like him. "If you know who I am, then you know what I can do."

Drake pulled himself up to his feet, leaning against the wall, his weight on one foot. He struggled to get every word out in between pained breaths. "Blaine, don't. I've stopped bullets before. I couldn't stop his. He's an aberration. He's like us."

Alpha's head whirled around at that comment to look at Drake again. The smile on his face was more terrifying than anything I had ever seen, "Like us? It would appear that Christmas has come very early this year. Three little aberrations, all here to join me or be my prisoners, how lovely."

"I'll never join you," I said, my voice finally sounding more defiant than terrified.

"No, I suppose you won't," Alpha said. He reached over before I could react and grabbed my chin. "You're weak. Having a panic attack over a few dead bodies. You won't be much use as an agent. Not for a long time, anyway. But I'm confident I can break you down and remould you. It might take a lot of pain though."

At that comment, all of Alpha's agents said, in unison, "Pain is good. It reminds us we are alive."

I flashed back again to that night. But it was different. I saw the two women who fired the gunshots. I remembered something more, something that I had hidden from myself. More than just the two people who were there.

They fired their gunshots. The man was in pain. He begged for mercy. "Please . . . it hurts so much . . . please, the pain—"

The two men then said, in unison, "Pain is good. It reminds us we are alive."

My memories of the night were coming back fresher than ever. I remembered the faces of those women who killed that man. They were right here in front of me. Alpha's agents. They were the ones that killed him. They were there that night. Alpha's people killed that man. He was responsible. If I hadn't been there, hadn't seen that man die, I wouldn't have moved. Wouldn't have met Sheila or Amber or learned about magic. Sheila would still be alive. It all led back to him. Back to Alpha.

"You—" I said, ripping Alpha's hand off of my chin. "You murder people for no reason and you expect me to work for a monster like you."

If I had thought Alpha would react to being called a monster, I was sorely disappointed. The look on Alpha's face wasn't anger, or even the psychotic laughter I could have expected from a monster. Instead it was a face of boredom and impatience.

"You are wasting my time," Alpha said, "so I'm done negotiating. You are coming with me. Now."

"What's to stop me from escaping?" I said.

Alpha grabbed my arm himself and replied, "Because I don't need the girl."

A half dozen guns pointed at Amber.

Amber stood up, trying to remain brave in spite of the guns, but anyone could see the fear in her eyes. "Yeah, well, maybe I have something to say about that . . . ."

Amber tried to use her magic, a spark appeared, but nothing else.

Alpha took a good look at Amber. On anyone other than a monster like him you would have every right to call him a pervert for the way he looked at her. He clasped his hands together and smiled, "A spark past three anti-mages? You're no aberration, but you're certainly better than the cannon fodder I regularly see. And I do need a new person to fetch my coffee."

"I'd rather be . . . ." but she didn't finish the sentence. I could see what she was thinking. Her eyes started to water.

"Weak," Alpha said, "I should do you a favour, Blaine, and kill her."

Alpha pulled out his gun and pressed it to Amber's forehead. "You're crying because you know someone who died here today, don't you?"

Amber's eyes flashed, but she controlled herself, and Alpha missed it.

"You're a bit too old for high school, and too young to have a child here," Alpha said, "younger sibling perhaps?"

Amber said, "Like I'd tell you."

"All the answer I need," Alpha said with a smile. "Search the bodies for residual magic. If the sister is a decent mage, odds are good the sibling has magic in them too."

"Don't you touch her!" Amber shouted angrily.

Alpha's smile widened. "Her? Thank you. Focus your search on girls."

It took them less than a minute before one of Alpha's men came out of the classroom with Sheila's body over his shoulder. I could see where the bullet had hit her chest.

My eyes started to water.

"What are you going to do to her?" I demanded as I willed myself to look at them taking her.

Alpha had clearly given up all pretence of being nice to us; he even seemed to be delighting in angering us, "Dead mages are almost as rare as live ones. And they are a good source for research. We're going to dissect it."

"Put her down!" Amber shouted.

"Or what?" Alpha said, the gun still pressed into Amber's

forehead.

I focused with all my might. What I was about to do was something I had never tried before. But it worked.

The gun from one of Alpha's agents disappeared from their hand and reappeared in mine. I pressed the gun nozzle underneath my chin.

"You want me alive. Leave Amber and Sheila alone, or I kill myself."

Alpha pulled the gun off of Amber's forehead and pointed it at me. "That's not a threat."

"But no one knows what will happen when an aberration dies," Ra said, speaking up for once.

"I do," Alpha replied. "And if you don't, then Odin is keeping secrets from you."

I could see Drake's eyes widen. My body trembled as I saw the excitement in Drake's eyes. It was the same enthusiasm he had when learning about how he and I were similar. I knew he wanted answers, but there was no way he wanted them badly enough to side with a monster.

"What happens?" Drake asked, desperation in his voice. "What happens when an aberration dies?"

"Work for me, I'll tell you," Alpha said, extending his hand out for Drake to shake.

And that's when Drake's eyes terrified me. He was considering it! He was actually thinking about working for that psychopath.

Why hadn't I seen that coming? Drake hadn't come because he cared. He came because I'm an aberration. Because I was the only aberration he knew about. Because he needed to understand how aberrations work, and he'd side with anyone who could tell him. It was stupid to think that he was my friend.

Alpha said, "I'll tell you everything I know."

Drake paused, a mischievous grin on his face, "Give me a sample. What are you good at?"

Alpha laughed. In an instant, there was a cup of coffee in his hand and he took a sip from it.

That was no illusion. He actually made it out of thin air.

Creation magic.

Alpha took another sip and said, "Fair trade, my friend? I've shown you mine."

Drake nodded and ripped the door off of a locker and let it float in the air for a couple of seconds.

"Mental," Alpha replied. But this time, it wasn't fascination or happiness in him. It was almost a look of horror. He was in such control though, that I couldn't understand why he would be scared when he discovered the truth about Drake.

"Epsilon, please see to the wounds of this boy, Drake, was it?" Alpha said, his charming psychopath demeanour returning.

A woman walked over to Drake and put her hand on his knee. It started to heal.

Amber shouted at Drake as she stood up. Sparks shot out of her, the start of a flame that couldn't get going. "Traitor! I should have burned you to ashes when I had the chance."

Drake gave Alpha a quick smirk. "Jealous ex."

Epsilon stepped away from Drake. Drake stood up on his leg. He wobbled a bit, but he was mostly fine. A bit of a limp was all he was showing from a shot to the knee.

"I'd prefer they weren't hurt," Drake said to Alpha, addressing him as an equal. "They're weak, but they both have potential. I don't have to explain Blaine, but Amber is less than a month away from getting her masters in fire, and she's only twenty. I personally know less than ten people her age with such skill. She's probably more powerful than half your people."

Alpha's eyes did not leave Drake as he replied, "Don't let your feelings for her get in the way. Or for Blaine."

"Blaine? I'm only interested in him because he's an aberration."

"Don't lie to me," Alpha replied, "But I do understand; there is a strong, immediate attachment the first time you meet someone like you."

The look in Alpha's eyes suggested there was a story behind the first time he met another aberration, but he certainly was not going to tell it today.

"Shall we leave?" Drake asked.

"For you to betray me?" Alpha responded, "I don't think so."

214

"What?" Drake said.

"Teleportation and Illusions are down with Blaine and Ra here. If you block all Mental then we can't make people ignore us. We would have no way to hide out in public, and Blaine is a wanted man. Did you really think I was that stupid?"

Drake's eyes gave him away. So he had been trying to come up with a plan to get us out of here. And Alpha had seen right through it.

Alpha raised his gun at Drake. Drake dropped to the ground, the shot missing. A telekinetic wave struck Alpha's people and sent them tumbling to the ground. Amber took advantage of the moment and hurled a pair of fireballs at Alpha while his anti-mages weren't focused.

Alpha created a solid thick wall of stone between himself and the fireballs. Drake practically flew over to me as he shouted, "Blaine, drop your ward, grab onto Ra!"

I grabbed Ra, as did Amber and Drake. Ra pushed the teleport button on his watch, and we were gone. I could still hear the sound of Alpha's bullets and scream of anger as we disappeared.

30| AMBER

WHEN MY EYES READJUSTED TO WHERE I WAS, I SAW WE WERE OUTSIDE of the city.

Drake's plan had actually worked. That wasn't something I really liked saying. Or thinking.

Drake smiled and looked right at me. He was in my head.

"Get out," I thought at him.

"Best I don't," Drake replied in my head, "If Ra here is the aberration of Illusions, then he could make you see things. Best to keep me in your head so that you'll know for sure what's real."

"Fine," I replied angrily, last thing I wanted was him in my head. "But if I feel even the slightest itch of thinking about my shower this morning, your body will be burned beyond any hope of identification."

"Please. I don't need to sift through your memories for that image. Now focus."

I pulled up my detection magic to pay more attention to my surroundings. I saw what Drake meant by focus almost instantly. Ra was trying to slip away. He had an illusion up to try and fool me. But he didn't get very far. Drake grabbed Ra and said, "Okay, you have some explaining to do."

Ra pushed Drake off of him, and got to his feet, looking squarely at Drake. "And how are you going to make me talk?"

I tossed a fireball inches from Ra's feet, "He won't, I will."

"Thank you," Drake thought, then said aloud to Ra, "Start talking. Who do you work for?"

Ra looked bored, "You couldn't ask a question Blaine doesn't already have the answer to?"

I slapped him as hard as I could. It felt good to hit the bastard who killed my sister.

He spat up a bit of blood before saying, "That your best? I've paid women to slap me harder."

I was about to slap him again when he let out a laugh and said, "Oh my . . . I know you. You're one of those dummies who actually bought into our bull about mind-wipes."

My hand stopped mid-swing. He couldn't have expected me to buy that. He was an illusionist, a trained liar.

"Your bull? Seems like we already found something you're willing to talk about," Drake said, stepping between Ra and I.

If Ra was letting the cat out of the bag, he sure didn't act like it. He had the hugest smile on his face, like he was happy to be talking about the plan. "You got me. We needed some way to start a rebellion in Atlantis. The biggest threat to magic users is having their minds wiped. So I faked some story about mind-wipes causing harm years ago, and idiots like you gobbled it up. Now our agents in Atlantis just have to say that Blaine did the shooting because of the mind wipe, and boom, anarchy."

I couldn't believe him. What he was saying was impossible. There was no way . . . .

"Don't believe me?" Ra said. "Take a look."

Ra's body started to change, a veil coming up over him. He looked just like Doctor McPherson. The man who published the paper claiming that mind-wipes were harmful.

"I see you recognize me, Amber," Ra said, "been a while since our last chat."

"But you . . . you were a student in the city. You lived in the city for ten years!"

"What can I say, my illusions are that good," Ra laughed as his illusion faded away.

My hand was shaking and my entire body was trembling. If he could do that . . . if he could lie for ten years, then what else could be a lie? Was I really that much of a fool?

"Amber, calm down," Drake said, putting his hand on my shoulder. "There is only one reason for him to tell the truth so easily, he's trying to get on your nerves. Don't let him."

"And you would know all about nerves, wouldn't you, mental master?" Ra said, changing the target of his talk to Drake.

"I'm surprised that you never found out about me if you were in the city for ten years," Drake said, pacing around Ra, ensuring he had no escape lane.

"What makes you think I didn't?" Ra's smug smile was becoming enough to make me want to rip his entire face off.

"You tried to recruit Blaine, but not me."

"Blaine's ideals match ours. Yours don't."

Drake had this calm fury to him. I've seen it before, when he gets furious there is a terrifying level of silence to it. "Ideals? You shot kids. I would have thought your only ideal was power."

Drake's tone of voice and the way that the ground shook subtly showed his anger. But I knew him well enough to know that Ra killing kids wasn't making Drake angry. What made Drake angry was that he couldn't read Ra's mind. That he couldn't know if Ra was lying. Ra had to be.

Blaine had been sitting aside, watching it all, a deep look of contemplation on his face. He finally stood up. "He's lying to you Drake. We need to move."

"What?"

Blaine walked over to Ra and dragged him to his feet. "He's stalling. He thinks we're going to get caught by his allies if we stay here. So he's going to keep spewing lies mixed with half-truths until they arrive."

Should have thought of that myself. But if he was an aberration I couldn't exactly check.

"You're right," Drake replied, clenching his fist, frustrated that Ra was playing him. "We have to get going."

"You're not going anywhere," Dwayne shouted as he dropped down from the sky. He had his gun drawn and pointed directly at Drake. Behind Dwayne were over a dozen members of Atlantis's military personnel, including General Cabrera and Matt.

"Well, I guess we wanted Atlantis to come to us anyway," Drake commented as he raised his hands. "I surrender."

Blaine wasn't ready to surrender though. He teleported and moved right beside Dwayne. His punch contacted Dwayne in the side of the head. Dwayne's head cocked to the right. He spun around and shot Blaine with a burst of electricity. Blaine tried to dodge the blow, but it didn't work. Dwayne's signature lightning was laced with anti-magic. The lightning hit Blaine square in the chest. He fell to the ground, spasming and unconscious.

Dwayne recovered quickly and repositioned his gun to focus on Drake, though his eyes gave the briefest glance to me. "Amber, what are you doing with them?"

"That's a question for Atlantis," Cabrera replied. "Take them in."

Drake shoved Ra in front of us. "Happy to be arrested. Take him, too."

"Who's that?" General Cabrera asked, tilting his head, his eyes squinting. Trying to see if he was seeing an illusion or having his mind tricked. But not coming up with anything. He grabbed a member of his team and said, "Anything funny about the man?"

"Nope, not in the slightest," the man replied, "He's real."

"He's behind the shooting. Not Blaine," Drake said as he got down on his knees and put his hands behind his head. He emphasized the words 'not Blaine,' making his case clear while he was being arrested.

Matt came over to grab Blaine. I think he was trying to whisper to Drake as he did so, I heard him with my detection magic. "You want to be arrested? I hope you have a plan."

Drake nodded at Matt's comment and laid down on the ground. I surprised myself by following suit. I got down on my knees and clasped my hands behind my head.

Cabrera grabbed me personally while Dwayne grabbed Drake. Dwayne was one of the best anti-mages around, if he couldn't stop Drake, odds of finding someone who could were pretty slim.

"Ship them up," Cabrera said. "We take them to the prison cells now. They will await judgement by the council of six. Hurry, we can push past Blaine's ward much easier when he's unconscious."

The cell they threw me in was pure white. Were it not for the fact that it was not actually padded, I would say that it looked more like a room in a psych ward than a prison cell. At least it had an actual bed. Well, a mattress, couple of pillows, and some bed sheets, anyways. Not much in the weapons department.

I spent several hours just waiting. Stuck in my cell. Alone. Blaine, Drake, and Ra were nowhere to be seen. Couldn't really say that surprised me.

I had two guards outside my cell. I could see them when I went to the door and looked out the small window I had. I tried talking to them, but they weren't interested in listening to me, and did a pretty good job of outright ignoring me. I tried to see what I could do with my magic, but the room clearly had anti-magic running through the walls. I couldn't even get a spark off.

When the door to my cell finally opened I already feared the worst, that they would mind-wipe me and come up with some kind of story to tell the rest of Atlantis, instead of this becoming a long and drawn out trial.

Instead, Dwayne stepped into the room, unarmed and in a business suit. Never seen him in one of those before. He looked really good. He was carrying a file in his hand.

"Dwayne? What are you doing here?" I asked, standing up to look at him.

"I'm the seventh for your trial," Dwayne said, acting incredibly professional while the guards outside closed the door.

"But you're not even a warden anym—" I cut myself off, answering my own question. "I'm not a warden anymore, am I?"

Dwayne was a friend. Having a friend on the council would be helpful. Having at least someone who would listen and believe me could make all the difference.

But Dwayne's face told me it wasn't going to be that simple. "Amber, you should probably sit down, what I have to say won't be easy to hear."

I took a seat on the bed. Dwayne looked around the room, like he was trying to find something to focus on other than having to look me in the eye. That wasn't a good sign.

"I'm here to make a deal with you. The President thought it would be best if this offer came from me." Dwayne said, his voice telling me that I would not like this deal.

"You're going to have all charges against you dropped. Your name will be cleared. You won't be allowed in the military, to take any kind of political job, or regain your position as a warden, but you will be allowed to stay in Atlantis and continue your training."

I glanced down at the floor instead of at him. There was no way this was coming without some strings attached. Even with losing my warden status, this was way too good of a deal.

"What's the catch"

Dwayne looked at the ground instead of me as he said, "Testify that Drake used magic to control you."

They wanted me to betray Drake? I may hate him, but I wouldn't go that far. Lie to protect the status and integrity of people in power. It was everything I stood against.

"And what about Blaine?" I said, biting my tongue to stop myself from telling him that he could forget about me lying.

Dwayne passed the file over to me. I opened it up to see Blaine's name and all kinds of medical charts and notes.

"What is this?" I asked, starting to read through the files. It was a dumb question. I could see what it was pretty clearly. Files on Blaine, from a psychiatric institution. It said that Blaine had been in a psych ward for six weeks over the summer, suffering from post-traumatic stress disorder after witnessing a murder in his home town. It said that he had lashed out violently several times at the end of his last school year. He wasn't mentally stable, if these files could be believed.

"The President wants you to claim that the school shooting happened because Blaine is crazy. The mind-wipes had nothing to do with it."

"You have got to be kidding me, Dwayne," I shouted, "There is no way you would ever agree to this. It's a load of bull, and you know it!"

"Is it, Amber? Blaine being unstable and Drake using you both seem perfectly reasonable to me. Besides, if what you say is true, it will just cause mass panic."

"And that's a good reason to lie? To keep the peace?"

"Yes," was all Dwayne replied, crossing his arms in front of him. The discussion was over, because he had stopped listening. I very much wanted to scream.

I wasn't going to turn on Blaine. Did the President think that just because a friend suggested it that I would say yes? I heard

Blaine out, I saw Ra and Alpha, I fought for my life beside Blaine and Drake. I even used my detection magic; they couldn't have slipped anything past me. My necklace was still on, I could feel it. Not even Drake could control me very easily with that kind of protection.

Time for a different approach.

"What about the other prisoner, Ra?" I asked Dwayne, ending the long pause between us.

"Mr. Brown is one of Blaine's teachers, and is confused and terrified by the whole incident," Dwayne began, "He just wants to go home. We told him that after the trial happens we will return him home without any memory of Atlantis."

A couple of sparks erupted from my hand. The door to my cell opened immediately and the guards were about to rush me when Dwayne stepped in front of them and said, "Relax. She didn't do anything to hurt me. We're fine. Now go back outside."

The guards hesitated, but a quick glare from Dwayne had them doing as they were told. No one would have ever done that while I was a warden.

"Ra did it," I repeated, "he killed my sister. He deserves to rot and die for what he did. And you want to let him go? No. Not happening. Whatever it takes, he is not getting away with this."

"Amber, be reasonable. Which is more likely: that some man from some secret society of mages frames Blaine for murder; or that Blaine, a boy with a file showing his mental instability, snapped and killed people? The story you and the others are trying to sell is completely ludicrous. Isn't it possible that Drake actually is in your head, making you think all these crazy thoughts?"

I reached for my pendant again, pulled it off my neck and showed it to him. "No, Drake can't be controlling me. This protects me from mind control. You should know. You made it for me."

Dwayne's eyes went wide for a moment as he looked at my pendant. I don't know what he was so surprised by. But he then said the words that shattered my world.

"Amber, there's nothing in your hand."

I looked at the necklace and the pendant at the end of it. No. It was there. It was real. I could see it. I could feel it. That couldn't be faked.

Dwayne got down on his knees and grabbed my hands in his, placing his hands underneath mine, cupping the pendant that I knew was there. "I know it's hard. I know you can see it right in your mind even now, despite being in an anti-magic cell and being nowhere near Drake. But there is nothing in your hands. Our anti-mages thought their magic prevented them from being controlled, but Drake used them to escape. He's too powerful, and Blaine is going to become his equal sooner rather than later. There is no shame in admitting that they manipulated you."

I was shaking. I couldn't breath. Couldn't think clearly. The words came out in a blurt, more from instinct than anything else. Trying to remain composed, and failing completely, "No... it can't . . . you're wrong."

Dwayne ignored my words and looked me right in the eyes. I felt like one of the drunk people I'd seen Dwayne help when I went on a ride-along with him. "Amber, I'm trying to help you. You're my friend. I've been there for you through everything, and I want to be here for you now. They are using you. There is nothing in your hands. Your pendant is gone. Just let go. Let go of the pendant, it's not even there. Can you let go of what you believe, just this once? Just this once, can you not be stubborn, and believe what a friend is telling you? A friend who only wants what is best for you."

I let go of the pendant. It felt so real, slipping out of my hands, I was sure that if I looked I would see it lying in Dwayne's palms. Dwayne reached up with one hand and tussled my hair for a moment, and I knew then that the pendant wasn't there, had never been there.

Dwayne pulled my hands closer, let go, and wrapped his arms around me. It felt good. I clung to him, tears filling my eyes. I was ready to burst. I think Dwayne knew that though. His voice was calm and reassuring, "Amber, I know how you feel. Sheila is gone and the world seems wrong. You've been tricked and lied to, but it's over now. You are safe. You will get through this. You have a friend by your side. I will never hurt you."

31| BLAINE

I WAITED IN MY CELL. AND WAITED. AND WAITED. I TRIED TELEPORTING, just inside my cell. I could manage it, but it was exhausting, and I was already in rough shape. There was strong anti-magic in the room, and probably anti-mage guards outside. Drake might have been able to break through all of this, but Drake's been learning magic way longer than I have. I wouldn't be pulling a breakout anytime soon, no matter how much I wanted to.

I hated these rooms. Too white for a prison. Too clean. Too much like being back in the psych ward. I wanted out, and I wanted out now.

I fidgeted. I unmade the bed. I tossed the sheets around the room. Anything to keep my body busy enough that my mind wouldn't overload from everything that had happened.

It wasn't working. I could feel the tears coming, felt my face getting wet. I crumpled to the ground and let it all out. I couldn't save Sheila. I couldn't save anyone. I wasn't strong enough.

I tossed the mattress at what I thought was the door. If it was, no one on the outside gave any indication.

Just before I had reached the point where I was ready to rip my own hair out, which was probably far less time than I should admit to, I started shouting at the guards.

"Hey!" I shouted as I banged on the walls to my cell. One of them had to be the side with the door.

The guards ignored me.

"Hey, I need to talk to General Cabrera!"

The guards continued to ignore me.

"Come on! I was framed."

One of the guards responded, "So you claim."

"It's the truth!" I shouted back.

"Everyone says they didn't do it."

"But I'm telling the truth!" I shouted again. I punched the wall in frustration. They were in danger, and they wouldn't believe me. Their stubbornness was infuriating.

I must have been waiting there for hours. Hours of tossing stuff around my room, punching walls, and screaming in frustration, before the door to my cell finally opened. General Cabrera, the President, and the rest of the council of six entered the room. Dwayne Cooper was with them.

"Get that traitor out of here!" I shouted at Dwayne.

The others glanced at Dwayne, who headed for the door, "If me leaving means he'll talk, then I'll go."

"No," the President replied, "We're not going to cater to the whims of a murderer. He doesn't want you, then that's exactly why you need to stay. Now, Blaine, start talking. Why don't you start with why you think Dwayne is a traitor?"

I wasn't sure if I should be relieved or infuriated. They were about to give me a chance to talk, but I don't think they were willing to believe a single word I said.

"Dwayne's working with the people who framed me for the school shooting," I wanted to punch Dwayne right in his lying mouth. My fists clenched, and I had to hold myself back from busting his jaw. Hitting him right now was not a good idea, no matter how satisfying it would be.

"Dwayne has been a respected member of the Atlantis community for twelve years, and has served as a warden for seven of those years. You were banished before for breaking our laws. What would ever make us trust your word over his?"

Fury rose in me. How could she not see through him? How couldn't she tell that he was lying to her, manipulating her? The President couldn't possibly be that stupid.

"Check the other prisoner, read his mind. You'll find what you need to learn there. You'll see that I was framed."

"We already have," the Lawyer responded. "He's just a teacher."

I almost screamed, but I restrained myself. I couldn't wrap my head around what they were saying. Ra was guilty. How could they not see that?

225

And then it hit me. Ra had a mind-lock in his own mind; probably all of their double agents, like Dwayne, had it too. Not even a mind-scan would detect their treachery. If they had just let Drake be around, then he could disable those mind locks, I'm sure of it!

"That can't be right. Ra is tricking you," I began.

I was about to continue when General Cabrera's face jerked at the mention of Ra's name. I was ecstatic. Ra's name meant something to Cabrera.

"What did you say?" Cabrera asked.

The President had a look of disgust on her face as she glared at Cabrera. "Don't tell me you actually believe him."

"Ra is an Egyptian god," Cabrera replied, matter-of-factly.

The Doctor, Lawyer, Teacher, and Master began to murmur at that comment. I couldn't make out what they were whispering, because the President spoke overtop of them.

"You can't seriously be talking about Odin. He died fifty years ago."

The President glared at Cabrera, a look that clearly told Cabrera that he was supposed to back down.

Cabrera met the President's glare with the steely ferocity of a man willing to stand his ground against an enemy he is uncertain he can defeat. "No bodies were ever found, Madame President."

"So, naturally, when the name of a god comes up, you assume that it means Odin is back," the President said before adding, "you're paranoid."

Cabrera stepped up to the President, his face at best an inch or two from hers as he replied, "Odin, and his former partner Alpha, destroyed *all* of the other magic cities. Camelot, Olympus, El Dorado, Asgard, all gone because of those two. Atlantis survived only because they turned on each other. And we never found a body for either one."

Now it was my turn to react. How could no one have told me that Odin and Alpha used to work together? And that they were responsible for the destruction of all the other magic cities? I guess Odin left that part out of his story, like he left out pretty much anything important I should have been told.

"A prisoner mentions the name of a god and suddenly you believe them?" the Master asked.

"Caution is my job," Cabrera responded, "Need I remind you that Odin and Alpha discovered ways to implant memories that could fool even the best mind-scanners we have. If that man has any affiliation with Odin, then everything we see in his head could be a lie."

He knew about the mind-locks. Cabrera was on my side. At least, he was entertaining the idea that I could be telling the truth.

"General," the President said in a tone so patronizing I wanted to punch her for Cabrera, "our duty is to dispense justice, not waste time with conspiracy theories."

"Fine," Cabrera said, "look in his mind. If what you find contradicts Mr. Brown, we investigate further."

The President nodded and reached over to place her hand on my forehead. I felt her hand, cold and wrinkled, pressing against my skin. But nothing else was happening. I couldn't feel her trying to get into my head. Could she really be that good? That I wasn't even noticing?

The President pulled her hand back and said, "He's guilty. I've seen it for myself."

I couldn't believe it. How could she not see that Ra was the killer?

Because I still had the mind-lock. She can't see Ra or any other citizens of New Asgard in my head. No! She couldn't find the truth.

"No! It's the mind-lock," I shouted, "it hides any memory I have of Ra or the mages of New Asgard."

"We mention mind-locks and immediately they become his defence. You've read the files, General. He's not right in the head. He would say anything if it would make you believe him."

General Cabrera left the room, uncertainty covering his face. The others were quick to follow suit.

I didn't know what to do. What could I do? If both mine and Ra's minds told the story that Ra wanted everyone to believe, then what could I hope to do against it? I'd need someone to believe me. Someone to believe every word I said and be willing to investigate if it was true. Drake's memories from Sheila were my only hope. It was the only thing that could save me now. Sheila hadn't been mind-locked.

I didn't get much of a chance to ponder that thought. It was less than five minutes after the Council of six left my prison cell that I was brought out of it in handcuffs and chains.

There were two dozen guards escorting me back to the stadium where I had been placed on trial before. Over half of Atlantis was watching me from their seats.

This seemed different though. Gone was the trial bar where the Council of six and the chosen seventh would sit. Replacing it was a row of chairs, and a podium.

The President, the other councillors, Dwayne, Amber, and Ra were up on the stage. All of them were sitting except for the President, who was at the podium.

"Thank you, citizens," the President began, "I know that over the course of today many of you received distressing news about former student, Blaine Allan, performing a school shooting and murdering dozens of minors. The deaths are, sadly, true. We lost one of our own in that school, Sheila Bennett, sister to Amber Bennett."

The President waited for a moment as that information went through the crowd in a collective amount of whispering and murmuring.

"However, what is not true is that this was caused because Blaine had his mind wiped. There is no no reason to believe that Blaine Allan performed these actions because of the effects of a mind-wipe."

I could hear the crowd murmuring, processing what had been said. Drake's powers would have been nice right about then. I would have loved to know what everyone in the crowd was thinking.

Where was Drake? He should have been there. Probably being escorted by a couple dozen guards up here, and giving them a heck of a time.

The President continued at the podium by saying, "To talk about this further, we have someone whom many of you are familiar with. Amber Bennett, formerly one of the leaders of the anti-wipe coalition, has agreed to talk today about the truth of what happened. We applaud her bravery to stand before us amid such a horrific tragedy."

My face was painted with confusion as Amber took the stage. What was she doing? Why was she up there? I wasn't sure if she was playing them, or if she had betrayed me, jumping back to Atlantis' side.

The President began to clap as she stepped back and let Amber take the podium. The audience started to clap as well. It was incredibly, thunderously loud. Thousands upon thousands of people clapping all at once.

Amber spoke into the microphone, "Hello." The sound of all the clapping died instantly.

"Today, my sister died. It's hard to be up here, talking about it. But this needs to be said."

Amber paused, clearly trying very hard to not think about Sheila. She, at least, wasn't faking anything here. Had she tricked them? And if not, what had they said to change her mind, to convince her? They wouldn't let her talk if they weren't sure she would say the right things.

"My first reaction on hearing that Blaine was responsible for this shooting was similar to many of yours," Amber continued, the stress she was under evident in her voice, "That the mind-wipe we performed on him six months ago had messed up his brain."

She couldn't have tricked them, could she? Convince them she would play ball for them, only to expose the truth?

"But then I realized that Blaine had always been messed up."

I felt my jaw drop to the ground. I couldn't believe what she was doing. She knew the truth. Why would she say that? What had they done to her? I needed to know. And they would pay for tricking her.

"Three months prior to joining Atlantis, Blaine was institutionalized," Amber said, sharing my secrets for all of Atlantis to hear. "He spent six weeks in psychiatric care to deal with post-traumatic stress disorder. The files say he was angry, even violent sometimes. That he lashed out verbally against priests and teachers in his hometown and physically assaulted several of his

229

peers. Blaine's actions today were not the result of a mind-wipe. They were nothing more than the result of a very sick and deeply disturbed child."

She had to be lying, or coerced. I know that Amber would never say those things. She trusted me.

It seemed that someone in the crowd thought so too. From the crowd I heard a shout of "LIAR!" The sound was amplified, louder than any person could talk.

This man in the crowd shouted again. "The President is lying. They've known all along that mind-wipes cause harm, and now that we have proof, they are trying to hide it. Amber would never say this! What did they do to her? Are we going to take this? Are we going to take being lied to?"

Another man in the crowd stood up, his voice booming too. "Sure, because a government conspiracy is more likely than that the kid is nuts."

The arguing went back and forth. The President went up to the microphone, shouting into it, "Settle down!" But to no effect. The audience was too loud, and not even the silencing power of the microphone seemed able to stop it.

It's hard to tell when something changes from being a large shouting match to a riot, but I think I saw it there. People started shouting, pointing fingers at one another, getting in each other's faces and doing some light pushing.

But eventually, the pushing stopped being so light.

And eventually the shouting turned into magic.

There were people flying around: some with their magic, others hit so hard that they were shooting through the air. Fire, lightning, shadows and more filled the sky.

The military moved in, trying to stop the fight. That was a mistake.

Chaos erupted in the stands. Humans transformed into tigers, bears, and lions. Swords and guns appeared out of thin air. Teleporting, super speed, illusions and more were making it impossible to keep track of everything. Flames, lightning, rocks, smoke, water, and more blurred the air in a fog of magical effects.

This is what war must look like for mages.

The military was trying to calm people down, but it was no use. Even with all of the anti-mages in the entire city, there was no way they could stop everyone.

All but two of my guards raced off to try and help with crowd control. General Cabrera was trying to escort the rest of the council out of danger. Dwayne Cooper seemed to be helping protect the council as a swarm of people from the crowd stormed at them.

That's when a group of a half-dozen people broke free of the military and ran at the President.

Thinking of the safety of the President instead of keeping me in chains, my final two guards left me alone. One quick teleport, and I was out of my restraints. The teleport was harder than usual though; I guess the cuffs and chains were designed to prevent that very thing. They just hadn't accounted for me.

With the cuffs off my hands, I looked for Ra. There was no way I was going to let him get away. To my complete lack of surprise, Ra was trying to run away. He probably had some kind of illusion up to hide from everyone else, because no one was going after him. Except me.

I chased after him. He would not get away. I wouldn't let him. Not after everything he had done.

I teleported after him, closing the distance. But I knew I couldn't just grab him after a teleport. So I ran. Maybe Ra should have gotten himself some more training too. He was huffing and puffing and sweating up a storm. He was right in front of me. My arm swiped out to grab him...and grabbed nothing but air.

He tricked me. Ra must have had an illusionist in the city. He wasn't there. Someone had already gotten him out. Gotten away with him. But who? How many people in this city were working for New Asgard?

The fight was getting worse. Blood in the stands, limbs bending in ways they should not bend, healers doing the best they could to keep everyone in one piece, and failing miserably. There were probably already a few dead people, not that I could tell who was dead and who was just unconscious in this mess.

Could this have been Odin's plan? They wanted everyone fighting over mind-wipes. But it seemed like it was too easy to get this started. They had manipulated everything else: that mind-wipes are harmful, that I was saving people in my lessons with Ra, that I was a killer. They had to be manipulating this. Just how many people within Atlantis were actually working for them?

I was paralyzed with indecision. Should I try to stop the fighting? Should I run, get away before they have a chance to throw me in jail like they did with Drake?

An answer to my questions appeared as I saw Dwayne. He and the President had been separated from the other councillors. Now it was only Dwayne escorting the President to safety. Or to her death.

I wasn't about to let him get the President alone.

I teleported right in Dwayne's face and punched him as hard as I could. I had been slowing down time to make the attack hurt even more, but Dwayne's head just jerked back, and he looked at me, completely fine. He reached out and grabbed me with one hand, moving just as fast as he would if I wasn't trying to stop him. I tried to teleport out of his grasp, but my teleport failed.

Dwayne had a calm look on his face as lightning spread from his arm and into my body. The lightning hit my body and I felt myself spasm. My limbs went limp. I couldn't move. I could barely scream, it was a struggle to get my body to say anything, to do anything.

"You won't get away with this," I shouted at Dwayne, taking more strength to say those words than anything else I had done that day.

Dwayne ignored my threat and continued walking, I heard him shout, "Madame President, let's get to your office. You will be safe there."

I could feel my joints finally willing to move as Dwayne and the President continued to run away, out of the stadium, and out of my line of sight.

I cursed myself for letting Dwayne get away on me. I had to think. Odin and his people wanted to start the riot. But why? What good was the riot going to do? They had to be trying something. But I had no idea what.

Almost getting roasted took me out of that train of thought. A fireball had landed only a couple feet away from me.

I looked up to see Amber, diving down at me, flames shooting.

I teleported out of the way, barely. I stretched and twisted my body as much as I could, but my joints did not want to move. My body did not want to move. Whatever Dwayne had done was making it next to impossible to move. But I could at least get my magic to work.

Amber was still coming after me. I slowed down time. I managed to get to my feet, though they pleaded with me the entire time, and I wound back a punch. It connected with Amber's face as she dove at me, and she went flying back.

I teleported as far as I could manage. It was a few blocks away from the stadium. Wasn't going to do me any good in finding Ra or Dwayne. But it got me away from Amber and the fighting.

Well, kind of. The fight had already erupted out into the streets. But no one was after on the streets, and that was the important thing. I needed to catch Ra, and Dwayne. I had no idea where Ra was. But I did know where Dwayne was going. I hated the thought of letting Ra get away. But at least I knew where to go to give Dwayne the beating he deserved and stop any plans he had. I focused a teleport to get me in front of the President's building. Tallest building in the city. Dozens of floors, a skyscraper like nothing I've ever seen back home. Easily a hundred stories high. And her office was at the top.

I couldn't just teleport to the top. From the bottom you can't see the top well enough to teleport, and all of the windows to the building are tinted and enforced with anti-magic anyways. What else would you expect from a building that has to protect the president?

I ran into the building, and it looked like I had gone to the right place. I saw an elevator close with Dwayne and the President inside it.

"Get him!" the President shouted to the people on the main floor. A dozen people looked at me, ready to fight.

I saw a swirl of water in the hands of one, a gun appeared in the hands of another, and I could feel two people inside my mind pretty quickly.

They wouldn't be in my mind for long.

I slowed down time. Half speed. Quarter. Eighth. Twentieth. One-hundredth. One telepath screamed as her nose bled and she fell to the ground. The other maintained herself for about a second or two more, my time, before falling down too, neither of their minds capable of handling mine when it was thinking a hundred times faster than normal.

I teleported to the man with a gun in his hand, grabbed the gun, pulled the clip out, and whipped him in the head with it, all in less time than it took him to blink. He didn't crumble that quickly from the blow, some invincibility training I'd wager, but he did fall none the less.

And then someone punched me.

I hit the floor, but managed to maintain my time-slow; knowing that if I didn't, I was dead.

I glanced at my assailant. A speedster. She was breathing heavily and running around the room, though she still looked like she was only going at half speed to me. Even at a hundredth her normal speed she could still move fast enough to tag me in my time-slow. I had to take her down, and fast.

I teleported in the direction she was running, ended up in front of her and punched her in the face. Her nose was bleeding as she fell to the ground. She wasn't unconscious or anything, but it was enough for me

I saw the light on the elevator door that signalled the floor it was at. The elevator had already made it to the fiftieth floor. But that should be impossible! The elevator would have been slowed down too. Unless....

Dwayne. Could his anti-magic be strong enough to stop me, by himself? I suppose it's possible. But he shouldn't be that strong. He's supposed to be weaker than Amber, that's why she took over from him as Warden.

I let out a heavy breath. I didn't have time for this. Didn't have time for these people. I had to get to Dwayne and the President.

I ran to the stairway and opened the door.

I looked straight up—it was a long way to the top, but I could do this in a few hops.

I teleported up to the fifth floor, but I felt myself breathe heavily again. I pulled the time-stop so that I could focus on teleporting my way up to the top. I had to get there and stop Dwayne. Whether she knew it or not, and regardless of my opinions of her, Dwayne had the President hostage and I had to save her.

Teleport after teleport, five floors at a time, seemed to be about the best I could do. Like something was holding me back. I could feel the anti-magic, it seemed to be emanating from the elevator itself. Dwayne was stopping all magic. But he wasn't good enough to stop me. Though I will admit he was making it harder.

I was gasping for breath by the time I made it to the top floor.

I could hear a male voice. It must have been Dwayne's, talking. "It's time the world learned the truth, Madame President."

Dwayne was going to get rid of the barrier—he was going to expose Atlantis to the world! I raced to the door of the President's office.

There she was, Dwayne beside her. The President screamed as I ran into the room. Dwayne fired a bolt of lightning at me, but this time I teleported out of the way.

When I reappeared beside Dwayne, I stumbled and fell to one knee. What was wrong with me? Why was this so hard?

Dwayne didn't have any trouble taking advantage though. He kneed me in the face. I crumbled to the ground.

"Oh, thank God," the President said, "you've saved me, Dwayne."

I struggled to get to my feet. I tried a time-stop, but it didn't work. I couldn't be that tired. I couldn't afford to be that tired. What was wrong with the President? Why did she say Dwayne had saved her?

"The problem," Dwayne began as he pulled me up by my hair, "with you aberrations," Dwayne continued as he punched me in the stomach, "is that it never occurs to you that someone," he punched me in the stomach again, "with a lot of training," two more punches to my stomach, "might actually be stronger than you."

I fell to the ground. I couldn't get up; my magic wasn't working.

"No one performs magic around me without my permission," Dwayne said, as he sent a surge of lightning through my body. The same way that he had done before, disabling my nerves, making me unable to move. "Not you, not Drake, not even Odin."

He just said Odin, right in front of the President.

I shouted at her, "You just heard him! He's the one you need to stop, not me! He's working with Odin!"

If I thought I was going to get any reaction out of the President, it was not the smile that I saw spread across her lips, nor did I expect to hear the words that escaped her lips, "You're assuming I don't."

I felt the blood rush out of my face. Odin couldn't have her. How was . . . how was Atlantis still a secret if the President had been in Odin's pocket the entire time?

"Why?" I shouted. "Why wait this long? Why now?"

"Because now we have someone to blame," the President responded. "Ra was right about you, day one. He read you like a book. Said there was no way you would go along with the plan. So we planned to use you. Atlantis will be revealed to the world because of the actions of a mage terrorist, isn't that right, Blaine Allan?"

"I'll never help you!" I shouted.

"You already have," the President replied.

Dwayne smiled. He then punched himself in the face. His nose started bleeding. The President smiled as she walked over to Dwayne. She punched Dwayne in the stomach. "Sorry, but it has to look convincing."

Dwayne nodded. "I know."

She hit Dwayne several more times. Punch after punch hitting Dwayne, and unlike my punches, they seemed to be hurting him, leaving bruises. Dwayne fell to the ground.

The President turned her face away from me. When I saw it again, it was a bit bloody. Injuries on her face, hair a mess. She had just changed how she looked on a whim. But the President didn't have power like that; she was a telepath. Not a shapeshifter.

A shapeshifter! Odin had replaced the President with one of his own! But when? How long ago did the President get replaced? Was it after my banishment? Before? Days, weeks, months, years? Was that why she wore several dozen mind-protection gems like the one Amber had? To make sure no one found out the President was a fake?

The Shapeshifter pressed several buttons on the desk in her enormous office. I could see it, see the outside. The gray barrier was disappearing—I could see the blue sky.

A screen came out of the desk, like a TV screen, but it seemed different. As it turned on I watched, I saw every single television channel in the world slowly appear, I saw dozens, hundreds, of websites flash through the screen. And then, all at once, they all changed, all showing the image of the President. Every single TV with cable or internet, every single computer, all at once, was broadcasting the Shapeshifter.

Like a trained actress, the Shapeshifter pretended to look terrified. She was starting to cry as she said, directly into the screen, "I-I-I am th-the President of the lost city of Atlantis. This me-message is for the p-people of Earth. A-atlantis is ready to come out of hiding, and join the world."

She'd done it. The barrier was gone; the world was informed. Atlantis was exposed.

I couldn't move, couldn't use magic. I was helpless. Completely helpless. I hadn't even stood a chance. Ra, Odin, Dwayne, I had never been a threat to them. I had never been strong enough. They just let me think that. Let me believe I was strong, knowing I was actually too weak to ever put their plans in danger. I lay there, seconds, maybe even minutes passed as I tried to process what had happened, and tried to get my body moving again.

After what felt like an eternity, I could finally feel my fingers again, could feel my entire body. My magic was still not working, but I was able to get to my feet.

It was at that moment that several officers burst through the door to the President's office. Before I could do anything but try and run for the window, they had grabbed me and restrained me.

"You're too late!" the Shapeshifter shouted, "I'm sorry. He...he tried to kill me, and I...I was so scared. He told me that I had to show Atlantis to the world, that Atlantis would pay for everything it did to him. He threatened my children! The barrier is down. The world knows about Atlantis."

I almost broke free of the men holding me in that instant of shock on their faces, but they managed to maintain their grip.

"Take him away!" the President shouted, crying as she did so, "Lock him up in the most secure way possible. He can never escape! He took our secrets. He destroyed our way of life. Lock him away, and make sure he never escapes!"

Dwayne got to his feet, and managed to speak, "I will escort him."

As I was dragged out of the President's office, I felt sick to my stomach, furious and unable to do anything about it. Odin had won. Atlantis was exposed to the world, I was blamed for it, and I hadn't done a single thing to even hinder their plans. Everything I had done, every last piece of it, they had planned for and countered. Ra was probably laughing at my naivety right now. Laughing his fat head off.

epilogue| RA

I AWOKE WITH A THROBBING HEADACHE. TRYING MY BEST TO IGNORE the drums pounding in my head, I thought about what had happened. I had been at the announcement in Atlantis, ready to see them change the world. The riot had begun. I was trying to get away and then....

I couldn't remember.

I tried to rub the sleep from my eyes. But my hands wouldn't move. I couldn't move. My only thought was that I must have gotten way too drunk.

I struggled again, but couldn't budge, not an inch. It wasn't telekinetic, and I could tell now that I was drunk. I've been drunk too often to know the difference. It felt like I'd been drugged or something. Drugged and then tied up. There were leather straps, plastic wrap, and duct tape all over me. I could feel it, though I couldn't see it.

There was tape over my mouth. Tape and plastic and a leather strap from a hospital table were securing my head down. I think the only part of my body not covered by the plastic was my face. It felt like one of those freaky things you see on all those crime shows, with the psychopath serial killers. The kind of thing Blaine would think I'm into. I almost laughed at that thought, but reminding myself of where I was quickly stopped that.

I couldn't see anything. There was a light above my head, blinding me to most of what was going on around me.

"Good, you're awake."

I tried to shake the grogginess out. The voice sounded familiar. I knew this person, but who was it? It hurt to focus, my head was killing me.

"I apologize, but I can't let you leave. I have so many

questions, and you have so many answers."

I felt something touch my face, a hand, wearing a black leather glove, reaching at the tape at my mouth. "If you scream, if you say anything other than answers to my questions, you will feel the other side of this."

I felt the flat of a knife against my cheek.

"Glance to the right if you understand."

I did as I was told. But I needed to think of a way out. I tried an illusion.

Nothing happened. I'd hit my head worse than even I thought. I couldn't do an illusion.

"Good," the voice said, ignoring my attempt to use magic.

The hand slowly peeled the tape off my mouth. It hurt, like hell.

"No screaming. Good work. Now, do you feel ready to answer my questions?"

"Yes," I said, trying to sound like I was better than I was, but even I could hear the groggy, out-of-it tone in my voice.

"How many aberrations are there?" There was a subtle clomp to the steps as the voice walked around the room. The voice was wearing nice shoes. Business shoes.

"Twelve, one for each school," Ra said.

"And you know this for sure?" the man said. Yes, I was fairly sure about that. The voice definitely sounded like a man.

"Yes," I answered; it was a lie, I didn't know for sure. No one does.

"Why are there twelve?"

"I don't know," I replied, cringing as I gave him the answer.

The man pulled the knife back, a friendly tone to his voice as he said, "I believe you."

"Oh, thank you." I need him to believe me.

"I fail to see why you are grateful. What do you think I am going to do with you once you are of no use to me?"

I screamed.

A new piece of tape was placed over my mouth.

I tried to create an illusion again. It worked—I could see the illusion.

240

"That won't work on me."

He could see through it. He was an aberration like me. I still wasn't sure who it was. The voice wasn't clear, not in my dazed state. Alpha seemed most likely though.

"Now, I need to thank you for everything you have done."

The voice was clearing. I could make it out. Not Alpha.

"You see, if you had not tried to contact Blaine, then I never would have found out that your organization has a half dozen aberrations in it."

My eyes finally adjusted. I caught a glimpse of the man. He was wearing a black dress shirt and had raven black hair.

Drake!

"Ah, the drugs must be wearing off," Drake said as he stepped into clear view. "Not that it matters."

Drake smiled as he continued pacing around the table. "When I met Blaine, I thought I wanted him right where I have you. In fact, I was certain of it. But then he was exiled and I was imprisoned. Of course, your decision to punish Blaine brought you to my attention.

"And I was ecstatic. You see, I like Blaine. That naïve, childlike, religious hick/idealist really grows on you if you give him a chance. But my research needed to continue, so I was going to have to strap one of the few genuinely good men in the world down on this table."

Drake pulled out a needle from one of the tables at the side of the room and flicked it a couple of times.

"Now then, the first step to studying you is a blood sample," Drake said.

The knife telekinetically cut a square in the plastic and duct tape, just enough for access to my right arm.

Drake pulled out a cotton swab and some rubbing alcohol. He rubbed the bare spot on my arm. He smiled as he plunged the needle in and took my blood.

I struggled, but that just made the needle hurt. I couldn't do anything in the position I was in. I needed to do something.

At least he wanted me alive. He was studying my blood.

"Perfect," Drake said, smiling as he looked at the needle full of my blood.

241

Drake placed the needle back on the table, "Now, you're probably wondering why I am so grateful to have you here. I mean, Blaine is my friend, I could have asked him for a blood sample. He's curious about this aberration thing like I am. He'd support my research."

I didn't like where the conversation was going. I struggled against my restraints.

Drake put his hands on both sides of the table and faced nose to nose with me. "Of course, there is one thing that I need to do. Something that I simply have to know. And Blaine, bless his pure and untainted heart, simply would not understand. But I have a few questions first. Question one: How many aberrations do you know of, including yourself?"

"Nine."

"Their names?"

"Drake, Blaine, Alpha, Lempo, Loa, Ares, Ishtar, Odin, and Ra."

"Many of those are code names, give me better," Drake said, easing the knife ever so closer to my right eye.

"Ishtar is Felicia Ohura, Ares is Maxim Korozin, Odin is Henry Hunter," I said, terrified as the knife slowly inched closer.

Drake did not stop, the knife slowly moved closer.

"I don't know Lempo and Loa's! And I know pretty much nothing about Alpha."

Drake paused for a moment, "Very well." The knife was put away. "Do you know why aberrations cannot affect one another with their magic?"

"No," I replied, no longer capable of hiding the fear in my voice. Drake was crazy.

"I see."

The knife on the table flew up out of the air, and came hurtling down to my leg. It stopped right after cutting through the plastic and tape. It just stopped, right above my knee. I could barely feel that it was there. I knew it was there, but it refused to hurt me.

"How interesting. I can control the knife telekinetically, but the moment that doing so would harm a fellow aberration, it doesn't work."

242

Drake moved to grab the knife in his own hand, no longer controlling it with his telepathy.

"But if I am holding that exact same knife in my own hand, rather than telekinetically," Drake said as he stabbed the knife right through my knee, "it works just fine."

I screamed. I couldn't feel my toes, he broke the bone!

I had to focus. Stop thinking about the pain. Drake hadn't bothered to put tape back over my mouth. That had to mean there was no one nearby. Drake wasn't worried about anyone hearing my scream, he was just looking for cooperation. There was no one anywhere near us.

"Now, you say that there are twelve aberrations. Are there always twelve?"

"You put a knife through my leg!" I yelled, all rational thought escaping me as I screamed at him. Stupid. I should know better.

Drake pulled the knife out of my knee, and plunged it into the other.

I did my best to stifle a scream. I wouldn't give him the satisfaction, not again.

"Please remember, you may only speak to answer the questions I ask. Now I repeat: are there always twelve?"

"I don't know."

Drake pulled the knife out of my right knee.

"I see. Well, that just adds one more reason to the list. You see, Ra, the biggest reason that I am grateful you have appeared in my life is because I like Blaine. I did not want to hurt him."

Drake ran the bloodied knife's flat edge along the plastic overtop of my stomach, a level of calm over him. He was not enjoying this, I could see it in his eyes. Hurting me wasn't fun to him. He wasn't a serial killer. This was research. I was nothing but a frog for him to dissect.

"My research must be thorough, after all," Drake said, "since Alpha claims to know what happens, and isn't dead, there is little reason to hold back. I simply need to know: what happens when an aberration dies? And because of you, I don't have to kill my friend in order to find out. So thank you."

I wanted to scream in pain as I felt the knife pierce my

heart; instead, nothing happened but blood coming up from my mouth. I tried to breathe, tried to keep going, but I felt everything vanishing. Could see my life fading before my very . . . .

As Ra screeched out his final breath, little yellow lights began pouring out of him. They spun around the room. Around and around. They spun for seconds, seconds that felt like centuries. The lights shot at Drake, entering into his body from every possible direction. Drake fell to the ground, overcome by the light.

Drake gasped as he spasmed on the floor.

After what felt like forever, he stood up.

"That hurt," Drake said as he looked around the room. Ra's dead body was laying there. No different than he would have expected. But those lights, they had left Ra, and entered him.

A thought occurred to Drake. "I wonder."

"Beach," Drake said aloud, and suddenly he could see a beach in front of him.

"Castle," Drake said, and an illusion of a castle appeared.

"Amber," Drake said.

Drake looked down at his hands, then over at the illusion he had created of Amber. A smile crept over Drake's face as he looked at the illusion.

"Fascinating."

| ACKNOWLEDGMENTS

Thank you to Xander Richards, who read my second draft, gave me advice, and made me believe I had written something worth reading.

To Ashley Pachkowski and Corey Schultz, who read my second draft and helped point me in the right direction.

To Gray Myrfield and Rissa Weitzel, who ripped my fourth draft to shreds yet also encouraged me to finish it.

To Audra Balion, Cover artist.

To Lindsay McDonald of I.Designs, for being a patient, understanding editor.

To Wes Funk and Jeff Smith, who offered advice throughout.

To my parents, Bob and Jan Hildebrand, for keeping me on track and helping me with the first batch of physical copies.

And last, but not least, thanks to you for reading.

Additionally, thanks to all those who helped with the creation of the One Spell Trailer including: Erich Jurgens, Gray Myrfield, Zach Greenhorn, Kole Dulle, Ashley Pachkowski, Slade McKee, Katee Polischuk, Corey Schultz, Damien Bartlett, Darren Zimmer, Dallas Thomas, Rissa Weitzel, Amanda Bristol, Andrew Donnison, and Heather Woytowich.

CPSIA information can be obtained at www.ICGtesting.com
Printed in the USA
LVOW07s1622280316

481071LV00002B/452/P

9 781364 806590